Evil Turns

Books by Jane Tesh

The Madeline Maclin Mysteries
A Case of Imagination
A Hard Bargain
A Little Learning
A Bad Reputation
Evil Turns

The Grace Street Mysteries
Stolen Hearts
Mixed Signals
Now You See It
Just You Wait

Evil Turns

A Madeline Maclin Mystery

Jane Tesh

Poisoned Pen Press

First Edition 2016

10 9 8 7 6 5 4 3 2 1

Library of Congress Catalog Card Number: 2015949287

ISBN: 9781464205217   Hardcover
       9781464205231   Trade Paperback

Poisoned Pen Press
6962 E. First Ave., Ste. 103
Scottsdale, AZ 85251
www.poisonedpenpress.com
info@poisonedpenpress.com

Printed in the United States of America

Evil Turns is dedicated to all my theater friends:
The Lenoir-Rhyne Playmakers,
the Surry Arts Players, the NoneSuch Playmakers,
and everyone at Elkin's Foothills Theater.
No matter what the show is about, there's always drama!

At dawn of day I ride away,
I'm here and there and everywhere!
At midnight hour, when none can know,
To join the witches' dance I go!

Hocus pocus witches' charm!
If you move, I'll do you harm!

Hansel and Gretel by Engelbert Humperdinck

Chapter One

You wouldn't think there'd be a lot going on in a small Southern town. After all, the weather is warm and muggy, the pace is slow, and people take time to say hello and ask about your family.

They also take time to murder each other.

I was sitting in my office this warm Thursday morning in May, the latest edition of the *Celosia News* spread out on my desk. "Man Found Dead in Local Vineyard" was the headline, followed by "Strange Markings Found on Body." The story continued with details of an unidentified man discovered at Phoenix Vineyards by the workers early yesterday morning. Cause of death was unknown, and the strange markings were stars and odd symbols the reporter had decided were linked to witchcraft. The police were questioning members of Darkrose, a group of young people whose names had been linked to a series of shady events around the neighboring city of Parkland.

This was one crime I hadn't been involved in and one I hoped Jerry wouldn't find intriguing. With his questionable past, his penchant for fake séances, and his ability to make anything into an adventure, a secret society and a body with mysterious signs on it might prove beyond tempting.

Too late.

My cell phone rang. It was Jerry, his voice brimming with excitement. "Mac, have you seen today's paper?"

"Looking at it right here."

"You've got to take this case."

"Unfortunately, no witch hunters have come to Madeline Maclin Investigations, demanding justice. I've been hired by the local post office to find some missing boxes and the head cashier at the Dollar Store suspects her husband of cheating and wants me to keep an eye on his activities."

"Small potatoes. We need to look into this Darkrose group. I'm almost through with breakfast."

Jerry Fairweather, my husband and reformed—I hope and pray—con man, is a slim handsome man with light brown hair and warm gray eyes, the same eyes I hope our child will have, should we ever have children. That's still up in the air. He'd bounced around several jobs in town before we realized what had been right in front of us all along. He was a morning person who loved to cook, and the owner of Deely's Burger World, a popular diner on Main Street, wanted to start serving breakfast. This arrangement had worked out very well, so much so that business was booming, and Jerry added buttermilk pancakes and waffles to the menu.

Who did we have to thank for bringing Jerry's culinary skills to our attention? A con man named Big Mike, who'd paid us a visit in October. As it turned out, Big Mike was Jerry's Con Master, a huge man who ran a secret College for the Dubious Arts. He'd taught Jerry all sorts of uncommon skills such as picking locks—although I'll admit that talent had come in handy during my previous cases.

"Let me know how things go with this cooking deal," he'd said. "I'm glad Jerry's interested in going straight."

Jerry's voice brought me back to the present. "Mac, are you listening? I can be there in fifteen minutes."

"Sure, come on." I didn't know if Jerry ever planned to go straight, but I kept trying. Wandering through the vineyards with him would be better than sitting in my office all day. Tracking elusive boxes and shadowing a possible cheating spouse weren't exciting cases but they paid the bills. And I'd discovered that the small town of Celosia, North Carolina, where Jerry and I moved when he inherited his Uncle Val's old house, had more than its share of murder. Celosia has only ten thousand people living in town and the surrounding rural areas, but most of those ten thousand people are always stirred up about something. It doesn't take much.

When Jerry arrived he brought a paper bag containing one of his delicious sausage biscuits and a big cup of iced tea. He had on jeans and a light blue shirt and one of his favorite ties, a yellow one with dancing hamburgers. He took a seat in the green and beige armchair I have for clients.

"So what do you think?"

"I think we can go have a look, but chances are the crime scene is off-limits, and you know Chief Brenner doesn't like me nosing around."

"I can call Del and see if he knows anything about Darkrose."

Del was one of Jerry's pals from his old life. I'd love to say former pal, but had to admit Del and his information had been useful in the past. And Del was a reasonable fellow, not the threat that some of Jerry's so-called friends have been. During my last investigation, I had to contend with yet another of Jerry's disreputable acquaintances from his Con Man school days. Fortunately, I'd been able to get rid of Honor Perkins by telling her I was pregnant, which I wasn't. Not yet. "Okay, but just Del."

Jerry's gray eyes were alight. "How about if I infiltrate Darkrose?"

"You may be good at disguises, but I believe Darkrose is all women."

He feigned being insulted. "I'll have you know I can be a very lovely woman."

"I'm sure you can be, but no."

"You do it, then."

"I might, if I had a client who wanted me to solve the murder."

"You need to find a client. This is too good to pass up."

"Don't you have something to do? Camp Lakenwood's grand opening? The writing of Celosia's centennial song?"

"Taken care of. Now, let's go catch some witches."

We stood up, then heard a quarrel outside my door.

The first voice was a man's voice, and whoever he was, he was highly annoyed. "But there isn't anything in Celosia's history worth writing an outdoor drama about!"

"Of course there is." I definitely recognized the second voice, the strident tones of Amanda Price, a very opinionated woman. She reigned over Celosia's Women's Improvement Society, a local club whose members were determined to keep Celosia up-to-date and one step ahead of other small towns in the area. Recently, the Society pushed for new streetlights and curbside recycling with Amanda doing most of the pushing. "Celosia is brimming with history. We'll call the play *Flower of the South*."

The man was not impressed. "But people who aren't from this area have never heard of the celosia flower. They call it a feather flower, if they call it anything at all. How can you possibly make a story out of that?"

"We'll tie it in with the hardships the settlers had."

"What hardships? Most of them came from Ireland and Scotland and did very well. Vineyards were huge business before tobacco took over. You want the opening number to be a bunch of Irishmen and Scotsmen drinking and smoking? That'll go over real well."

Jerry and I poked our heads out of my office door. Amanda Price and Harold Stover stood in the hallway. Harold, a tall dark man with a short bristly moustache, folded his arms and lowered his brow. Amanda, as usual, was fashionably dressed and looked supremely confident. She was tall enough to look Harold in the eye, which she did over the top of her jeweled-studded glasses, and swept back her dark hair.

"I say this whole drama should be based on the life of Emmaline Ross, that courageous woman who defied the odds to become one of North Carolina's first female vintners."

"How can that be important? Did she even live in this area?"

"I'm sure she did."

Harold held up both hand to wave, dismissing her idea. "This is ridiculous. We're getting nowhere. Let's scrap the whole idea and concentrate on a centennial park."

Amanda was not deterred. "Oh, everyone has a park. We could make a real contribution to the fine tradition of outdoor drama in our state."

"Or destroy it." Harold noticed me. "Madeline, Jerry. Sorry if we disturbed you."

Amanda pointed a perfectly manicured finger in my direction. "Now here's someone who will agree with me. I don't know if you've heard, Madeline, but the Women's Improvement Society is planning to produce an outdoor drama. Don't you think that would be a huge draw? We need something special to put Celosia on the map."

"We're on the map," Harold said. "Thirty minutes north of Parkland."

Amanda ignored him. "Would you like to be on the committee, Madeline? Perhaps help design the costumes or the posters? We need someone with your artistic talent."

I started to say I didn't think so when Amanda's eyes brightened. "And, Jerry, you are perfect to help with the music."

"It's going to be a musical?" Harold croaked, aghast.

"Why not? *Unto These Hills* has singing and dancing. So does *The Lost Colony.*"

"Those dramas are based on historical facts, not some legend of a milkmaid."

Amanda whipped off her glasses. "Not a milkmaid, Harold! A vintner! A creator of fine wine! Why are you so against this?"

"Where are you going to get the money to mount a production like this?"

"Fundraisers, of course—car washes, bake sales. We'll get the whole town involved."

He gave a derisive snort. "I can tell you right now the Baptist churches won't support a show about wine."

"This isn't glorifying alcohol. This is celebrating our history."

"A centennial park makes much more sense and would be thousands of dollars cheaper. And where are you going to have this outdoor drama? We don't have an amphitheater. Are you going to pitch a tent in somebody's field?"

"That's a very good idea, Harold. I'll bet someone would be proud to let us use a field."

"And clean up after all the people? You're dreaming, Amanda."

"At least I have dreams! Nothing would get done in this town if I didn't push!"

She looked as if she'd like to push Harold over and stomp on his face. I held up a hand. "If I could make a suggestion." They turned to me expectantly. "Why not have a centennial celebration featuring a short musical play about Emmaline Ross? That way you could have both things and probably have the production at the community theater."

Harold looked interested, but Amanda shook her head. "No, Emmaline's story deserves much more, something that can be an annual event."

Harold threw up his hands. "There's no reasoning with her. Go on. Bankrupt the city with your insane ideas." He stalked off.

Amanda watched him go and then turned to me, arms spread wide. "Bankrupt? Can't he see this will be a goldmine for Celosia? People will come from all over the state, all over the country."

Personally, I couldn't see anyone outside of the greater Parkland area coming to a small-town history show, but from the short time Jerry and I had lived in Celosia, I'd learned not to make snap judgments about my new home and its inhabitants. Compared to the sequined glitter and glamour of a beauty pageant where a contestant might present a truly horrible YouTube-worthy talent, the saga of hardworking pioneers in drab cloaks and shawls singing about their misfortunes would not be an attraction. But Celosians had fooled me before.

Amanda replaced her glasses and fixed a keen glance on Jerry and me. "So, Madeline, will you be on the drama committee? Jerry, will you write the music?"

Jerry readily agreed. There wasn't a chance he'd miss out on what would most likely be a real drama, not just an outdoor one. I was more cautious. Getting a project this size up and running would be like trying to lift a dinosaur. "I'll think about it," I said.

"I know you're not busy. No one's murdered anyone lately, have they?"

At least she didn't say, "And we never had so many dead bodies until you moved to town." Did I mention I'd solved four murder cases? From the way Harold Stover looked at Amanda Price, I'd say chances were looking good for number five.

"Not lately."

"Well, there's a little something you can do for me."

"Please come in."

"Is this a private matter?" Jerry asked. "I can step out."

"A few concerns of mine, nothing personal. You can stay, if you like."

Amanda came into my office and sat down in the client chair. Jerry perched on a corner of my desk. Amanda looked around and gave a little sniff, as if the space didn't meet her high expectations.

I loved my office. When I worked for a large agency in Parkland, I was stuck in a hot little cubicle in a huge featureless building. My Celosia office was light and cool with a view of the red and yellow swing set in the yard next door. The room had been very neutral, light pine paneling and a beige carpet, but I'd been working on it. I'd decorated the walls with a mural of leaves and flowers in bright greens and yellows so the effect was of stepping into a spring garden. The carpet would be the next to go, but for now, I'd added a multi-colored area rug. The bookshelves were filled with personal items, including the frog my grandmother had made out of patchwork, seashells from my honeymoon in Bermuda, and several of my small paintings, including an abstract swirl of rainbow colors and my favorite sketch of Jerry sitting on our front porch.

None of this impressed Amanda Price. She took off her jeweled glasses and set them on my desk while she hunted in her pocketbook for her phone. "I was on my way over to see you when I ran into Harold and thought I'd better set him straight about plans for the Celosia Centennial. That man doesn't have a scrap of imagination. A park with benches and a fountain! How lame is that? I don't know why he's on the planning committee."

I settled back in my chair. "Do the other members of the committee support his idea?"

"Oh, I can persuade them, I'm sure." She found her phone and searched through its menu. "Larissa Norton told me what a fine job you did clearing her of her ex-husband Wendall's murder. She wasn't a fan of yours before, but you certainly won her over. Oh, here we are. If I don't put things on my calendar, I lose track of what I'm doing. Can you provide security at my garden party tomorrow afternoon from two to four at my home on Sunnyside Lane? I know it's short notice, but I've been so busy with my plans for the drama."

This was a new one. "Security? You mean make sure your guests don't run off with the silver?"

"Exactly. And this will be an undercover operation, so I hope you have something suitable to wear."

Jerry and I exchanged an amused glance. Amanda must not have been aware of my pageant past. I'd lived my mother's beauty queen dream from the time I was a baby, and as a teenager, grudgingly used pageants to make money for school. Although I'd gladly given up that life to become a private investigator, I still had a couple of stunning cocktail dresses shimmering in the back of my closet. "I believe I can find something."

"Good! I want everyone to think you're an invited guest."

This was insulting on so many levels, I called upon my best competition smile and let it ride. "Anyone in particular you suspect?"

"Eloise Michaels has had her eye on my silver centerpiece ever since I bought it out from under her at an estate sale, and I know Gloria Goins covets my Waterford crystal candlesticks."

I wrote this down. "Anyone else?"

"Just watch the guests, and if anyone does anything suspicious, politely escort them out."

So I was the bouncer, too. "Okay."

She crammed her phone in her pocketbook and wedged out her checkbook. "I really appreciate this, Madeline. If all goes well, I'll recommend you to my friends."

"Thank you." Madeline Maclin, Security to the Suburbs. I told her my fee, and she wrote a check.

"Oh, and one other thing. I'm missing a very expensive Louis Vuitton purse. While you're on duty, see if you can learn anything."

"Where did you last see your purse?"

"I can't remember!" She gave a little laugh. "I have so many purses, I didn't miss this one until recently. I suppose I could do without it, but it's one of my favorites. It's beige with a brown handle and a lovely sparkly design of brown on beige. A subtle design, of course."

Of course. "I'll see what I can do."

"Thank you. I'll be in touch. Jerry, you can go ahead and get started on songs for *Flower of the South*."

He gave her a little salute. "Yes, ma'am." As soon as she was gone, he turned to me, grinning. "Security detail for her garden party. Do you get to frisk the guests? I'll come help you."

"You heard her. I get to dress up and blend in."

"I've seen you dressed up, Mac. There's no way you're going to blend in."

"You are perhaps the nicest husband I've ever had."

"Thanks." He leaned over the desk to give me a kiss. "Witches and murder can't possibly compete with the story of brave Emmaline Ross and a fancy purse, but I still want to check out the vineyard."

◇◇◇

Phoenix Vineyard and Winery was one of many that had sprung up around Celosia in the past five years. As Harold mentioned, vineyards were big business way back during North Carolina's settling days until the Native Americans showed Sir Walter Raleigh how to smoke the local tobacco leaves. Now that cigarettes and smoking had become unpopular, vineyards and wineries were making a comeback.

Jerry and I had found a reasonably priced used red Jeep for a second car. Now that he had a steady job, having two cars made life much easier. We took the Jeep out to the Phoenix Vineyard but were stopped at the gate by a stern-looking policewoman.

"Sorry, folks, employees only today."

The only thing we could see past the gate were rows and rows of grapevines, each one marked with a rose bush to lure bees to pollinate the vines, and the imposing building that housed the winery, an upscale restaurant, and a gift shop.

I knew a lot of the local police, but I didn't recognize this officer. "Can you tell us anything about the incident that happened here? Do you know the identity of the victim, or what exactly happened to him?"

Her face was a well-schooled blank. "It's an ongoing investigation, ma'am. As soon as we know anything, we'll have a report for the news agencies."

"The paper said something about Darkrose. What's that?"

She wasn't budging an inch. "As soon as we know anything, we'll pass that information along."

There was nothing to do but thank her and head back to town. Jerry took out his cell phone. "I'm calling Del."

"Go ahead."

"If Chief Brenner had been here, I'll bet he would've let you have a look around."

"You'd lose that bet. The chief is not happy with me."

"Why? Because you solve all the murders?"

"I think he's gotten a little flack from other departments about me. I'm trying to keep a low profile."

"*The Beauty Queen and the Chief.* Sounds like a hit sitcom to me."

Jerry left a message for Del and then received a call from Deely, saying one of the fry cooks was sick and asking if Jerry could come help with the lunch service, so we drove to Deely's Burger World.

A popular spot in Celosia since its early days as an ice cream parlor, Deely's still had its original gray-and-white Formica counter tops, silver stools with red cushions, red plastic booths that made squishing sounds when you sat down and stuck to your legs in summer, and faded slogans for Coca-Cola in the yellowed wallpaper. Jerry kept his cooking clothes in the Jeep, so he changed into his old jeans and tee-shirt, grabbed an apron and headed for the kitchen. Sitting at the counter, I listened to the hum of conversations around me. As usual, news in Celosia spread faster than a dancing cat video on Facebook. Not only were people speculating on the vineyard murder, but they were talking and arguing about the centennial and the outdoor drama.

Young waitress Annie Vernon stopped by for my order, one of Deely's finest cheeseburgers, fries, and a Coke. She had dyed her hair a strange shade of green, and three earrings dangled from each ear. Her newest piercing was a nose ring, which made her look like a thin, yet friendly, cow. "Are you going to try out for the play, Madeline?"

"Has the show been written yet?"

Annie plucked a straw from her apron pocket, revealing a small black rose tattooed on her wrist. She had several flower tattoos, but I hadn't seen this one before. "All I know is it's called *Flower of the South*, and it's about Emmaline Ross. I want to try out for the part of Emmaline. Her family came over from Scotland, and she was about my age when she started her own vineyard. She managed to make it work, even though everybody said a girl couldn't do it. I can relate to that."

"How do you know so much about her?" I asked.

"We studied her in school."

"And she lived in Celosia?"

"Not exactly in Celosia. She lived where Camp Lakenwood is now."

Hmm. This could be a problem. "I don't remember seeing any sort of historical marker at the camp."

"I think there's the remains of a cabin in the woods somewhere." Someone called for Annie. "Gotta go," she said as she hurried back to help another customer and join the discussion about tryouts for the drama.

I wondered if Nathan Fenton knew about this. With my help, Nathan had solved a mysterious riddle and received his inheritance, which included Camp Lakenwood. It would be just like Amanda to insist the drama be held on the sacred Emmaline

Ross site, if there really was one. Open house for the camp was Saturday. I'd ask Jerry to check with Nathan and see if he knew anything about Emmaline.

Across the diner, voices raised in another argument. A few months ago, Celosians had been fiercely divided over a movie about Mantis Man, their local legendary monster. Some people wanted to cash in on the craze, while others thought the whole idea cheapened the town's image. Then a few months later, when Wendall Clarke came to open a new art gallery, the local Art Guild had argued constantly over who should run the gallery and whose artwork should be displayed. This time, the discussion was about the body found in Phoenix Vineyard and the complainers were a group of old men Jerry had nicknamed the Geezer Club, who always sat in a corner of the diner to hold forth on their opinions.

One of the men settled his John Deere cap firmly on his head. "Bunch of crazy kids practicing Satanism. They come over from Parkland and think they can start something here."

His friend took another pinch of chewing tobacco. "Kids are wild today."

"Police said the man was all covered with these weird signs and tattoos. Probably a cult ritual."

"Why they want to cover themselves in tattoos, anyway? It looks stupid. In my day, the only people with tattoos were sailors and criminals."

Annie, coming with my bill, paused when she heard this. "Did you want a refill, Madeline?"

"No, thanks." I indicated the Geezer Club. "Don't pay them any attention."

"Oh, I don't. They go on like that all the time. What they don't get is I'm not just a waitress here. I work two jobs to support myself and I'm saving money to attend the University of North Carolina at Parkland."

I realized I'd been guilty of thinking of Annie as just the Waitress at Deely's, too. "You support yourself?"

"Yeah, my mom kicked me out when I was sixteen. Her new boyfriend and I didn't get along. I'm better off on my own, believe me."

"Must be tough, though."

She shrugged. "I manage."

"Is that a new tattoo?"

She held up her wrist where the black rose was artistically carved. "Yeah." She gave the Geezers a dark look. "And I'm not a sailor or a criminal."

When the lunch rush was over and the diner had settled down, Jerry passed his apron to Deely and came out front. "Ready to go?"

"All set."

Jerry took the last drink of my Coke. "I think an outdoor drama is a neat idea, especially one about wine. I already have an opening number in mind."

"What about the centennial song?"

"Oh, that's done. Want to hear it?"

Before I could say no or stop him, he stood up in the booth. "My fellow Celosians! May I have your attention, please!" When he had the attention of everyone in the diner, he said, "You proud and lucky few will be the first to hear your centennial anthem!"

"Sing it!" someone shouted. They gave him a round of applause to get him started, he put his hand over his heart, and he sang in his reasonably tuneful baritone,

"Fair Celosia, in this special hour,
One hundred years of strength and glory,
We grow and flourish like our namesake flower,
Long may the world tell our story!"

It was actually not bad, and everyone reacted with cheers and loud stomping of feet. Jerry took several bows and sat down.

"Where did all this songwriter talent come from?" I asked. "Please don't tell me you conned someone into writing that for you."

"That was my own sheer God-given talent," he said. Then he lowered his voice. "But I borrowed the tune from an old beer commercial."

Chapter Two

Jerry said he'd drive out to Camp Lakenwood and talk to Nathan. I went back to work. After making several phone calls, I found the missing post office boxes. The Rotary Club had used them to haul food drive collections to the local food pantry, and the boxes had been mistakenly stored with the regular boxes. Check that one off. The Dollar Store cashier's husband worked at the bank, so I waited until almost closing time and stopped off to have a little chat with him. He beamed at me and showed me the array of travel brochures on his desk. Turned out he was sneaking around to plan a huge anniversary surprise for his wife, which included a two-week cruise to the Bahamas.

"That's great," I told him. "I know you'll both enjoy that."

Back in my office, I called my worried client and assured her everything was okay. "It's definitely not what you think."

"Did you confront him? What did he say?"

"Be patient and you'll be glad you did. An opportunity is coming up for you to have a long talk with him."

"Thanks, Madeline. He needs a long talk."

No, you do, I wanted to say, if you don't know your husband well enough to trust him. But maybe this was unfair. I trusted Jerry, but I didn't trust some of his ideas, or any of his friends.

Jerry arrived soon after. He plopped down in the armchair. "Nathan didn't know anything about Emmaline Ross, but he said we could look for the cabin whenever we like."

"Good timing. I solved both my cases today. Although I haven't located Amanda's pocketbook."

"Well, that was impressively fast. They'll have to write an outdoor drama about you. I heard from Del. He said the *Pagan Desires* series plays a big part in the Darkrose Coven."

It was hard to escape the bombardment of commercials, interviews, and previews for *Pagan Desires*, the latest young adult craze. I'd seen the book and its sequels, *Dread Desires* and *Demon Desires*, prominently displayed in bookstore windows, including Celosia's own Georgia's Books, but I hadn't read them.

"Other than speculation, is there a connection to the body in the vineyard?"

"Del didn't know anything about that. He said in Parkland it was a popular teen pastime to dress up as the characters and hang out near graveyards."

"Maybe this isn't the same Darkrose, or someone is using the name. Maybe someone is taking the pagan thing too far." I wondered briefly about Annie's black rose tattoo, but couldn't imagine the hardworking young waitress as a member of any kind of coven, much less one based on a wildly popular book.

"Del said he'd get back to me if he remembered anything else." He checked his watch. "Don't you have an appointment with Dr. Wallace today?"

"Tomorrow." I'd been adamantly against the idea of having children, but that was with Bill, my ex. Having a child with Jerry as the father was beginning to sound like an appealing idea. The patient young doctor I was seeing in town told me everything was in working order.

"Sometimes things take longer than we plan," she'd said, "but stressing about it won't help."

Had I waited too long? Jerry tried to cheer me up. "Look, we know there's nothing wrong with your inner workings, and there's definitely nothing wrong with mine, so I predict we'll have twins or triplets any day now. Then you'll wonder why you ever worried."

"I've got to worry a little."

"Mac, I believe we've discussed your control issues."

Recently, a revealing conversation with my mother made me realize I had more in common with her than I ever suspected. All during my childhood, she'd managed every facet of my life, and I'd let her, until I went off to college and discovered I could manage myself. Meeting Jerry and being exposed to his carefree lifestyle had opened my eyes to all sorts of new possibilities, but down deep, I liked being in control. Now I was in control of my career and my art—or at least it seemed that way, and the fact that a baby wouldn't show up when I wanted it to was really annoying.

Jerry hopped up. "Okay. The graveyards of Parkland await."

"I don't know about the graveyards, but we could ask around about Darkrose."

We were ready to go when Harold Stover knocked on the door and came in, his moustache bristling with indignation. "Sorry to disturb you, Madeline, but you know I argued with Amanda Price earlier today, and do you know what she has done now?"

"Staged a coup and declared herself Queen of Celosia?"

"She might as well! She's already set up tryouts for this fool outdoor drama she thinks she's going to write, and people are lining up to audition! The Centennial Committee never approved this. You've got to stop her."

"I don't believe she's committed a crime, Harold."

"She'll listen to you. Tell her she's got to follow proper procedure. She can't run over everyone like this."

Actually, running over everyone was Amanda's specialty. "Is she at the theater?"

"Yes, twisting Evan's arm. The woman's impossible."

I tried to calm him down. "I know you're worried about what this would cost the city, and I understand an outdoor drama would be expensive, but Amanda's a wealthy woman. She has resources."

Harold wasn't giving up. "Yes, but if she has this drama on city property, she has to follow the rules. Will you come talk to her?"

I looked at Jerry and knew he was thinking the same thing I was. We'd have to postpone our graveyard trip.

"If nothing else, we can rescue Evan," Jerry said.

Evan was no match for Amanda in full force. "All right. Let's see what we can do."

◇◇◇

Jerry and I had met Evan James, director of Celosia's community theater, when we first moved to town and became involved in a murder during the Miss Celosia Pageant. The community theater performed in the Samuel Baker Auditorium, an imposing brick building that resembled a high school built in the Thirties. The exterior was old-fashioned, but inside, the auditorium had been remodeled. Ancient squeaky wooden chairs had been replaced by rows of plush red seats, and the sad-looking beige plaster walls had been scraped and repainted a soft gray that matched the new gray carpet.

Amanda set up a table at the double front doors and supervised a line of people as two other members of the Improvement Society assisted her with the audition forms. Evan stood to one side, his ever-present handkerchief out, mopping his brow. A thin, neatly dressed man with sparse brown hair, Evan was a champion worrier. This sudden takeover of his territory was unsettling.

He came right to me. "Madeline, do you have any idea what this is all about? Amanda said she and the Improvement Society wanted to hold auditions here for an outdoor drama. I really had no reason to refuse her request, but what's going on? I haven't heard of any outdoor drama."

"It's still in the planning stages. I'll see what I can find out."

Amanda saw me and waved me over. "Have you come to sign up? Jerry, don't go anywhere. I want to talk to you, too. Isn't this a wonderful turnout?"

How long had she been planning this? "Amanda, do you have the play written?"

She tapped the side of her head. "It's all in here. I just need to write it down."

"You might want to run it by the Centennial Committee first."

"Did Harold put you up to this? Of course he did." She glanced in Harold's direction. "There he is, scowling, as usual. Look at all the people! Don't you see how excited they are to be a part of history?"

"This has not been approved," Harold said. "Evan, don't stand there wringing your hands! Tell her she has to go through proper channels."

Evan quailed beneath Amanda's fierce glance and stammered for a reply.

Amanda answered for him. "The theater isn't being used right now, so Evan kindly volunteered to let the Society use it."

"Volunteered, my a—"

"Harold, there's no need to be vulgar. If you aren't going to sign up to audition, you can leave."

"Oh, no. I'm going to find out exactly what you're doing." He appealed to the crowd. "Don't let this woman fool you. There is no outdoor drama. There is not one word put to paper."

Amanda smiled at him and tapped her head again. Looking as if he'd like to tap her head, Harold took out his cell phone and marched off, no doubt to report to the committee.

Amanda dismissed him with a wave. "Now then, who's next?"

I'm sure Amanda planned to start auditions right away, but Harold's phone calls must have alarmed Bill Finster, another committee member, who arrived and informed Amanda she'd have to wait.

She stared at him as if she'd never heard of the word. "Wait? And deprive these people, some of whom have stood in line for hours, the opportunity to try out?"

No one had been in line more than twenty minutes, but Finster, the poor fellow, wasn't as brave as Harold and managed to answer that the committee needed time to meet and discuss the outdoor drama, and would she please consider holding auditions another night?

She gave a theatrical sigh. "Very well. I suppose we can wait until tomorrow night. That will give more people a chance to sign up."

"Ha!" Harold said in triumph. "You'll see you can't walk over the rules."

Amanda wasn't fazed by this set back. "Round one to you, Harold, but this is only the beginning."

Harold waited until she had flounced away and then turned to Finster. "Where are the others?" Jerry and I heard him say. "We all have to stand up to her."

Finster looked harried. "Harold, I read through the bylaws, and there's nothing in them that says a group of people can't put on a public performance."

"But she's not planning to have it in the theater. Isn't there a law against doing a show outside? Doesn't she have to have a permit of some kind?"

"You can put on any sort of show, as long as it doesn't obstruct traffic, isn't lewd, doesn't have profanity, and doesn't feature nudity. I checked. Haven't you seen the kids in the park having puppet shows and all that fantasy role-playing?"

"Amanda's thinking much larger than that, plus she'll charge admission. Do you have any idea how much a project like this is going to cost? Expenses will be astronomical!"

"That's something we can discuss, Harold, but for now, as long as Amanda does her show in the theater, she's in the clear, and if she builds another theater somewhere, then she can do what she likes unless she decides to have naked people running through the grapevines. Then you can call the cops on her."

Harold kept protesting, but Finster had had enough. We didn't hear their parting remarks. Finster got into his car and drove away. Harold stood and fumed for a few minutes and then stalked off. It didn't sound as if he had a case.

"Looks like Amanda's going to get her way," Jerry said. "Although I think a nude romp through the vineyards would really bring 'em in."

I noticed that despite the drama between Harold and Amanda, no one got out of line. Someone called to Amanda and asked if there was a problem.

She laughed. "Not at all! Even if there are a few little legal things to work through, you don't want to miss this opportunity, do you? Of course, you don't! Sign up now and we'll hold auditions tomorrow. Next, please."

◇◇◇

While Evan dithered in the background, Amanda continued to sign people up to audition for her nonexistent show. Jerry and I stayed for a while, and when Harold didn't return with the police or the FBI, we decided the drama was over for today, and we'd try to get to Parkland tomorrow. I got into my light blue Mazda, Jerry got into his Jeep, and we went home.

Our home, the Eberlin House, was about a mile from town. The two-lane road wound past sleepy farms and meadows filled with wildflowers, with the occasional cow leaning over a fence to gaze as we passed by. Jerry finally accepted some of the Fairweather family fortune from his younger brother Tucker to pay for repairs, so nowadays, the house looks like an old-fashioned country home instead of a haunted mansion. The big oak trees gave the front porch plenty of shade, and the windows gleamed with new panes, replacing the original glass that had been cracked and covered with spider webs.

We weren't surprised to see waiting on the porch Austin Terrell and Denisha Simpson, two neighborhood children who had adopted us. Well, mainly they had adopted Jerry as their big brother and playmate. Austin, a sturdy little white boy with hair carefully sculpted like porcupine quills, was wildly enthusiastic about everything. His best friend, Denisha, was a self-assured little black girl who enjoyed keeping Austin in line. They had an uncanny ability to show up around meal times.

Austin bounded up as soon as we got out of our cars. "Jerry, guess what! My dad bought me a four-wheeler!"

"Congratulations!" Jerry looked around. "Where is it?"

"He's already wrecked it," Denisha said.

"I did not, Denisha! It had a flat tire, that's all. It's got stripes and everything, Jerry. My dad said he'd take me to the mud track on Saturday. You want to come? You can ride my uncle's. He's not going to go."

"I can't this Saturday. It's open house at camp."

Thank goodness. Jerry's Jeep made me nervous enough. As accident prone as he was, the last thing he needed to do was get on a four-wheeler. I could see him sailing over the handlebars to land headfirst in the mud.

"Aren't you coming to the open house?" he asked Austin. He'd made sure Austin and Denisha were able to attend Camp Lakenwood.

"This'll be after. You could come then."

"I have to stay and greet everyone. I'll go another time."

"What about you, Madeline?"

"Thanks, but I'm working on a case."

His eyes gleamed. "Another murder?"

"I hope not."

The kids followed us into the house. Stepping inside lifted my spirits. I loved the transformation we'd been able to accomplish. The living room had been gray and somber, filled with heavy dark furniture. A paint job had done wonders. Now the room was a light blue with white trim, and the furniture was white and modern, a sectional sofa decorated with pillows in shades of sapphire and midnight, glass end tables with crystal lamps, and a large, square glass coffee table. In the kitchen, Uncle Val had modern appliances, and we'd kept the solid square white wooden table and curved-back chairs. Again, the color scheme was white and blue, a more cheerful skipper blue for the chair cushions. This blue was echoed in the tiny willow leaf pattern in the tiles of the white floor. White lace curtains billowed at the windows that ran the length of the back of the house, giving us a full view of the meadows and woods beyond.

Denisha sat down at the table. "What are you cooking tonight, Jerry?"

He searched in a cabinet for the frying pan. "Liver and turnips."

"You are not."

"You're right. I'm making snails au gratin."

This caught Austin's attention. "Does that mean rotten snails?"

He opened the refrigerator. "And tofu with owl gravy. Now where did I put that owl?"

"He's kidding, right, Madeline?"

"Is supper not served at your house?" I asked.

"Sure, but we like to see what you guys are having." He pulled out a kitchen chair and took a seat. "What's your case about?"

"Some people in town are deciding what to do for Celosia's centennial celebration. I'm going to try to keep them from killing each other."

Denisha took the napkins from the basket on the table and passed them around. "We already heard about the celebration. There's going to be a special park, isn't there?"

"Or an outdoor drama. Or both."

Jerry put eggs and cheese on the counter. "Or none."

Austin wasn't interested in any sort of drama. "Jerry, did you know there was a witch in the neighborhood?"

With the recent talk about Darkrose Coven, Austin's remark put me on alert.

Denisha rolled her eyes. "He means Ms. Underwood. You know, the lady who sells dried flowers? Austin, she isn't a real witch."

"How do you know?"

"Because my aunt buys stuff from her all the time, and we're not dead."

"What kind of stuff?" I asked.

"Seeds, mostly, and sometimes soap and candles. She makes her own. She comes to the farmers' market sometimes. That's where I've seen her."

"Why do people think she's a witch?"

"She talks funny, like you used to, Jerry, all about the spirits and how they know stuff we don't know."

He cracked the eggs into a bowl and scrambled them. "She sounds like somebody I ought to meet."

The kids decided they didn't want omelets. Austin reminded Jerry he'd promised to take them to the latest super hero movie when it came out, and he and Denisha hopped on their bikes and rode off.

I poured two glasses of iced tea and set them on the table. "Well, that was enlightening. I need to find and talk to this Ms. Underwood."

"Told you I wanted to infiltrate the coven."

I came up behind my husband to give him a hug. "I'm glad Denisha said you used to talk funny. Used to, as in no more."

Jerry turned the omelet and added cheese. He gave me a grin and a kiss. "Now I can take up witchcraft."

Chapter Three

No witchcraft was performed that night, unless you count some pretty magical things happening in the bedroom. Friday morning, I was awakened to the sounds of *Hansel and Gretel*, one of Jerry's many opera CDs. He'd been exposed to opera at an early age and was still fond of it, although he usually preferred more offbeat compositions.

I yawned and rolled out of bed, wondering why in the world I'd married a morning person. Jerry was up and singing away as the smell of coffee and toasted bagels wafted up the stairs.

I pulled on my robe and ran my hand through my dark tousled curls. Still yawning, I wandered downstairs to the kitchen and eased into my chair at the table. "Don't tell me. Let me guess." He already had a mug of coffee ready. I grasped it thankfully. "*Hansel and Gretel* is your salute to Darkrose Coven and the witch in the woods."

"Yes, but you've also got to hear this." He turned off the CD, and despite my protests, pulled me to the parlor where he sat down at the piano and began to play and sing.

"I'm Emmaline, I'm Emmaline,
And I am feelin' mighty fine,
I'll squash my grapes and make a brew
That's filled with alcohol for you!"

He finished with a triumphant chord. "That's the opening number. Then here's the sad number after the crop has been ruined." He switched to a minor key.

"My grapes! My grapes! O Cursed blight!
Through all the cold and windy night
The heavens rolled and waters boilt,
And now I see my crop is spoilt."

"I'm not sure 'boilt' is a word," I said.

"I'll bet it was back then. And here's the closing number, when the grateful settlers see all she's done for them." He swung back into a cheerful tune.

"Brave Emmaline, we trust in you!
You've taught us all that we should do.
Now we as neighbors will join hands
And make NC a better land!"

"I can't wait for Amanda and the committee to hear this. It's beyond poetry. When did you have time to be so creative?"

Although Jerry insisted his older brother had all the musical talent, I thought differently. True, Des was a wonderful pianist who gave concerts all over the world and made CDs that sold very well, but Jerry could take any song and put his own spin on it. All these songs he made up were really good, even though the words sometimes needed editing.

"Last night was pretty inspiring." He winked. "I think it would be cool to have a chorus of grapes that get louder as they ripen. Want to hear their dance music?"

"I need more coffee."

Accompanied by happy grape music, I staggered back to the kitchen and refilled my cup. I usually wasn't up this early. When Jerry finished his ode to the vineyards, he came into the kitchen.

"I'm off to feed the starving hoards of Celosians." He kissed me. "Your breakfast should pop up soon. See you later."

My breakfast did pop up soon after he left, but I wasn't quite ready to eat. I relaxed and gazed out the kitchen window at the pleasant scene of the fields behind our house. Pleasant scenes made me very happy. For most of my younger years, the only scenes I saw were hotel rooms and hotel ballrooms as my mother hauled me around from town to town and state to state to Little Miss Pageants. Even now the smell of certain carpets took me back to that stale, insulated experience. College dorms and classrooms weren't much better. Then I was stuck in the hot dry office I shared with other struggling investigators at one of the agencies in Parkland.

But now, I saw wildflowers were thick among tall grasses, white Queen Anne's lace, daisies, and the occasional bright red stab of a poppy. Bugs whirred and cheeped. I often spied deer far off at the edge of the woods that separated our land from the neighbors' fields. This morning, a flock of starlings swooped up into the trees and disappeared into the leaves. The sweet smell of honeysuckle drifted in on the breeze. Peace. Sunlight. Lots of green.

I never thought I'd enjoy living in the country. I never thought the Eberlin House could be livable. Several rooms still needed remodeling, a spare bathroom had plumbing difficulties, and questionable parts of the attic lurked above, but repairs were coming along pretty well. The only problem at the moment was a strange scratchy noise coming from one of the chimneys. Maybe it was mice. I kept forgetting to call Nell to come check whenever she had a chance. Nell Brenner, the police chief's daughter, was an excellent handywoman. She'd been able to get most of the house in great shape, but Nell was in demand, and we often couldn't afford her. Things were looking up financially. Jerry's job at Deely's, plus his time at Camp Lakenwood would bring in needed cash.

I pulled out my laptop and set it between my breakfast and my coffee. I looked up the online *Celosia News* to see if there were any further developments in the vineyard case. The victim had yet to be identified, I learned, and found several close-up photographs of the signs and symbols found on the man's body.

Besides the expected crescent moons, stars, and pentagrams, was a straight line with a U and an upside down U intersecting the line. I searched the Internet for the U symbol and discovered it was a symbol for money. I also found out that the rose was a powerful Wicca symbol representing the female parts—"the sacred gateway where everything in the universe is born."

Like the two U's in the symbol for money, were all these witchy elements intersecting in Celosia? Did Celosia have its own branch of the Darkrose Coven? Maybe the mysterious Megan Underwood would know if I could find her. Maybe Annie would tell me the meaning of her rose tattoo. I called Deely's and found out Annie wasn't working the breakfast shift but would be in after lunch to help clean up. So, I decided to spend some time getting a little artwork done.

I'd converted Uncle Val's upstairs parlor into my art studio. Gone were the overstuffed and uncomfortable Victorian chairs, heavy gray draperies, and Uncle Val's collection of books on bats. I kept the marble-topped table and fancy rose glass lamp and the other books, leather-bound copies of the classics. The old draperies had given the parlor all the charm of a dungeon, and as soon as they were down, the room came to life with the perfect light for painting. After confronting the critic who had trashed my first show, I'd regained my confidence and my enjoyment in creating art, and painting was a nice balance to the intensity of my investigator job. My works in progress were propped along the walls—landscapes, abstracts, and portraits.

As soon as I was fully awake, I spent the morning working on my latest landscape before preparing for Amanda's guard duty. Thanks to Jerry's insistence—well, thanks to one of Jerry's tricks—and a successful showing at the Weyland Gallery in Parkland, I had several commissions, the landscape and two modern paintings for a client's mountain home. My best painting, *Blue Moon Garden*, was back in the Weyland for an exhibition of impressionistic flower paintings, and the curator reported that prints of my work were selling well. I had also been commissioned to paint a portrait of a friend's young daughter. The three photographs he'd given me to work from were on my desk. One showed the little girl in her Sunday best. One showed her having a tea party with her dolls. One showed her smiling up at her mother. She was a sweet-faced child with blond pigtails. She'd be a joy to paint.

Water, leaves, and trees grew beneath my brush as I spread colors across the canvas. I even added a little brown sparkle to the leaves in honor of Amanda's missing Louis Vuitton. Subtle sparkles, of course.

Amanda's purse. I really hadn't been looking very hard for it. Okay, to be honest, I hadn't been looking at all. It was difficult to take Amanda seriously as a client. No doubt she had lots of expensive pocketbooks.

Come on, Madeline, be professional, I told myself. Find the purse. Play security guard. But first, I had my doctor's appointment, and after the garden party, I would have a talk with Annie.

Dr. Kathleen Wallace was a petite woman with short brown hair and a cheerful disposition. I always enjoyed talking with her, despite her less-than-cheerful diagnosis.

She finished her examination, I put my clothes back on, and we sat down in her office. Kathleen fixed me with her most earnest expression. "Madeline, I see no reason why you can't get pregnant, but sometimes we have to leave these things to Mother Nature."

"I know. I like to plan, and having this major event in my life up in the air is driving me crazy."

"You'll have plenty of time to set up your nursery. Nine months, to be exact." She paused and toyed with her pen, as if pondering what to say. I thought there was something unpleasant and baby-related she was reluctant to tell me, but her next words surprised me. "I should probably make an appointment to come see you, Madeline."

"What can I do to help?"

"I hesitate to even mention it. It's a little ridiculous."

"Believe me, I've dealt with some very ridiculous cases."

"And you've handled some very sensitive matters in town, too." She reached into her desk drawer and took out an envelope. "This is both."

She slid the envelope across to me. I opened it and took out two photos. One showed a younger Kathleen in shorts and a skimpy tank top chugging a glass of beer almost as big as she was. The second photo showed her dressed in a robe and standing in the middle of a pentagram, surrounded by candles.

More witches? "Do you know who sent these? Is someone blackmailing you, Kathleen?"

"Not exactly."

"Were these on Facebook?"

"Thank God, no. One of my sorority sisters took these."

"Some kind of initiation?"

"No. The one with the beer is the ridiculous picture. I can deal with that. But the other one, not so much."

"Doesn't look good."

"Oh, it's not Satanism. I was interested in all kinds of alternative medicines, natural healing, the wiccan lifestyle."

"But to someone looking at this picture, the pentagram might say witchcraft."

"Foolish, I'll admit."

"You weren't part of the Darkrose Coven, were you?"

"No, no, it wasn't any kind of coven."

It would have been an amazing and convenient coincidence. "You said not exactly blackmailing you. Is it the sorority sister? What does she want? Are there more copies of these pictures?"

"I'm sure there are copies, and I need you to get them before she posts them all over the Web."

I considered her problem. "You know what your best course of action is. You post the pictures. Make a joke out of it before she does. Say it was for a bet, or a Halloween party. Everyone does stupid things. If you're upfront and admit it, people will understand and forgive you."

She looked doubtful. "I don't know, Madeline. How would you feel if awful pictures of you appeared on the Internet?"

"You don't know about my pageant past, do you? I can show you hundreds of ridiculous photos of me in my Little Miss getups, and there's a really embarrassing video of the time my violin string broke in the middle of the talent competition and smacked me in the nose."

She managed a slight smile. "Yes, but that's a beauty pageant. Forgive me for saying so, but that doesn't have the same impact on a career. I can't make a joke out of these pictures. I just can't."

"What do you think this sorority sister of yours wants to accomplish by sending you these pictures?"

"I don't know. We haven't spoken in years. I don't know what she wants, or why she decided now is the time to harass me."

"Have you considered contacting her?"

"And end up begging and pleading? No, thank you. I'd prefer it to be handled by a professional."

"All right. Give me this woman's name and address, and I'll see what I can do."

Kathleen wrote down the information on a piece of paper and handed it to me. I almost dropped the note. "Your sorority sister is Olivia Decker?"

"What's wrong?" Kathleen asked. "Do you know her?"

"Oh, I know her." I couldn't believe it. "She almost married Jerry." Olivia Decker, a hard-as-polished-nails blonde who wanted to run every aspect of Jerry's life, the tough little gold digger who almost turned the Eberlin house into a B&B. This sounded exactly like something she would do.

"Is it going to be a problem, Madeline?"

I looked at Kathleen's worried face. I would not mind going a few more rounds with Olivia, especially if I could foil another of her schemes. "A problem? Oh, no, not at all."

Chapter Four

At one-thirty, I cleaned up and put on my fanciest cocktail dress, a little number in red lace and a skirt layered in overlapping panels that hugged my figure and showed off my legs. Gold metallic high heels completed the outfit. I rarely wore much makeup, but for today, I made sure it was perfect. I added a pair of small gold-and-diamond hoop earrings and a gold bracelet. I was ready to blend in.

Amanda had divorced her husband, and apparently she got everything. Her house on Sunnyside Lane was a huge Colonial-style home with a landscaped yard and a four-car garage. The party was in the backyard on a wide gray stone terrace overlooking tennis courts and a swimming pool. The terrace could've easily been a centennial park. A fountain sparkled in one corner, surrounded by massive white and green ceramic flower pots filled with decorative ferns. In another corner near a rose garden was a large table with a lacy white cloth; a silver centerpiece filled with pink and red roses; silver platters piled high with little sandwiches, cookies and cakes; and a crystal punchbowl with heart-shaped ice cubes floating in pink punch.

My appearance caused quite a stir. Everyone in town was used to seeing me in casual clothes, even jeans and tee-shirts as I went around investigating. There hadn't been an occasion for me to go all out, and from the looks I was getting, I'd surprised the crowd. I resisted the urge to give them a pageant wave. I really hadn't paid much attention to the Improvement Society, figuring it was like the Garden Club or the Art Guild, so I expected to see older women in the Society, but, oddly enough, there were two women my age and two in their teens.

"Madeline, so glad you could come!" Amanda made a big show of greeting me and showing me around. She introduced me to her guests, most of whom I knew, including Constance Tate, her second-in-command. Constance was a tall aristocratic-looking woman with short silvery hair and pale blue eyes.

She gave me an approving glance. "You look wonderful, Madeline. I didn't know you were interested in joining the Society."

"I'm thinking about it."

"What do you think of our latest project?"

"It's very ambitious. Do you have an idea how to finance it?"

Before Constance could answer, Amanda moved me along to the next two women. "This is Eloise Michaels, and I want you to be sure to meet Gloria Goins." Her underlying tone said, "Keep an eye on these two."

After meeting the rest of the group, I worked my way around to the teens. They looked up from their cell phones and introduced themselves as Britney Garrett and Clover Comer. Clover. Now there was a name I'd have to tell Jerry. Britney's long dark hair was streaked with light lavender strands. She wore a sleeveless white-lace top and a very short white skirt. Clover was blond, dressed in another tiny white skirt with a blue top with a design of butterflies. Both girls had on gold bangles and many earrings. They admired my dress.

"Where did you find it?" Clover asked.

"This is leftover from my pageant days."

"You look great." Britney pointed to my shoes. "Those are fabulous. And I love your eye shadow. Is it Plum Perfect?"

"Smoky Plum."

"It's amazing."

"Thanks. It's nice to see younger people interested in the Improvement Society."

"Yeah, well, it sounded cool."

I did not for a minute believe that these young ladies were in any way interested in being a part of this group, and as we chatted on about fashion, I became convinced they were here because someone made them come. Then the breeze lifted Britney's long hair, and when she brushed it out of her face, I saw the black rose tattoo on her wrist.

"That's a nice tattoo."

She gave it a glance and shrugged. "It's okay."

"Annie who works at Deely's has one just like it."

"Lots of people do. It's kind of a thing right now."

The siren call of their phones pulled them back into the Internet, and I continued my round of the terrace. No one took anything, although Eloise did give the silver centerpiece longing looks. Checking out the guests, I realized the older women were among the wealthiest in town, and when the discussion turned to *Flower of the South* and what it would cost to pay for the production it occurred to me that this party was a fundraiser for the outdoor drama.

It must have occurred to Harold Stover, too, because halfway through the party, he showed up uninvited.

Amanda met him as he crossed the terrace to confront her, a little half-smile hinting she was ready for battle. "Well, what a nice surprise. Care for some tea, Harold?"

Harold got right to the point. "I know what's going here, and I've come to put a stop to it."

She gestured with her glass of punch to the groups of women who had stopped talking and nibbling cakes to observe the impending fireworks. "You're against garden parties now?"

Harold had obviously been doing more research into the matter. He waved a piece of paper in her face. "You cannot have an outdoor drama on city property unless you have all the proper permits and a majority of votes from the commissioners."

"Nonsense! We're merely a group of private citizens who want to put on a show. There's no law against that. And who says we're going to have it on city property?"

Harold was dangerously red in the face. "There is no money in our budget for this!"

"It's not going to cost the city anything."

"Are you going to pay for the lights? Garbage pickup? Parking? Seats? Concessions? Programs and posters and advertising? If your drama is on city property, you're responsible for these things and more."

"And what if it isn't? We could have it in a field somewhere, or in someone's backyard."

"There's still the issue of crowd control, insurance, emergency vehicles if someone gets sick, or a fire breaks out."

She waved him away. "Details, details."

"This is your last warning!"

"Would you care for some punch?"

"Don't fight me on this, Amanda!" He threw the papers down and stalked off. He looked so angry, I wasn't sure he should get behind the wheel, so I followed him to his car where he turned on me. "I thought you were going to do something!"

He'd been angry at my office and at the theater, but this was approaching unreasonable. "You'd better calm down, or you're going to have a stroke. Amanda's baiting you, can't you tell?"

"I'm so mad at her, I could—" He brought his hands up as if gripping Amanda's neck. "She doesn't have one shred of business sense!"

"Why don't you wait and see how this turns out? Right now, you're the only one so dead-set against the idea. If enough people in Celosia want an outdoor drama, they'll find a way to finance it."

He jerked a thumb toward the party. "Like all those rich biddies in there."

"It ultimately helps the town, doesn't it?"

He'd cooled down a little. "I suppose."

"Why don't I call you after the party and let you know what they decided?"

"I'd appreciate that, thank you." He glared at the house. "One of these days, I'm going to kill Amanda."

"Not the smartest thing to say, Harold."

This brought a slight grin. "Not to you, anyway."

He drove off, and I went back to the party.

"Such a wet blanket," was Amanda's comment.

"He's concerned about Celosia." I didn't expect her to under-stand Harold's point of view, and she didn't.

She shrugged. "If he were truly concerned, he'd be behind this project instead of trying to derail it."

"Have you actually thought through all the details?"

"I've got members of the Improvement Society working on everything. We're planning a full presentation at the next town council meeting."

"Why didn't you tell Harold that?"

"Did he look like he would listen to anything I said? Or believe anything I said?"

I had to admit he didn't, and he didn't sound as if he believed me, either, when I called him after the party.

"She's up to something, Madeline. I don't trust her one inch."

"If you can hold on until the next town council meeting, Amanda plans to give a full presentation."

"So she intends to bulldoze over any objections, as usual." He gave an exasperated sigh. "Sorry to sound so cranky, Madeline, but I'm under a lot of stress lately. I've got business deals to tend to, and I guess I'm projecting a lot of my own financial concerns onto this outdoor drama."

"Would an outdoor drama be that bad for Celosia?"

"It's ridiculous. We have, what, seven thousand people here? Closer to ten, if you count the surrounding communities. But that's still not enough to support an outdoor drama. It would be a huge commitment."

"It might pay off, though. Increased tourist trade, maybe new businesses selling souvenirs."

"Like Emmaline Ross bobbleheads? I know the kind of things Amanda is capable of. This business with Roger Price, for instance. He was a fool to marry her. She almost took him for everything he had until he finally caught on and got out. If

I hadn't helped him, he'd be sitting on the street corner selling pencils."

Maybe this was the underlying source of the Amanda/Harold feud. "What did Amanda think about you helping her ex?"

"Oh, she wasn't happy, but I wasn't going to let a friend of mine go under. And I'm not going to let Celosia go under, either. Didn't I hire you to stop her?"

"Not exactly."

"Name your price."

"Harold, I want you to relax."

"I'll relax when that woman is out of my life." He hung up.

The party finished around four o'clock with an announcement from Amanda that auditions were at the theater tonight.

"In case you were wondering, I have permission," she told me. "I went by the municipal building this morning. You know, the mayor is so excited about being in the play. Everyone is, except old Stick-in-the-Mud Stover. I hope we'll see you and Jerry there."

I assured her we wouldn't miss it.

When I stopped by Deely's, Annie was sitting at one of the booths, refilling the ketchup bottles.

"Wow, look at you," she said. "What's the occasion?"

"Amanda Price's garden party. Security detail."

She grinned. "That outfit doesn't work as well for an undercover job, and I don't think you could chase bad guys in those heels."

"Fortunately, no one ran off with the silver."

"What can I get for you?"

I sat down across from her. "I need a little information. Do you know Britney Garrett or Clover Comer?"

She took a napkin and wiped a blob of ketchup that had escaped. "Oh, yeah, I know them. We all graduate this year."

"They don't seem to be the kind of girls who'd be interested in the Improvement Society."

"Yeah, they said they wanted to do something for the town. I think Britney's aunt is in it."

"Britney has a rose tattoo like yours."

Annie kept her eyes on the ketchup bottles. "Uh-huh. Lots of the girls got one."

"Lots? How many would you say?"

"I don't know."

"May I see yours?"

She turned her wrist. The black rose looked very much like the rose I'd seen on the Wicca symbols site.

"What's the deal, Madeline? Are you thinking of getting one?"

"Have you ever heard of Darkrose Coven?"

"No. Why?"

She'd answered very quickly. "There may be a connection to the body found at Phoenix Vineyard."

"You think I'd have something to do with a thing like that?"

"No, of course not. But I think someone in the coven might."

Annie remained defensive. "I know you're always snooping around for clues, and you've solved murders here in town, but there's no coven, okay? We like this rose design, that's all there is to it."

"Who's 'we'?"

She sighed as if I'd asked her the world's toughest question. "Me, Britney, Clover, and about three other girls. You want their names and addresses? They'll all tell you the same thing."

"Yes, please."

She pulled her pad from her apron pocket, tore off a piece of paper, and began to write. Harold Stover came in the diner, saw me, and interrupted.

"Excuse me, Annie. I need to talk to Madeline."

"No problem." She moved to the counter where she continued to write, her body language suggesting this was an arduous task and I'd better be grateful.

Harold took her place in the booth. "I want to apologize. My temper got the best of me, and I want you to know that's not how I am."

"It's okay, Harold. Amanda brings out the worst in everyone."

"I don't know why I let her get to me. Even if she had the money, there's no way she can get this project of hers off the ground. Another show about our pioneer ancestors? It's dull and pointless. I think she has another motive, and that's what I'd like for you to find out."

I did have a hard time imaging how such a socialite as Amanda would find a tiny historical event intriguing, or why she'd want to spend her time and money on such a project. "I can do that."

"Thank you."

Calm, reasonable Harold was smiling and pleasant. It occurred to me I didn't know what he did besides sit on the city council. He'd said he was under stress with business deals and had financial concerns. "What line of business are you in, Harold?"

"I run several nonprofit organizations, mainly for the preservation of endangered animals, as well as animal rescue." He brought out his wallet and handed me a few brightly colored cards that said Pandas, Incorporated; Rustling Waters Fish and Bird Sanctuary; Peregrine Falcon Rescue and Rehabilitation; and Parkland Cat Shelter. "Those are the main ones. I have a few smaller organizations I run, as well. As you can imagine, we always need contributions. Things have gotten a little tight lately. I guess when I see someone like Amanda throwing her wealth around on a silly outdoor drama when she could be using her money for something useful, I get a bit annoyed."

"She has a right to spend her money as she likes."

"I know. I need to sit back and take a deep breath. Several deep breaths."

Annie brought her completed list to me and plopped it on the table. "Here."

"Thank you."

"Bring us a couple of Cokes, would you, please, Annie?" Harold asked. As she stalked off, he said, "Is she having a bad day, too?"

I glanced at the list. "She thinks I accused her of a crime. I only asked a question."

"A crime?"

"Have you ever heard of the Darkrose Coven?"

"Darkrose Coven. Now there's a name I haven't heard in a long time."

"You know something about it?"

"Oh, years ago some girls were out in the woods playing like they were witches and everyone got upset. They called themselves a coven, but they were only harmless."

"Are you sure about that?"

"I thought they were harmless, but other people accused them of holding Satanic rites, killing animals and possibly worse, but nothing was ever proven. You know if an animal had been harmed, I would've known about it."

Possibly worse. Maybe founding members of the coven were still at large. "Who could I talk to about this?"

"Lauren Garrett would know. She was a free spirit if there ever was one. Not so much now. She's an associate pastor at the Methodist church."

"Does she have a daughter named Britney?"

"Yes. A very pretty young woman."

With a black rose tattoo. "Thanks, Harold."

Annie brought our Cokes, put them down, and walked away. I'd have to leave her a big tip.

"Why the interest in Darkrose Coven?" Harold asked. "I thought Jerry had given up all that kind of stuff."

"There may be a connection to the man who was found at Phoenix Vineyards."

"Oh, are you on that case?"

"No, but I can help you with Amanda."

Again, a big, relieved smile transformed his face. "Any help will be appreciated."

Chapter Five

I stopped by the Celosia Methodist Church office and asked the secretary if Lauren Garrett was in. I was directed to another office down the hall and greeted by Lauren, an older, shorter version of Britney. She had the same pretty features and long dark hair. Her desk was situated in front of a stained-glass window, so she was framed by a Technicolor scene of Jesus carrying a lamb. Not exactly your standard evil coven shot.

"Hello, come in. It's Mrs. Fairweather, isn't it? Or do you prefer Maclin?"

"Either one's fine," I said. "But please call me Madeline. Would you have a few minutes? It's about Darkrose Coven."

She made a comical face of mock distress. "Better shut the door."

I did, and she motioned me to a chair. "That bad, huh?"

"My past comes back to haunt me," she said with a chuckle. "No, just some extreme silliness. How in the world did you hear about it?"

"The paper mentioned it in connection with the vineyard murder."

"Oh, that's right. I did read that. Are you involved with the case?"

"Indirectly."

"Well, it has to be another Darkrose. We gave up that nonsense years ago." She sat back in her chair. "You know how you do stupid things when you're a kid, play with Ouija Boards, try to mix up love potions, pretend you can make things happen. That's all it was."

I'd spent most of my childhood pretending to be a perfect little doll, so I sort of understood.

"The farmer whose field we were playing in took offense, so we moved to the woods near Peaceful Meadow. Nothing ever happened."

Peaceful Meadow sounded more like a picnic spot. "No animal sacrifices? No calling up spirits?"

"We found a dead deer once and performed an elaborate burial service. If anyone saw us, I'm sure they misinterpreted the whole thing."

"So your congregations wouldn't be shocked if they knew you were once a member?"

"Maybe some of the older folks would be uncomfortable, but as you can see, I've seen the light." She grinned and gestured to the Bibles crowding her bookshelves, the crosses on the walls, and the statue of Jesus on a table by the door. "Completely reformed."

"Does Britney know?"

"Oh, yes. If you try to keep secrets from your kids, they find out anyway. Might as well be up front with them to begin with."

Lauren Garrett sounded like a sane and reasonable mother, but I was curious about something else. "I was a little surprised to see Britney and her friend Clover at Amanda Price's garden party. It's great that they want to take part, but I didn't think girls her age would be interested in the Women's Improvement Society."

"I didn't, either. Her Aunt Eloise had invited her several times, and she always refused, but then Amanda came by one day and invited her personally, and she said yes."

"Was Clover personally invited, too?"

"I believe she was."

Why would Amanda want teens in her group, and why specifically these two young women? "It's nice to have a little diversity in any group. Are there any other members of the original Darkrose Coven still in Celosia?"

"I don't think so. Most of them wanted to get out of Celosia as soon as they could." Again she gestured around her church office. "I defected to the Other Side."

I gave her one of my cards. "If you think of anyone, please give me a call."

She agreed, we shook hands, and I was in the parking lot unlocking my car when a white convertible screeched to a halt beside me and Britney Garrett jumped out, her face twisted in anger.

"How dare you rat on me! You told my mother about my tattoo, didn't you? You should mind your own business!"

Whoa, what a reaction. "Hold on. Yes, I came to talk to your mother, but no, I did not come to tell her about your tattoo."

She tried to calm down. "You better not have."

"Would she be that mad about it?"

"She said I couldn't have one."

"I won't tell her."

Britney took a few steadying breaths. Tears trembled on her eyelashes. "Sorry, Madeline. I saw your car, and we'd just talked at Amanda's, and I didn't know why else you'd be here."

"That's okay. My mom was very strict, too." If Lauren had once been part of a Junior Witches Club, I didn't see the problem with her daughter having a flower tattoo, but then, I wasn't a mom or a pastor, at that. "I came to see your mother about something else. She said Amanda herself invited you to join the Improvement Society."

"She did."

"And your Aunt Eloise is Eloise Michaels?" Coveter of the silver centerpiece?

"That's right."

"Amanda must have had a convincing argument."

Britney looked uncomfortable. "I guess." Her cell phone jangled with the sounds of a current pop tune. "Excuse me."

She walked off, phone to her ear. I got in my car. What had Amanda said to Britney to get her to join the Improvement Society? I'll tell your mother you have a tattoo? Judging from

Britney's reaction, I'd say that was a possible answer. And why would Amanda care, unless there was more significance to the black rose than I'd discovered?

◇◇◇

Before heading for home, I stopped off at Georgia's Books and bought a paperback copy of *Pagan Desires*. According to the description on the back cover, a group of daring young girls, led by flame-haired Lissa, formed a coven called Darkrose to protect themselves from evil forces and to meet hot young angel boys, two of whom became rivals for Lissa's attention. The book appeared to be standard young adult fiction popular today. Vampires and zombies were still going strong. Why not add a few angels? But this series was not around during the original Darkrose days. The name of the coven must be a coincidence.

Something else puzzled me, though. If Lauren Garrett had been a member of the first Darkrose Coven, wouldn't she have a black rose tattoo? Or was that something only the new members had?

Georgia's Books also had today's *Celosia News*. Hoping to find something about the body in the vineyard, I bought a copy. On page two, I read that the body had been identified as Eric Levin, age twenty-six, of Copeley. He had died from a combination of stab wounds and poison. The investigation was ongoing. Still no explanation why witchcraft symbols had been left on the body.

I got home around five-thirty, just as Jerry got back from camp. Nathan drove up behind the Jeep in his green SUV. Both men got out, Nathan slamming his car door with more force than necessary.

"Everything ready for the camp's open house?" I asked Jerry.

"Ready as we can be," he said, "but Nathan's about to pop."

Nathan's reddish hair was on end, and his little round glasses were steamed over. Nathan usually reminded me of one of my history professors—neat, tidy, and put together—but today, in his camp shorts and tee-shirt, he looked like a frazzled Boy Scout leader who had lost his troop. "Madeline, I need to talk to you. Amanda Price is still pestering me about using the far side of the camp for her outdoor drama. Does that woman not know how to take no for an answer?"

"I don't think she does."

"I don't need that kind of stress right now."

I invited him up on the porch. "Come sit down. You look like you could use some tea."

"I sure could."

Nathan and Jerry sat down in the rocking chairs. I got everyone a glass of tea and took another rocker. "Has she been calling you?"

"Worse than that. She came to the camp. She charged in around four-thirty, wouldn't you say, Jerry?"

"She must've rushed over right after her party. She cornered Nathan and wouldn't let up."

Nathan's face was still red. He took off his glasses and wiped them on his tee-shirt. "I swear, I don't often lose my temper, but something has to be done about that woman." He settled the glasses back on his nose. "She hasn't one bit of proof that Emmaline Ross or anyone, for that matter, ever lived on that piece of land."

"What exactly does she want to do?" I asked.

He took a large swig of tea in an attempt to calm down. "She wants to build an amphitheater on that land, bring people in from Celosia in covered wagons, and ferry them across the lake. Talk about an insurance nightmare! And who in the world wants to ride ten miles in a covered wagon?"

Jerry put his feet up on the porch railing. "Amanda said it would be a total frontier experience."

"It would be an experience, all right! I told her I owned that land, and she could not do anything to it. She replied that the amphitheater would bring hundreds more people to the camp and make it a huge success. She had the nerve to say I would be allowed to put on camp productions there. Thank you very much, Amanda!" He took another gulp of tea, choked, and sputtered as Jerry patted him on the back. "It's like talking to a wall!"

I rescued Nathan's tea glass before he dropped it. "I'll talk to her. You know if she refuses to leave you alone, you can have her arrested for trespassing."

"I certainly will. I told Jerry I finally understand what it's like to want to kill somebody."

"You'll have to get in line."

Jerry steered the conversation back to Camp Lakenwood and Nathan's plans for the open house celebrations. Once we felt Nathan had calmed down, we let him drive home.

I settled back into my rocking chair. "That's the second person who's wished Amanda dead today."

Jerry sat on the porch rail. "He tried his best to be polite to her."

"I'm sure he did. Poor Nathan. But she can't build anything on his land without his permission."

"So who was the first to wish her dead?"

"Harold, of course. He crashed the garden party, correctly suspecting that it was a fundraiser for the outdoor drama."

"Well, it would be quite an undertaking for Celosia."

"And as we've seen many times in the past, a wonderful opportunity for people to take sides and squawk."

A thundering noise echoed across the front meadow, and Austin came roaring up on his four-wheeler with Denisha following on her bike.

"It's fixed!" Austin announced. "Want to try it?"

Of course Jerry wanted to try it. I stood on the porch with Denisha, my phone ready, my finger poised to hit nine-one-one, while Jerry sped off across the meadow. He and Austin took turns until Denisha reminded them they were tearing up the yard.

"You're right," Jerry told her. "We'll take it to the track next time."

Austin took off his helmet and brushed his hair back into its little spikes. "Whew! You got any Coke or anything, Madeline?"

He followed me into the kitchen to wash his hands and to scope out any snacks. I gave him a Coke and another to give to Denisha. On the way back to the porch, he spotted Jerry's *Hansel and Gretel* CD.

"There's an opera about that?"

"Yes, and wait till you hear the composer's name. Engelbert Humperdinck."

Austin burst out laughing. "You made that up!"

"No, it's true."

"Humperdinck!"

"Turn it on," Jerry called from the porch.

Austin especially enjoyed "The Witches' Ride," and Denisha liked "The Children's Prayer." She called it "The Angel Song." I'd forgotten how beautiful the melody was.

When at night I go to sleep,
Fourteen angels watch do keep.

Denisha listened closer as Hansel and Gretel continued their duet. "That boy's voice is really high."

Jerry let her in on the secret. "Actually, it's a girl."

"A girl plays Hansel?"

"And a man plays the witch. In this production, anyway. Also, a woman plays the Sandman."

The little beads in Denisha's hair clicked as she shook her head. "Opera's crazy."

Austin's mother called, looking for him. He and Denisha thanked us for the Cokes and rode away.

I turned to Jerry. "Now for the big news of the day."

"Bigger than the outdoor drama? Bigger than a new four-wheeler?"

"Olivia Decker."

"Eek. What about her?"

"I went to see Dr. Wallace, as scheduled. Everything's fine, by the way. We're still in a holding pattern. Kathleen has a problem, though, and hired me. Seems unflattering pictures have surfaced, thanks to an old sorority sister. Kathleen wants me to retrieve the extra copies before they go viral. Guess who has them?"

"Olivia. What evil plan is she cooking up now?"

"That's what I get to find out."

"Well, give her my love and a big sloppy kiss."

"Sure thing. It'll go right along with *Pagan Desires*."

"Now that sounds intriguing."

I showed him the copy of the book, and explained about my visit to Lauren Garrett, former member of the original Darkrose Coven, and how Britney Garrett had freaked out when she thought I'd told her mother about her tattoo.

Jerry was pleased by the news of a local coven. "So there used to be a group of witches here, and it may be starting up again. You get a black rose tattoo and you're in."

I took out the list Annie had made for me. "Here are the names of the girls who have the same tattoo. It may be only a fad, as Annie said, or it may be something more sinister."

As if on cue, the music changed to a deep foreboding tune. "What's the plan?" Jerry asked.

"I'll start with the names on this list. Maybe some of these girls will be at tryouts tonight. Annie was planning to audition. And here's the latest news about the man found in the vineyard."

I handed him the newspaper and he read the article. He raised his eyebrows. "Poison? That sounds witchy."

"Let me see if the online report has anything new."

The report had the latest findings on the case, which included the origin of the poison, which was, surprisingly, rhododendron.

Jerry looked even more surprised. "Rhododendron? We've got those growing around the side of the house. I didn't know they were poisonous."

The large bushes with their purple blossoms were everywhere in Celosia. "Let me Google it."

Sure enough, along with azaleas, oleander, and mountain laurel, all parts of the rhododendron bush are poisonous with such horrible effects as paralysis, seizures, and coma. Even sucking nectar from the blossoms or eating honey from bees that had frequented the bushes could cause a life-threatening reaction.

"Jerry, this is a poison anyone could get his hands on."

"Anyone who knows his deadly plants, and that sounds even more witchy."

I remembered I hadn't told him about the meaning of the symbols found on Levin's body. "Speaking of witchy, I looked up the witchcraft symbols. The U's intersecting on a line stand for money."

"Money. There's a crime right there. Maybe someone in Copeley would know. Where is Copeley, anyway?"

Back to the Internet. A few clicks and I had my answer. "It's about an hour from here."

Jerry folded the newspaper and handed it back to me. "These road trips are piling up, Mac."

"We'll get to Parkland, I promise. Let me see if Eric Levin had a Facebook page."

Eric's page was filled with pictures of Eric. Eric on a motorcycle, Eric on a jet ski, Eric on a surfboard, looking tough and surly, many shirtless selfies, revealing a muscled physique, and pictures of Eric with his arm around a succession of young women. "He didn't have a problem with self-esteem." I read a few of his posts. "Oh, and he likes to brag about how many women he's dated. He even has a rating system. Amber gets four stars, lucky girl."

"Sounds like a charming fellow."

"What would you say the chances are one of these lovely scantily clad ladies didn't approve of her rating?" I read on until I was disgusted with Eric's vanity. But being conceited wasn't a crime. He didn't deserve to die.

Chapter Six

With *Hansel and Gretel* still sounding forth, Jerry and I had dinner and then went back into town to check out the auditions for *Flower of the South*. Jerry wore a green tie decorated with goofy-looking grinning daisies. Over the next hour and a half, with Harold Stover fuming at the back of the theater, Amanda and two members of the Women's Improvement Society listened to songs and dramatic recitations and conferred in excited whispers. Jerry and I sat in the middle of the auditorium with Evan, whose handkerchief was worn to threads as the tryouts continued.

"Madeline, I had no idea this wasn't the committee's plan. Amanda asked if she could use the theater this evening, and I said yes. I never wanted to get in the middle of a controversy. Has she thought about costumes or props or sets? Where is she going to have this drama? We don't have an outdoor venue unless you count the band shell, and it's not very big."

A woman sitting in front of us turned around. "I heard we're using the old drive-in."

This made Evan sit forward. "The Night Owl? She can't use that. It's been sold."

The woman's friend turned to join the conversation. "I heard the city's building an amphitheater."

The distress was piling on for poor Evan. "Where did you hear that? We don't have the money for that sort of project!"

I thought I'd better say something before Evan dissolved.

"Amanda likes to talk big, remember? I'm sure things will work out."

Then the two women gasped, and one pointed to another woman walking down the aisle. "Is that who I think it is? What's she doing here?"

"What's going on?" I asked them.

"That's Megan Underwood."

Jerry poked me. "Austin's witch."

"Why is everyone whispering?" I asked the women.

The first woman was reluctant to answer. "She's…different."

"Evan, do you know her?"

He gave the woman a glance and sighed as if the sight of her added to his troubles. "She's somewhat of a recluse and rarely comes into town. She lives out in the woods somewhere and raises herbs. I can't imagine why she's here."

Megan Underwood was a dreamy-eyed woman with long pale corkscrew curls decorated with beads and feathers. She wore an ankle-length multicolored skirt and an old-fashioned blouse with puffy sleeves. She carried an elaborately carved walking stick with a dragon's head, complete with jeweled eyes. Her appearance caused a hush in the auditorium. Amanda and her Society friends drew back.

She struck a pose. "I'm here to audition."

I'd never seen Amanda speechless. After a long moment, she regained her composure. "All right. Is there any particular role you're interested in?"

"The lead, of course."

This set her back for another moment. "What makes you think you're qualified?"

Megan Underwood made a large graceful gesture with the walking stick. "I am the reincarnated soul of Emmaline Ross."

Jerry leaned forward in his seat. "Let's see where she goes with this."

After Megan filled out the audition form, Amanda handed her the short speech she'd written. "Whenever you're ready." Her voice could not have been more discouraging.

Despite her strange appearance, Megan Underwood was a fine actress with a clear voice that carried to the back wall of the auditorium. She managed to convey all the pride and courage one would expect in a pioneer woman. When she finished, there was a flurry of whispering from the committee members, and then Amanda said, "Thank you."

Megan bowed and drifted out.

"Be right back," Jerry said. He got up and followed her.

"What is he doing?" Evan asked. "She won't talk to him. That's the first time I've ever heard her say anything."

I was pretty sure she'd talk to Jerry, especially if he introduced himself as a warlock, so I was surprised when he returned shaking his head. "Like any good witch, Megan disappeared."

"That fast? She must have kept her broomstick running."

Evan was still baffled. "Why on earth did she come to audition?"

"You heard her," Jerry said. "She's Emmaline Ross, reborn. She must tell her story to the world."

"She doesn't live in town. How did she hear about the play, though?"

"I guess the spirits told her."

Several more young women did their best, but no one came close to Megan's portrayal of Emmaline. I dared Jerry to try out. "You could be Emmaline's crusty but devoted father, or the villain who tries to ruin her crop."

"I'd rather be the guy who gets to sample all the wine."

Evan glanced up the aisle. "Oh, dear. As if this evening couldn't get any more dramatic."

I turned to see a large woman with a determined air coming down the aisle.

Evan lowered his voice. "That's Joanie Raines. She tries out for everything, and if she doesn't get in, she gets very upset. I think you can see why she isn't right for every part." He wiped his brow. "I can't tell you how many times I've had to deal with her. She's a nice woman, but, to be as tactful as possible, she doesn't always fit a director's vision. She didn't understand why she wasn't chosen for Dorothy in *Wizard of Oz*, or Laurie in *Oklahoma*, or Tinker Bell in *Peter Pan*."

"But she might be just right for a part in this show."

"She'll want the lead. She always does. The theater world is all about appearances. Unless Emmaline Ross was a large woman, I don't think Joanie has a chance." He wadded up his handkerchief. "I can't take any more of this tonight. Jerry, if you and Madeline are staying for the rest of the auditions, would you make sure all the doors are locked?"

"I'll take care of it," he said.

Evan thanked him and left. I turned my attention back to Joanie. She looked grim. "Pioneer women were big and strong, weren't they?"

Joanie read Emmaline's part very loudly with many expansive gestures. It wasn't what you'd want in the theater, but for an outdoor drama, it could work. She definitely wouldn't need a microphone. In the bright lights, she was a very attractive woman with round blue eyes and long brown hair tied back in a ponytail. She wore a bright pink shirt and dark jeans that enhanced her full figure.

Halfway through her audition, Amanda cut her off with a dismissive "Thank you." Joanie looked insulted, but gave a little bow and walked off the stage. As she steamed up the aisle past us, she stopped.

"You're Jerry Fairweather, right? The fellow who holds séances?"

Jerry had promised no more séances. "I'm sort of out of the business."

"What about voodoo? Are you any good at curses?"

"Not exactly my style."

"Too bad. I'd have a job for you."

Joanie's voice was causing people to turn around in their seats and stare.

Jerry motioned toward the lobby doors. "Why don't we talk outside?"

We stood on the front steps of the theater while Joanie unloaded all her grievances. "I know what Amanda Price is doing.

She's setting up all this so she can be the star. Never mind she's way too old to play Emmaline Ross. It's her game and we have to play by her rules."

"She might not get this play off the ground," I said. "There are a lot of things to consider."

Joanie made a sound like "Huh!" "You haven't lived here long enough to know that if Amanda wants something, she finds a way to make it happen."

"If you didn't think you stood a chance, why did you try out?"

"To show people what a real actress can do. I'm the best choice for Emmaline, and everyone knows it."

"What about Megan Underwood? She read very well."

Joanie's blue eyes went wide. "Megan Underwood was here? I don't believe it. She's totally undependable. Drifts in and out of town like an old plastic bag. If Celosia wants to have a successful outdoor drama, then I'm the only one who can deliver." She turned to Jerry. "No curses, you say? How about reading my palm? Can you do that?"

When she held out her hand, palm up, Jerry and I both saw the black rose tattoo on her wrist. It was faded, but it was very similar to Annie's and Britney's. We exchanged a quick glance that Joanie didn't see.

She pushed her hand forward. "Look at that lifeline. Don't tell me I'm not destined for great things."

"I'm sure you are."

"Well?" She wasn't going to leave until Jerry did something paranormal.

He took her hand, and gazed at it for few moments. "Your heart line is long and curvy which means you freely express your feelings and emotions. Your head line is curved which denotes creativity, your long lifeline reflects your vitality, and this fourth line is called a fate line. Not everyone has this. Yours is joined to your lifeline, showing you're a self-made individual."

Joanie nodded in satisfaction as he spoke. "That's remarkable, and it's all true. I'll be Emmaline Ross. I know I will."

"You've had a life surrounded by the supernatural. Even as a young woman, you were fearless, joining other women to get in touch with the spiritual world."

Joanie cocked her head, curious. "You see that?"

"The dark rose guides me."

She rubbed her wrist as if to erase the tattoo. "This old thing! It's nothing."

I decided to be direct. "Were you a member of the Darkrose Coven?"

For a moment, her considerable assertiveness was shaken. "Good lord, where did you hear about that? That's ancient history."

"What can you tell us about it?"

"There's nothing to tell. Kids playing games, that's all."

"You must have been more than kids to get tattoos."

"Okay, so maybe we were teenagers. Spur of the moment, we all decided to get a tattoo. My mother flipped out, I was grounded for a month, and that was the end of that."

"Could you tell us who else was in the group beside you and Lauren Garrett?"

"Why would you want to know that?"

"I'm just curious. The paper mentioned a Darkrose Coven."

"They meant the one in Parkland. Maybe you're too curious, Madeline."

Yep, I am. "Is there anyone in town who could tell me more?"

"No." Joanie seemed unnecessarily upset. "I don't see why you have to always be poking your nose where it doesn't belong. Did someone hire you to solve that man's murder, the one they found in the vineyard?"

"No, but I'd still like to find out who killed him."

"That's the police department's job. And as for what happened years ago, you don't have to know everything that goes on in Celosia. Did you ever stop to think it might not be any of your business? You're not even from here. Thanks for the reading, Jerry. I've got to go."

She made a grand exit, every inch stiff with disapproval. "Hit a nerve there," Jerry said.

"Joanie's the second person today to tell me to mind my own business. I'm beginning to think everybody in town has a black rose tattoo."

"And a secret to go with it."

"Another big secret is why Amanda continues to steamroll this outdoor drama idea and how she's going to pay for it."

"But my songs are great. You want them to go to waste?"

"Tell her you want payment up front and see what she says."

Back in the auditorium, tryouts had finished. Amanda stood and straightened the stack of audition forms. "That's all for tonight. Thank you, everyone. The cast list will be posted on Monday."

As people filed out of the auditorium, I expected another attack from Harold, but when I looked for him, I didn't see him. "Guess Harold had enough."

"He might be waiting outside in the bushes," Jerry said.

We came down the aisle to hear more intense whispers as Amanda and the Society members discussed Megan Underwood.

Amanda spoke in tones of disbelief. "The nerve of that woman! We can't have someone like that representing Emmaline. She's nothing more than a vagrant and a flaky one, at that."

Constance divided the audition forms into three stacks. "But she gave a very good reading."

Amanda wasn't having any of it. "You know we can't depend on her. What if she decides she can't perform on the night of the full moon, or some such nonsense? We have another whole night of tryouts, and there's bound to be someone perfect for the part." She turned to Jerry. "Jerry, I understand you've written a few songs for the play. We'll hear them in just a minute. We've got a show to cast." She took the first stack of audition forms and spread them on the table. "We have our work cut out for us. We really need an Emmaline."

I wanted to know more about Megan. "What about Megan Underwood? I thought she was great."

"She had a good audition, I agree, but she's so flighty, you never know if she'll show up."

"Joanie Raines was good, too," Jerry said.

"I'm thinking of Joanie as Emmaline's mother."

That would go over well. "She'd be a strong Emmaline," I said.

"Yes, but physically she doesn't fit the role. If we can't find someone, then I'll play Emmaline."

Exactly what Joanie had said.

"Now, we've got two people who would be perfect for Emmaline's father and grandfather, and the rest of these people can be farmers and settlers and members of the rival vineyard. What are your songs like, Jerry? I hope they're simple enough for everyone to learn in a short time. I want the show up and ready in four weeks."

Four weeks? Even I knew that wasn't possible.

Jerry went to the piano in the orchestra pit and played through his songs. I wasn't surprised that Amanda took them seriously.

"Excellent! Could you write a few more, one for the vineyard workers to sing and one for Emmaline's parents?"

"I can probably come up with something here in a few minutes."

I got Amanda's attention. "Nathan Fenton wanted me to remind you that you can't have your production anywhere on his land."

"I tried to explain things to him. He's missing a golden opportunity."

"He doesn't see it that way. If you insist on coming onto his property, he can have you arrested for trespassing."

This made her pause for only a moment. "I would prefer to have his cooperation. It's important that we have the show on or near the site of Emmaline's cabin."

"Do you know for certain where her cabin was?"

"Not exactly."

"Could someone from UNCP's history department find out for you? Seems to me that would be the answer."

"I suppose."

Jerry played a fanfare on the piano to announce the next songs. "This one's for the workers.

"We tireless band of laborers, who toil amongst the vines,
We work in sun and wind and rain, creating finest wines."

"That will do nicely," Amanda said.
"And Emmaline's mom and dad sing this:

"Our lovely daughter, Emmaline, we sing our pride for thee.
Following your path through scorn and doubt,
Tending the grapes through storm and drought,
Finding your place in history!"

"Splendid!" Amanda said, and the committee members clapped.

"I'll record everything and send you a copy," Jerry said. "But I'll need payment first."

This didn't faze her. "Of course. Write him a check, Constance."

Constance took out her checkbook. "We haven't completed the budget. Did you have a figure in mind?"

Amanda waved a hand. "Oh, five hundred should do it, I think."

"Five thousand," Jerry said. "That's for the songs. The orchestra arrangements will be more, of course, and I'm cutting you a really good deal because it's for Celosia."

I knew he'd named a ridiculously high amount to see how Amanda would react. Constance glanced at Amanda as if for permission. Amanda gave her a curt nod.

"I'll take half now, if that's easier," Jerry said.

Constance wrote the check, tore it out of her checkbook, and handed it to him.

"Thanks."

"No, thank *you*," Amanda said, overly sincere. "We'll expect those orchestrations within the week."

Jerry folded the check and put it in his pocket. "No problem."

No problem because he didn't intend to write orchestrations. Something very strange was going on here. "Amanda, I don't see how you can have this play ready in four weeks."

"Then what if I told you I had applied for a grant that will take care of all expenses?"

I wouldn't believe you. "That sounds wonderful, but you still can't have the show up and running in such a short time."

"Of course we can! Where's your pioneer spirit?"

Where's yours? I wanted to ask. What sort of game are you playing, and what are you planning to get out of it?

"Do you suppose Constance is underwriting the whole show?" I asked Jerry as we drove home. "I know she's wealthy, but this doesn't make sense."

"I'll bet you anything Amanda's got something on Constance."

"And on Britney and possibly Clover and the rest of the Society?" I hadn't seen either of the girls at auditions. I hadn't seen Annie, even though she'd seemed keen to try out for Emmaline.

"Maybe they're all witches, and Amanda saw them poison Eric Levin," Jerry said. "She videoed them all dancing naked in the forest and threatened to put it on YouTube."

"So she makes them put on an outdoor drama? Can you say 'farfetched'?"

"Okay, so she makes them do something else. I'll join the coven and find out."

I knew he wouldn't give up that idea. "Nice palm-reading, by the way. It sounded very authentic."

He grinned. "Got it off the Internet."

"It convinced Joanie, that's for sure. Tomorrow I suppose I'll go around town checking every woman's wrist for a black rose."

"I dare you to check Amanda's wrist. And tomorrow we go to Parkland. You owe me a night in a graveyard."

At home, we sat on the porch and listened to the cheeps of the insects and the warbling of little frogs from a nearby pond. The warm spring air smelled of honeysuckle and a slight hint of perfume from the roses we'd coaxed to grow up along the porch railing.

"Look at that beautiful view." Jerry spread his hands. "I can see Amanda setting up a big old amphitheater right there."

"Amanda's single-mindedness reminds me of my mother," I said. "She's determined to have her way, even if it flattens everyone in her path."

"She's certainly made a lot of enemies. Before this is over, I wouldn't be surprised if you were called in to solve her murder."

"I've thought about that, too."

"Let's see if murder's in your future." He reached over, took my hand, and turned it palm up. "Hmm, a nice long lifeline. Heart line just like Joanie's, long and curvy, so you freely express all those emotions. You've also got a fate line, and what's this I see? Little children frolicking in the meadow."

"That would be Austin and Denisha."

"And Hortensia."

Hortensia was the name Jerry had originally picked out for our phantom child. In the real world, we were considering Rose for a girl and Jackson for a boy, but that didn't stop him from finding more creative choices.

"Or how about Madeline, Junior? We could call her M.J. I like it."

My cell phone rang. "Hold that thought." I dug it out of my pocket and checked the caller ID. "You're not going to believe this. It's Chief Brenner."

"Uh, oh."

"Uh, oh, is right. Do you suppose Harold's made good on his threats?"

I braced myself to hear that Harold had strangled Amanda, so for a moment, I couldn't understand the frantic woman's voice.

"Madeline, you have to help me! Harold's dead, and the police think I killed him!"

In the background I heard Chief Brenner's voice. "Now, Amanda, calm down. We have to ask you some questions, that's all."

"You need to come right away! This is all a horrible mistake!"

"Let me talk to her," Chief Brenner said. Amanda began to cry, and the chief reclaimed his phone. "Madeline, Amanda insisted on calling you."

"What happened?"

"As you know, Harold and Amanda have been at odds over this outdoor drama Amanda cooked up. It's my understanding she came to his house to discuss the matter."

"He was dead when I got here!" Amanda wailed in the background.

"We haven't accused her of anything. We're trying to determine what happened."

"Madeline, help me!"

I couldn't ignore her plea. "Tell her I'm on my way." I ended the call. "Amanda went to Harold's house to talk about the drama and found him dead. She's asked for my help. The police have to question her, but it's possible Harold died of natural causes. He always looked as if he were about to have a heart attack."

Chapter Seven

"He was murdered." Chief Brenner met Jerry and me outside Harold's home on Park Street. The chief was a big man with close-cropped blond hair and sharp blue eyes. "A blow to the head. Looks like someone came in the back, and Harold must have confronted the intruder."

"So it couldn't have been Amanda," I said. "I can't imagine her doing anything so untidy."

"Unfortunately, we found her purse near the body."

"A beige purse with a brown handle and a sparkly design?"

"How did you know?"

"She hired me to find it. She said it was missing."

"Well, we found it. Right by Harold."

"You're sure it's Amanda's?"

"Had one of her credit cards in it."

My glance to Jerry said, This looks bad. "Where's Amanda now?"

"She's sitting on the porch with one of my officers who's trying to calm her down. You might have better luck."

Despite her trauma, Amanda managed to look perfectly put together. "Oh, Madeline, I am in such a state! I thought I'd stop by and explain everything to Harold, and now this awful thing has happened. Will you find out who killed him? It wasn't me, I swear. I know the police found my purse by Harold's body, but someone must have stolen one of my cards and planted it to frame me!"

"Who would do that?"

She paused, and I knew she was thinking practically everyone in town, including members of the Improvement Society who were jealous of her wealth or held grudges against her for her less-than-subtle methods of intimidation. Was this someone's twisted idea of revenge?

"You'll have to make me a list, Amanda."

"But murder Harold to get to me? That's crazy!"

"Tell me exactly what happened."

"After we finished at the theater, I decided to come over and talk to Harold and explain what the Improvement Society planned to do, down to the last little detail. I was even going to offer him a part in *Flower of the South*. I thought he'd be splendid as Emmaline's cranky grandfather. Don't you think so? Wait, what am I saying?"

"Focus, Amanda."

She took a deep shuddering breath. "I came by around ten o'clock. He didn't answer when I rang the bell. His door was unlocked, so I went in. He was lying on the floor in the hallway, and I could see a lot of blood, so of course, I completely freaked out. Then I was shaking so bad, I couldn't find my phone in my purse, so I used the phone in his kitchen to call nine-one-one."

"You didn't see anyone else in the house? Hear any noises?"

"I told you I freaked out. Any noises would have been me screaming. I couldn't stay in the house, so I ran out here until the police arrived."

"No! Did you notice your other purse?"

"I'm surprised I had sense enough to make a phone call." She reached over and grabbed my hand. "Please help me. You've solved other murders. You've got to solve this."

I untangled myself from her grasp. "I promise I'll help you. But you have to tell me the truth."

Chief Brenner came up the porch steps. "Amanda, you need to let Officer Lester take you to the station. I'll be along in a minute to get your statement."

She gulped. "All right. Madeline, I'll call you." The officer escorted Amanda to a patrol car.

"Could I have a look in the house?" I asked the chief.

"No."

"Have you found the murder weapon?"

"No, we're still searching."

"How about the purse? Anything in that?"

"Only her credit card."

"It's possible the murderer stole the purse and left it here."

"Anything's possible. You know that. Did she hire you?"

"Yes."

The chief's face was grim. "All right, Madeline, I'll be very plain with you. It ends here. You can talk to people in town, but you are not to interfere with the police in any other way." He gave Jerry an equally hard look. "No tricks. I know I've been lenient in the past, but not this time. Eric Levin, the man found in Phoenix Vineyard, was murdered, and now Harold is killed. Do you understand my position?"

"Yes, of course," I said.

"I realize we've shared information before. I also realize in some cases you've withheld information." I started to protest and he held up a hand. "To your credit, it's worked out. But I repeat, not this time."

"Amanda hired me, so I need to be able to investigate."

"As I said, you may ask questions. Keep away from any crime scenes."

"May I ask if Harold had any family?"

"He's got an aunt in Knoxville. We've already contacted her, and she's on her way. It will not be necessary for you to talk to her. Are we clear?"

"Clear."

Chief Brenner thanked me for my cooperation and stepped back into Harold's house.

"Well," I said, "that complicates things."

Jerry wasn't discouraged. "It just means we get creative. You know I can get you into Harold's house any time you like."

As I've mentioned, I'd relied on Jerry's lock-picking skills several times, but I had second thoughts. "I don't know. I've been warned off this case, but there's still the mystery of Darkrose Coven. What if I find a connection? Solving Levin's murder might lead to solving Harold's."

"You've been warned off that case, too."

"Chief Brenner said I could ask questions, right? Who knows more about what goes on in town than anyone?"

"Nell Brenner."

"Yes, and if she's a member of Darkrose Coven, then problem solved." I didn't really believe the chief's daughter was a member of the coven, but it was true she knew everyone and everything that had to do with Celosia. I had the perfect excuse to call her. "I want her to check on the chimney. Something's scratching around in there. Might be mice."

"Maybe it's bats." Jerry's Uncle Val had studied and filmed bats, and we often saw the little creatures flying around the house at twilight. "Mutant bats leftover from Val's secret experiments. That would be too cool."

"Whatever it is, it's our path to finding out what she knows about Darkrose Coven."

I called Nell and asked if she could come check on the chimney in the morning. She said she'd stop by. I spent time that night reading *Pagan Desires*, hoping to find a clue among all the angst and forbidden love. But all I could really think about was Harold and his animal charities. What would happen to them now? Had Harold made provision for them in his will? Did he even leave a will? Then I thought of Amanda and how I hadn't taken her seriously as a client. I had to take her seriously now. She was power-crazy and probably had a scheme going for who knows what reason, but was she a murderer? If she could use her wealth and clout with the members of the Improvement Society to walk all over Harold and his concerns, why murder him?

I felt the answer was tied to the Darkrose Coven, past and present. Death in a vineyard? An outdoor drama about a vineyard? Was that a coincidence? Annie, Britney, Clover, and three other girls had a dark rose tattoo, and so did Joanie Raines. I had to see if Lauren Garrett had one, if Megan Underwood had one, if Amanda had one. What about Kathleen Wallace? What about any one of a hundred women in town? Maybe every Celosian of a certain age had one. Then what? Having a black rose tattooed on your wrist didn't mean you were a murderer.

Saturday morning, Jerry and I were finishing breakfast on the porch when Nell Brenner arrived in her white van. She got out and opened the back of the van to get her toolbox. Like her father, Nell was big and blond. Her white overalls were clean but forever splattered with all colors of paint, and a sprig of blond ponytail poked out from her baseball cap.

She climbed up the porch steps.

"Morning. Time to see what's rustling around in your chimney."

"Thanks for coming today," I said.

"No problem."

"Before you get rid of our chimney invaders, I want to ask what you know about Darkrose Coven."

She set her toolbox down. "Now that's a touchy subject."

"What's the story?"

"Not much to do around here, especially for young people, unless they got a car and can go over to Parkland to the clubs. 'Bout twenty years ago, maybe twenty-five, bunch of gals got bored and decided they'd try calling up spirits. Like you did, Jerry, only they were serious about it. Decided to call themselves a coven, even though it was only four or five of them. Parents and churches got all upset, which, of course, made the girls even more determined to play witches. They'd been meeting out near the commune at Peaceful Meadow, but they retreated further into the woods before they finally quit."

Lauren Garrett had mentioned Peaceful Meadow. "There was a commune there?"

"Yeah, this being Celosia, not a very big one, and it didn't last long."

"Where is Peaceful Meadow?"

"Out past the Gatewood pasture on your way to the West-berry community."

"Is it close to the woods where the coven met?"

"Right next door to it. It butts up against the edge of Nathan's property."

So Emmaline Ross' phantom cabin wasn't the only thing that might be near Camp Lakenwood. "Lauren Garrett told me she was a member of this coven, but she said there was nothing to it, just some kids playing."

"She was more than a kid. Sixteen, maybe, twenty."

"And Joanie Raines got very defensive when I asked about her coven tattoo."

"I'm sure most of 'em would like to forget it, on account of the baby."

"Whoa, hang on, what baby?"

Nell took off her cap to tuck in a sprig of hair that had escaped. She put her cap back on. "That's the thing. One of those gals got herself in trouble and had a baby, but its body was never found. Now think about that for a minute."

Think about it. That's all I could do. A secret group meeting in the woods, pretending to be witches, and a missing baby? No matter how you looked at it, this was bad news. I found myself unable to talk, but Jerry asked the next question.

"How did anyone know about the baby?"

"One of the women broke down and told Dad. He and other officers went looking, but they never found a trace of it. Nobody in the coven ever told whose baby it was. They must have made a pact, because to this day, nobody knows."

"So the baby might have been Lauren's or Joanie's."

"Or Constance's."

"Constance?" I'm sure I sounded surprised. "Constance Tate?"

"Yeah, she was a little older than the others, but she was a member."

I took a few moments to process this information. If Constance had been a member of the Darkrose Coven and somehow

Amanda found out, was this the leverage Amanda needed to control Constance? If the missing baby had been Constance's child, and Amanda knew this, too, then Constance didn't have a chance. "Nell, Britney Garrett, Clover Comer, and Annie at Deely's all have black rose tattoos that are similar to the ones the original members of the Darkrose Coven have. Are they holding secret ceremonies in the woods, too?"

"I haven't heard of anything going on like that."

Were the girls just uberfans of the *Pagan Desires* series? Or was one of them secretly pregnant? I knew now why Joanie had been upset, but why had Lauren laughed the coven off as if it had been a merry prank from her past? I had a lot of people to talk to. "Does everyone in town know about this?"

"No," Nell said. "It was a huge embarrassment for all the families concerned. They managed to hush things up pretty well."

"But *you* know," Jerry said. "How do you get all your information, Nell?"

She indicated her toolbox. "I'm in and out of peoples' houses all day. After a while, no one notices me. Maybe I'm painting in the next room, or putting up new window screens, and they talk, and I can't help but hear what they say. Plus I was born in Celosia, went to school here. My dad's a policeman. He taught me to listen and not to blab about everything I hear."

"Speaking of your dad," I said, "he's warned me away from investigating Harold Stover's murder."

"Yeah, I know about that, too."

"I figured you did."

"He appreciates your help, but there's something different about this case. Harold was a good friend of his. He doesn't want anything to interfere with finding the killer."

Another reason the chief had looked so grim at the crime scene. "I had a chance to talk to Harold about his animal rescue work. I'm sorry I didn't get to know him better."

"He really worked hard raising money for those organizations. To have somebody like Amanda Price bullying people into giving her money for a vanity project really upset him."

She picked up her toolbox. "So to have him dead and Amanda still walking around doesn't make much sense, does it? Let me see what's made its home in your chimney."

She went into the house, and Jerry looked at me, his gray eyes dark with anger. "I hope to hell nothing evil happened to that baby."

I was trying not to think about the missing baby and what a group of desperate and delusional women might have done, but my emotion must have shown on my face, for Jerry caught me in a comforting embrace.

"I don't have to go to the camp's open house today."

"Yes, you do. Nathan's counting on you. I'll be okay. I need to talk to the other girls on Annie's list and have another talk with Lauren Garrett. I need to find out if any of Nell's information ties to Eric Levin's murder. Now more than ever, I want to solve this."

I wanted to solve everything.

Chapter Eight

During breakfast at Deely's, the diner was buzzing with the news of Harold's murder. I sat at the counter so I could watch Jerry scramble eggs and fry bacon for the customers crowding in for takeout orders. Everyone had a theory, including one involving a serial killer who had wandered over from Parkland. The Geezer Club gathered in their same corner booth and held forth that Amanda always looked as if she could murder someone, while people who worked in the stores and banks along Main Street decided Amanda was set up.

"Any idea who might do that?" I asked one young woman as she reached around me for her bacon biscuit to go.

She tugged an extra napkin from the holder. "From what I hear, Amanda's got plenty of enemies in town. Quite frankly, I'm surprised someone hasn't killed her."

"I'd talk to Joanie Raines," said another woman further down the counter. "She was very unhappy with the way she was treated at tryouts."

"Hey, what's going to happen to the play now?" someone else chimed in. "Are they still going to have it?"

"I don't know," I said. "Solving Harold's murder might be more important."

This set off another firestorm of argument between people who agreed with me and people who were appalled by the thought of losing their chances to be in an outdoor drama. I ate my own bacon biscuit and drank my coffee. Amanda had plenty of enemies. The question was, did Harold?

After the breakfast rush was over, Jerry put on his khaki shorts and green-and-yellow tee-shirt and headed out to Camp Lakenwood's open house while I drove over to Amanda's house. If anyone thought Harold's murder would halt production on *Flower of the South*, they were wrong. When I arrived, Amanda was meeting with Constance Tate in her kitchen, a vast room gleaming with stainless steel appliances, as cold and sterile as an operating room. It looked as if the kitchen had never been used. No cheerful canister sets, trivets, dishcloths, or any of the items that generally decorate a kitchen. Either Amanda was a neat freak, or she always ate out. The cast list for *Flower of the South* spread out on one of the granite counter tops. Constance was making notes on another sheet of paper.

Calm, icy Constance. Was it possible the baby had been hers? Was there any way to see if she still had her coven tattoo? She never said much, probably because Amanda did all the talking. When Amanda left the room to take a phone call, I told Constance I was surprised the show hadn't been postponed.

She wasn't concerned. "It's absolutely shocking what happened to Harold. But he would've wanted us to move forward with centennial plans."

"Which would be the construction of a centennial park."

"Everyone knows that's a dead issue." She had the grace to look embarrassed. "That didn't come out right, sorry. We're going to have an outdoor drama, and we can dedicate the opening night performance to Harold."

Just what he would've wanted. "So the show must go on?"

"I'm afraid so."

"May I see the cast list?"

"Of course. My original copy is on top."

The neatly handwritten list confirmed my suspicion that Amanda had indeed cast herself as Emmaline. Joanie Raines was Mrs. Ross. I didn't know a lot of the names, but it looked as if most people who tried out got a part. Whether or not they'd be happy with their roles was another matter.

"Constance, do you know anyone who had a serious grudge against Amanda?"

"Other than Harold? I suppose first on the list would be her husband's ex-wife, Tammy Henderson. She never forgave Amanda for 'stealing Roger away,' as she put it. Let's see, there's sales manager at Reynaldo's. She and Amanda are always arguing about fashion. Then there's the chef at Mamie's, her hairdresser, who is a wonderful woman by the way, and does my hair every Friday. I have absolutely no complaint about Delores, then there's her cleaning woman, her—"

I held up a hand. "Hold on. Does Amanda aggravate everyone she comes in contact with?"

"She's such a perfectionist, she's impossible to please."

Amanda returned, scowling. "The *Celosia News* can't stop pestering me! I don't want to talk to them. Why aren't the reporters out looking for the real murderer? Can't they see someone's trying to frame me?"

"What about your husband's first wife?" I asked.

"Tammy? I seriously doubt she had anything to do with this."

"It's my understanding she's not too fond of you."

"Yes, but when I divorced Roger, he went right back to her, so she won. Lucky girl."

"All right. Can you think of anyone else? A member of the Improvement Society, or maybe a member of the Centennial Committee?"

She turned briefly to give Constance a smile. "I've been friends with Constance and the others for years. What motive would they have? And as for the Centennial Committee, that was Harold and four others."

"I'm curious, Amanda, why is someone as wealthy and as fashion forward as yourself living in a small town like Celosia? Why aren't you cutting a swath through Parkland, or Greensboro, or even Charlotte?"

She made a dismissive gesture. "Been there, done that. Celosia needs my guidance. Can you imagine what this place would be like without me?"

Someone wanted Celosia to be without Amanda. And without Harold. Was getting rid of both of them part of the murderer's master plan?

Amanda's phone rang again, and with an exasperated sigh, she left the room.

"No," we heard her say, "I am not cancelling the show."

Constance sat back down at the counter and continued making notes on the cast list. Try as I might, I couldn't see the underside of her wrist.

"Constance, this is a completely different subject. Were you a member of the Darkrose Coven?"

She lifted one silvery eyebrow. "I beg your pardon?"

"About twenty years ago?"

"There is a Darkrose Coven," she said, and for a moment I thought she was going to tell all, "but it's in a book called *Pagan Desires*. That must have been where you heard of it."

"No, I'm talking about the original one, the one with Joanie Raines and Lauren Garrett and a few others."

Nothing cracked her composure. "You must be mistaken."

"You wouldn't mind showing me your wrists, would you?"

She stared at me as if I'd made an improper noise in church. Then she turned over both hands. An expensive silver watch was on one wrist, its thick band covering where a tattoo might be. A pearl bracelet dangled on the other. She took off both pieces of jewelry.

No tattoo.

"What's this all about, Madeline?"

Could Nell have been mistaken? Of course, tattoos could be removed or covered with makeup. "Nothing, thank you."

Amanda returned, complaining at the top of her voice. "Can you believe Evan James had the nerve to call and ask me if I was cancelling the show?"

I really didn't believe Evan had the nerve. "Did you get the grant money?"

"It's due any day now."

"Where is the money coming from?"

"The Hunter Hardin Foundation, an exceptionally generous group, and it was no problem to fill in the form."

"How generous?"

"One hundred thousand dollars. That, combined with our local contributions should be enough to get us started. Is there anything else, Madeline? I'm really very busy, so you need to get out there and clear my name."

To be on the safe side, I looked up the Hunter Hardin Foundation. It was legitimate, and the grant form was not complicated. So Amanda was telling the truth about that, at least.

Of the three young women on Annie's list, one was out of town, and one had broken her leg rock-climbing and was still in the hospital. Her family didn't want her disturbed. That left Renee Hedley, who met me at Deely's and obligingly put down her cell phone to show me her black rose tattoo. Renee had black hair chopped in a short shaggy style, a nose ring like Annie's, and a wealth of tattoos, including a thorny vine circling her arm blooming with skulls, and a fanged serpent running down her other arm. I'd offered to buy whatever she liked, and she opted for a cheeseburger and fries. She sat sideways in the booth, one red-sneakered foot up on the seat. When Annie brought her order, they gave each other a nod, and Annie moved on.

"Have you read *Pagan Desires*?" Renee asked me.

"I'm on chapter five." Lissa had been kidnapped by the demon Arzarath and had fallen under his spell, but the angel Rigel was coming to the rescue. All very dramatic.

"Are you up to the part where Arzarath takes Lissa to his chamber? Hot stuff."

"Looking forward to it. So you and Annie and the others got a black rose because Lissa has one?"

"Yeah, that's pretty much it."

"You don't meet and act out scenes?"

She laughed. "You mean like a LARP? Hell, no. That's for kids."

"LARP?"

"Live Action Role Play. Some people are into it, but it's too much trouble. I mean, you gotta find costumes and a place that'll let you play. I'm just into the books. The movie's coming out next year, and I can't wait. Hope they don't screw it up."

"Did you ever hear of another Darkrose Coven around Celosia?"

She spoke around a mouthful of cheeseburger. "Nope. There's one in Parkland. You could probably find a ton more if you looked online."

Annie approached cautiously, as if Renee were spilling deep dark secrets. "Need a refill?"

"No, thanks."

"Anything for you, Madeline?"

"Sit down for a second," I said. Renee moved her foot, and Annie slid in beside her. "Okay, ladies, I need your help. There have been two murders in the neighborhood, and I'm unofficially investigating both of them. It's unusual that the name Darkrose Coven has come up, whether it's the old one that was around years ago, or the new one associated with *Pagan Desires*. Both of you please let me know if you hear anything that might be a clue."

Renee looked interested, but Annie looked uncomfortable. "I don't think there's anything to it."

"I know somebody in the Parkland group," Renee said. "Maybe I can go to their next meeting."

"Let me know when they're going to meet, and I'll get in."

She gave me a critical glance. "You probably could."

"Annie?"

"I think you should leave it alone, Madeline. It's nothing. Just fans of the book."

Renee gave her a friendly shoulder punch. "Ah, come on. It'll be fun infiltrating the coven."

"You can go if you like. I'm not interested."

Renee's phone chimed with a text message which she read and quickly answered. "Gotta go. Give me your number, Madeline, and I'll let you know if I find out anything."

After she'd gone, Annie's look of disapproval spoke volumes. "What?" I said. "You don't think I can pass as a teenaged witch?"

"You do whatever you like, Madeline."

Annie's mood was puzzling, but Renee was eager to help. Maybe once I knew more about Parkland's chapter of the Darkrose Coven I'd be able to figure out why Annie was being uncooperative.

I wasn't sure that Amanda's chef, hairdresser, or housekeeper would have any useful information, but Tammy Henderson Price might have something to say about Amanda.

A phone call later, I was talking to Tammy Price's young daughter who said her mom wasn't home, but she'd give her the message to call me. I thanked her and then checked my watch. Time for open house at Camp Lakenwood.

Chapter Nine

The camp was ten miles away near a little farming community called Westberry, the same Westberry that Nell had said was near Peaceful Meadow. I turned off Chandler Road to Camp Lakenwood Trail. Nathan had repaired the twisting gravel road, as well as the wooden rail fence and faded welcome sign. The archway still said "Camp Lakenwood, Established 1954," but the letters had been repainted in bright yellow and green. So had the camp bus and the yellow arrows pointing to the main cabin where Nathan met me. Like Jerry, he had on his official outfit, khaki shorts and bright yellow and green camp tee-shirt. His eyes gleamed behind his little round glasses as he spread his arms wide.

"What do you think, Madeline? Quite a difference, isn't it?"

The last time I had been to Camp Lakenwood, it was in sad shape. Now all the cabins had been cleaned and repaired, new silver rowboats and green and yellow canoes bobbed at the repaired dock, and smooth concrete replaced the old cracked basketball court.

"It looks fantastic, Nathan. The kids will love it."

"Now what's all this about Harold Stover being found dead? What's going on?"

"That's what I intend to find out."

"You're on the case? Who hired you?"

"Amanda Price."

"What? Why?"

"Because she's a suspect."

When he was railing about Amanda yesterday at our house, Nathan's face had turned bright red. Now he looked ashen, and his voice quavered. "Why would the police think that?"

I hadn't seen Nathan this upset since we'd been in a time-crunch to solve his uncle's riddle and win Camp Lakenwood. "Nathan, what do you know?"

He swallowed hard. "I went over to Harold's house last night to talk to him about Amanda, but he wasn't home. At least, he didn't answer the door."

Uh, oh. "When was this?"

"I didn't get finished here at camp until nine. Nine-thirty, maybe? He didn't answer his phone, either, so I thought he might already be in bed."

Amanda had come by at ten and found Harold's body. "Nathan, you might want to talk to Chief Brenner."

He took a step back. "And have him think I killed Harold? No way!"

"You might have seen or heard something useful. Harold was dead when Amanda found him. You might have just missed the killer."

"Or just missed being killed by Amanda. I can't think about this now, Madeline. I've got an open house to run." He hurried off to greet arriving campers.

This was interesting news. Nathan was as mild-mannered as they come, but he'd been furious with Amanda. Could he have picked up a handy branch, hoping to smack her, and hit Harold instead? He was at the house at nine-thirty. Amanda said she came by at ten. Would Nathan go to such lengths as to kill Harold and frame Amanda? I didn't know the relationship between the two men, but from my short time in Celosia, I'd untangled a Gordian knot's worth of relationships. I didn't think Nathan was lying to me, but my past cases had involved a lot of secrets and lies, not all of them intentional. I'd better have a long talk with Nathan.

The camp was filled with children and their parents check-ing out the cabins and all the activities. I found Jerry playing basketball with a group of ten-year-olds. Other camp counselors gave guided tours of the crafts building and showed children how to build campfires, climb ropes, and paddle canoes. Austin helped younger boys dig worms for fishing. Denisha assisted little girls through the obstacle course.

I wandered around, greeting people I knew. I admired the tiny fish the boys yanked out of the water. I cheered for the girls as they managed to conquer the tire run and the monkey bars. Then I sat down at one of the picnic tables in a shady spot near the lake. I'd decided Nathan would be too busy today to discuss his problem, when he suddenly came up and sat down across from me.

"Madeline, I need to talk to you."

"That's convenient. I need to talk to you, too."

He took off his glasses to wearily rub his eyes. "I've already told Jerry. Chief Brenner called. He wants to see me as soon as open house is over today. A neighbor saw me knocking on Harold's door last night."

"You don't have anything to worry about. You didn't go in. Or did you?"

"No!"

"Now's not the time to hide anything."

He set his glasses firmly back on his nose. "I promise you I did not go in."

"You didn't try the back door?"

"No. I knocked on the front door and rang the bell. When Harold didn't answer, I figured he'd already gone to bed, and I left." He clasped his hands together. "It gets worse. Remember when I stopped by your house and vented about Amanda? I'd done the same thing here at camp when she came by. The other counselors heard me. They saw how angry I was. Brenner wants to talk to all of them, too."

"It's standard investigation procedure."

"There's more. Brenner said Harold was killed by a blow to the head with a piece of wood similar to a baseball bat. Look around. I've got a camp full of murder weapons."

He was getting way too upset. "Okay. You leave here with a piece of wood, go into town, and smack Harold over the head. What's your motive? You're mad at Amanda. Why not smack her over the head? Why attack poor Harold?"

"I don't know! This whole thing's got me so rattled!"

"Calm down. Cooperate with the police. I'm going to solve this."

"I need to hire you, don't I? I need you to clear my name!"

"Nathan, it's going to be all right. First of all, Amanda's already hired me, so I'm on the case. Second, unless you're lying to me, and I don't think you are, your name doesn't need clearing. You don't have a reason to want Harold dead. Or do you?"

"No, of course not. I don't have a thing against Harold Stover."

"No leftover resentment from Celosia High? He didn't bully you or stuff you in a locker?"

"No, no. We weren't even in the same class. I knew who he was in town, but we rarely came in contact."

"Then you need to calm down."

He took a few deep breaths. "All right. I'll try to keep it together."

"Show me what's going on around camp."

Giving me another tour and talking about all the events he'd planned helped Nathan steady himself. At the end of the open house, he blew his whistle and announced it was time to go. "Thank you for coming, everyone! If you haven't already signed up for the summer session, please go by the main cabin. Those of you riding the camp bus, make sure we have your address. We'll see you Monday morning."

While Nathan made sure everyone had a ride home, I met Jerry at the campfire site.

"Here's what I found out today," I told him. "According to Constance Tate, who may or may not have a black rose tattoo hiding under her watch, Amanda has difficulty getting along with people because she's such a perfectionist."

"Not the word I would've chosen, but go on."

"Two members of Harold's committee told me Harold had no enemies. I couldn't get in touch with two of the girls on

Annie's list, but the third, Renee Hedley, is going undercover in the Parkland coven, despite Annie's protests."

"Damn, I wanted to go undercover."

"You may still get your chance."

"Don't you think Annie knows more than she's telling?"

"I've felt that from the beginning."

"I've been busy, too. Nathan says to get to the edge of his property on the Westberry side, you cross the lake and go through his woods about three miles until you come to a fence that separates his woods from the woods that border Peaceful Meadow. He said we could explore whenever we liked."

"Good. Oh, two other things. I left a message for Amanda's ex-husband's wife, Tammy, to give me a call. And the murder weapon was a heavy piece of wood."

"That's what Nathan told me, when he was coherent. That phone call scared the hell out of him. He said he never should've lost his temper in front of the other counselors."

"Yes, but you know how provoking Amanda can be."

Amanda was beyond provoking.

Then Nathan joined us. He'd just gotten off the phone with Amanda. "That woman's completely insane! She wants to come out here and hunt for Emmaline's cabin. I told her if she set one foot on Camp Lakenwood, I'd call the police. She's not going to find anything because I won't have her put that stupid play of hers on my land. Tell her to find another place for her drama. There will be no drama here!"

Oh, I was sure there would be drama. "Jerry and I will look across the lake, anyway. I'll be sure to tell Amanda we didn't find any historical sites."

Nathan motioned toward the dock. "How are your rowing skills? Do you want to use one of the canoes?"

Jerry and a canoe had "overboard" written all over it. "How about a rowboat?"

"Take what you like. I've got things I have to do in my office. Do you have a compass? How far into the woods are you planning to go?"

I didn't want to upset Nathan by mentioning that the woods bordering his land had been the site of a coven. "To the edge of your property. How far is it?"

"Close to three miles."

"Is there a path of any sort?"

"No, but if you walk straight in you should come to a fence."

At the dock Jerry and I chose one of the sturdier-looking boats. We sat beside each other in the boat and rowed out across the lake. The water was as calm as a bathtub with a few ripples as ducks got out of the way.

When we first saw Camp Lakenwood, an obstacle course and some ancient teepees had been on the opposite side. Nathan moved the obstacle course to the main area of the camp, but teepees still poked up from the trees on the far side of the lake. Even with our amateur rowing skills, it took less than fifteen minutes to cross the lake. We pulled up to the sagging dock, which was a bit shaky when we stepped up onto it, but held our weight.

Jerry tied the rowboat to one of the dock's warped posts. "This is the next thing Nathan's going to fix. He said the campers can stay at the main camp this year until he decides what to do with the teepees. They've been here since the Fifties." He paused. "I thought there were six of them."

Five faded and dilapidated teepees stood in a circle at the edge of the woods, the remains of an ancient campfire in the center of the circle. Thick grass had grown in and around the teepees. As we approached, a startled rabbit fled from the grass. A few feet away, the forest was slowly reclaiming the land, vines reaching out from small saplings and leaves and pine needles thick on the ground.

Growing up in Pageant Land, I didn't spend much time outdoors. Jerry had had the extensive grounds and woods of the Fairweather estate to play in and needed his forest skills later in life when running and hiding from people who failed to appreciate his attempts to separate them from their money. So when he took an experienced look at the sun, said, "This way," and charged on ahead, I naturally followed.

Further in, the trees were older and thicker, mostly pine trees, but a few I recognized as oaks and sycamores. I was ready for us to fight our way through the underbrush, but except for tangled groves of thorns, we didn't have any trouble.

Around one stand of trees Jerry pointed out a clump of rhododendron bushes. "Look out. Evil rhododendron."

"If it grows all through the woods, the witches would have easy access. Tell Nathan not to let the campers chew on it."

"We're not letting the campers chew on anything."

A large fallen log blocked the path, and after checking for snakes, Jerry said it was safe to climb over. "A hollow log is good snake territory. Now that the weather's getting warm, they're coming out."

"You are so handy." The forest stretched off in all directions. I was already turned around. "If we find it's too far, we might reach the coven site from the other side."

"I don't mind being out in the woods with you."

"I'm glad you're along. All these trees look the same to me."

"If we come across the coven site, what are you hoping to find there?"

"I think the younger witches are using it."

"Would they have a reason to poison Eric Levin? Or have a connection to Harold's murder?"

"The men may have discovered their secret place and threatened to expose them. All this is conjecture, you understand. I really don't know what's going on, but that has not stopped me before."

We'd walked about half an hour when we saw a tall, saggy triangle of cloth propped between two large pine trees.

"I think we've found the missing teepee," Jerry said.

A walking stick with a dragon's head rested against one of the trees. Little pots full of fuzzy plants sat under a clothesline draped with gauzy scarves and wind chimes. We could hear a woman's voice singing about flowers and rainbows.

"And Megan Underwood's hideout. Hello!" Jerry called. "Anyone home?"

Megan came out of the teepee, still dressed in her bohemian flowing skirt and blouse, her long curls in disarray and wound about with daisy chains. She didn't seem alarmed or surprised to see us. "Greetings, friends."

"Greetings," I said. "I'm Madeline Fairweather, and this is my husband, Jerry."

"Madeline." She took my hands in hers and stared into my eyes. "You are a seeker of truth and a creator of beauty. Welcome to my home." Then she caught Jerry's hands and held them for a long moment. "You have a delightful, playful soul, but there has been great tragedy in your life, tragedy you were finally able to overcome. I'm so glad for you."

Jerry thanked her, giving me a brief frown. His parents had died in a fire, and for years, he'd mistakenly thought it was his fault. I'd found out the truth, and he was able to overcome the tragedy. "That's quite a gift you've got there, Ms. Underwood."

"Yes, yes, a gift and a curse."

"How long have you been living here?" I asked.

"For years. Centuries. Time has little meaning for me."

"You do know you're on private property that belongs to Nathan Fenton."

She waved a hand as if to dismiss this minor detail. "The forest belongs to everyone."

"No, this particular part of the forest belongs to Nathan."

She smiled at me as if I were a small child. "No one can own nature, Madeline. It's like trying to contain the wind. It must blow as it chooses."

"That's something you need to discuss with him."

"I need to be where Emmaline Ross lived and breathed. I need to feel her presence in the roots of my soul."

"Is this where her cabin used to be?"

"I have called upon the half moon to communicate with the spirits of the moon."

"Did they know?"

"We must wait till the moon is full."

"Jerry, you try."

He stepped forward with his best smile. "Ms. Underwood. May I call you Megan? I have also spoken with the spirits in séances. My guide is a lovely enchantress, very much like yourself, who helps me contact those who have passed on to other realms. What led you to this particular spot?"

I could tell Megan liked being described as a "lovely enchantress." She toyed with one of her many beaded necklaces. "There was a strange element in the atmosphere. I'm not sure how to explain it."

The smell of spectral grapes, perhaps? I wanted to ask.

She closed her eyes. "I was drawn to this place as I was drawn to embody Emmaline. The peace, the serenity."

"That's about to change," Jerry said. "In case you didn't know, on Monday, Camp Lakenwood is open for business, and dozens of small children will be yelling, splashing, and screaming all day long for six weeks."

Her eyes opened wide. "Is this true? Will they be coming over here?"

"Not at first, but eventually, yes."

"Dear me."

"Maybe we could help you move your things to a more receptive place?"

"I must go deeper into the woods."

"No, Nathan owns the forest, and he's planning to let the campers use all of it."

Megan thought it over. "Perhaps it's time for me to move on."

"Do you have a place to stay?" I asked.

"I'll go where the wind takes me."

"If you get a part in the outdoor drama, you'll want to be closer to town," Jerry said.

I followed his lead. "And if this is the site of Emmaline's cabin, no one should disturb it. Why don't you gather your things? Jerry can take me across the lake and then come back for you."

Megan agreed to this plan. While she wedged the little pots of herbs into a large worn shoulder bag with ragged fringe, Jerry pulled me over to one side. "Something else is going on here, trust me."

"What?"

"Think about it. She called you a seeker of truth and a creator of beauty, so she knows you're an investigator and an artist. And all that about great tragedy in my life? Easy enough to look up on the Internet."

"Is she conning us?"

"Of course she is. But she probably doesn't see herself as a con artist. She uses the same tricks to make people think she's magic. So what's she really doing out here?"

I glanced back at Megan, who was rolling up the wind chimes in the scarves. "Good question."

"Check her for tattoos."

I'd already decided that Megan was an ideal candidate for the original coven. "Let me help you with that, Megan. What lovely bracelets you have. Did you make them?"

She lifted and turned her hand so I could admire the bright beads and seeds strung together on twisted pieces of string. "I did. It's so comforting to be touching nature. All these were woven from plant fibers dyed with natural dyes." She held up her other hand and twisted them both, making the bracelets dance.

No tattoo. I glanced at Jerry and shook my head. He raised his eyebrows in surprise. "Megan, let's see about getting you home."

Chapter Ten

Jerry and I rowed over to camp, and then he returned for Megan and her treasures. Everything she owned fit into the oversized shoulder bag.

Nathan was not happy to learn she'd been squatting on his land. "Ms. Underwood, you did not have my permission to camp over there. I would be liable if something happened to you."

She apologized. "I must have taken a wrong turn. I didn't know that part of the forest was Camp Lakenwood. I was following my instincts."

"Did your instincts lead you to any real proof that Emmaline Ross lived there?"

"No, but who needs proof when the truth lies in the heart?"

"I do," he said. "Please find somewhere else to camp."

When I asked Megan where she'd like to go, she said she needed to meditate on the answer, so she spent the trip to Celosia singing softly in the backseat. We heard "Flower days, dancing sunbeams, and rainbows, loveliest place in the universe" until I had a sugar rush.

Jerry grinned and spoke over his shoulder to Megan. "What is that lovely song?"

"Oh, we sang it all the time in Peaceful Meadow where I grew up. It was like our national anthem."

"Do you mind if I sing along?"

"Please do."

Even my fiercest glare couldn't keep him from joining in. When they'd finished, I said, "Were you trying to get back to Peaceful Meadow?"

"Yes, but I had to stop and enjoy the forest."

A forest that led to another forest before reaching the meadow. Had she really been that turned around?

In town, Megan asked to be let out at the park. "Thank you very much for the ride. I can tell you are sensitive souls who are grateful to have found each other. Let me give you this gift." She rummaged in the bag and handed Jerry a pale leather circle with an open weave design in the center. Beaded fringe and feathers dangled from the end. "It's a dream catcher. May it catch all the bad dreams and let the good dreams through."

Jerry thanked her. I tried again for more information. "Megan, is there any other reason besides this connection you feel with Emmaline that you wanted to be in that part of the woods?"

Her dreamy eyes gazed off in the distance. "What more reason do I need?"

"Maybe you were looking for the site of the Darkrose Coven."

If I was hoping for a reaction, I didn't get one. "Oh, no. That's long gone."

"Were you a member?"

"No, I had no interest in casting spells."

"When you lived in Peaceful Meadow, did you ever see them?"

"They weren't very friendly. When they came out there, they stayed in the woods."

"No one from the commune objected?"

"We should all strive to be kind to one another. Live and let live, I say. Thank you for the ride, my friends."

That was all we could discover. She gathered her shoulder bag and got out of the car.

Jerry watched her drift away. "She's got the whole act going, though, the wild hair, the beads, the reincarnation."

"If it's all an act, then what is it for? She didn't have a black rose tattoo, but that doesn't mean she didn't have one in the past." I checked my watch. "Our little encounter with Megan set our coven search back."

"Plenty of daylight left. We could try it from the Peaceful Meadow side."

We were halfway there when my phone rang. It was Joanie Raines.

"Madeline, can you come to my house right away? There's a policeman asking all sorts of questions, and I need you to explain things."

"What's the trouble?"

"Apparently, a lot of people heard me complaining about Amanda Friday night. She's insisting someone set her up for Harold Stover's murder, but it sure as hell wasn't me! Come tell the police that. I live on Viewmont Road next to the Methodist church."

"Be right there." I ended the call. "First Amanda, then Nathan, and now Joanie Raines is a suspect and wants me to talk to the police." I turned the car around. "There's something to be said for being the only detective in town."

For such a large woman, Joanie's house was tiny and dainty. Everything was pink and ruffled, including the mailbox, the bird bath, and the welcome mat. Joanie and the policeman were standing in the narrow foyer. Jerry and I squeezed in. The policeman was a fellow I'd met before, but I didn't get a chance to say hello before Joanie demanded I set him straight.

"Tell this officer exactly what happened Friday night and what I said."

"To the best of my knowledge, you said Amanda was setting everything up so that she could be the star of the outdoor drama. It was her game and we had to play by her rules."

"And that we hadn't lived here long enough to see that what Amanda wanted, Amanda got," Jerry said.

"Yes, that's it." She glared at the policeman. "How does any of that make me a suspect? It makes me sound jealous, and that's what I am. I'm not a killer, or some criminal mastermind."

The policeman looked as if he couldn't wait to finish here. "I'm interviewing everyone who was at tryouts, ma'am."

"Amanda singled me out, didn't she? She sees me as a threat. She knows I'm a better actress."

"Tell me where you were Friday night, ma'am, from nine until ten."

"After tryouts, I came home."

"Can anyone verify that?"

"No, I was by myself the rest of the evening."

The policeman wrote this down. I knew he was thinking, you had time to sneak out, kill Harold, and get back to your house before Amanda came by, because I was thinking the same thing. He asked a few more routine questions and then thanked her for her time. Jerry and I moved to the living room so he could get by. It was also small and pink, pink walls, pink flowered sofa and chairs, and pink ruffled curtains. Joanie's collections of cups and saucers, spoons, decorative plates, and knickknacks crowded every possible surface. White ceramic rabbits sat on the window ledges and peeked out from behind baskets of paperback books. With the overabundance of pink and flowers, I felt as if I were inside one of those decorative Easter eggs.

Joanie followed us, furious. "Talk about a setup! Amanda set me up for this! I'm going to give her a very large piece of my mind."

Not a good idea. "That's the last thing you should do. Get into a shouting match with Amanda, and you'll definitely be a suspect. Is there anyone who can prove you were here all Friday night? Did anyone call or stop by?"

"No, and if they had, I wouldn't have let them in. I was so annoyed at being cut off during my audition, I didn't want to talk to anybody."

I tried another angle. "How well do you know Tammy Price?"

"There's an excellent suspect for you. She hates Amanda for stealing her husband."

"She got him back, though."

"She still could be angry. I never met her."

Joanie was so angry she didn't offer us a seat, which was a good thing. I was afraid if I sat down, I'd be swallowed by ruffles and never get out. "What about Megan Underwood?"

"Exactly what I told you before. I don't understand her, at all. Why would she want to be in a play? You have to be completely dedicated to commit to a show. She won't do that." Joanie held out her hand to Jerry. "You can see I didn't kill Harold, can't you? Take a good look and tell me I murdered him."

Jerry obligingly checked out her palm. "No matter what I see, I'm afraid palm-reading doesn't hold up in court, Ms. Raines."

She balled her hand into a fist. "All this makes me so angry! Now there might not be an outdoor drama, at all! You've got to solve this, Madeline. I'm not missing my big chance. I want to hire you."

"Amanda's already hired me," I said, "and I believe she's innocent."

Joanie put her hands on her hips and declared in her best theater voice, "Well, I'm innocent, too."

Jerry and I managed to wedge out of Joanie's house. He side-stepped a large ceramic duck holding a flower basket. "So Joanie's innocent? And Nathan? And Megan? Everybody's innocent. Looks like Harold hit himself over the head."

"I say we ride by Harold's house and try to get a look inside."

Jerry brightened. "No *try* to it. I'll get you in."

Harold's house was in an older neighborhood, built in a Thirties style. The house was surrounded by yellow police tape, but we didn't see a guard or a police car on the street. I drove to the end of the street and let Jerry out. He disappeared behind a tall hedge that bordered several homes. I parked the car and strolled down to Harold's as if I were out for a late afternoon walk. We'd timed our caper well. On a mild Saturday night like this, usually there'd be at least one or two people sitting on their front porches, but it was suppertime, so the neighbors were inside their homes. After another quick look to make certain no one was watching, I slipped around Harold's house to the back door where Jerry waited to let me in.

Harold had lived alone and very simply. Except for a massive grandfather clock ticking quietly, the rooms were sparsely furnished—a dark leather sofa and chair in the living room, a heavy-looking dark wood table and thick wooden chairs in the dining room—and except for the bloodstains in the hallway, very clean. Newspapers and copies of *Dog Fancy* were stacked by the sofa, along with a pair of Harold's shoes, large books about African elephants and famous battles of World War II, and a book of crossword puzzles. Open on the chair was a book about Siamese cats. Above the fireplace was a painting of three graceful Irish setters.

When I took a closer look at the painting, I saw a small black box on the mantel. The label said "Dusty" in gold letters. His dog's ashes. Tears stung my eyes. I recalled Harold's beaming face as he told me about his many charities supporting the preservation of pandas and fish and falcons. Did this overwhelming desire to help all animals ease the sadness of his loss?

Jerry pattered down the stairs. "Nothing in the bedroom but clothes and natural history books. I never would've guessed Harold was so interested in animals."

No, there wasn't any way to know what really went on inside a person until he was dead and strangers were snooping in his house. I'd been anxious to find clues in Harold's house, but now I felt as if I'd invaded a sacred space.

We walked down the hallway to the back door and looked out across Harold's backyard, a plain square of grass with large oak trees. Leaves and branches lay scattered on the lawn.

"Chief Brenner told Nathan the murder weapon was a piece of wood similar to a baseball bat. The murderer could've had a spur of the moment decision and used one of those branches. Then he or she could've tossed the branch back into the yard with dozens of others, and off they go, although, more than likely, they took the branch with them and burned it."

"Or chopped it up for toothpicks," Jerry said.

"Do any of these branches look strong enough to kill?"

"I suppose if you swung it hard enough, and the victim fell and hit his head."

"I can't see Amanda picking up a large dirty piece of wood under any circumstances."

"But we both know Amanda wouldn't leave an expensive handbag behind."

I'd seen all I needed to see, so Jerry and I left the house by the back door and made our way back to my car. I was becoming more convinced that Amanda had been set up.

At home, Nell left a note on the door.

"Baby owls found in chimney. Moved them out."

"Too bad we didn't get to see them." Jerry hung the dream catcher Megan had given us in our bedroom window. "Maybe it's a clue catcher. Maybe it'll tell you who done it."

I called the shower first, and afterwards, gave my reflection a good long inspection, particularly the side view. So far, no sign of a baby. I couldn't decide if I was relieved or disappointed. Not for the first time I wondered what my life might have been if Mother hadn't had pageant fever. Would we have forged a strong mother-daughter bond, or drifted even further apart? Now that I'd had success as an investigator, our relationship was improving, but it had a long way to go. Would a baby solve that problem? If anything, raising a child, especially a little girl, might become a real battlefield if Mother decided her granddaughter had to be Little Miss Perfect.

Jerry peeked in. "All done? What are you doing, admiring yourself? Because that's what I'm doing."

I put on my robe. "Checking for babies."

"And?"

"Nothing yet."

"That's okay. When the time is right, Hortensia will make her presence known."

Jerry sang in the shower, first, his medley of tunes for *Flower of the South*, and then a rousing rendition of the Celosia National Anthem. When he hopped into bed with me, I commented again on his ability as a songwriter.

"Thanks," he said. "I'm still curious about Megan Underwood, though. How did she get over to that side of the lake? Nathan's new rowboats and canoes have been stored until now, and all of them have been on the camp side."

"Good question."

"And if Denisha and her aunt see Megan at the farmers' market, how does Megan get to town and bring soap and candles? Camp Lakenwood is ten miles away."

"Good question number two."

"And how did Megan hear about the auditions and again get to town and back to her teepee? I didn't see a broomstick, just that sad-looking dragon walking stick with one eyeball and broken teeth."

"Are you sure about that? I think it had both eyes at the theater."

"One eyeball."

"And broken teeth. Do you suppose that cane is the murder weapon?"

"She was in town Friday night for auditions."

I considered this possibility for a few moments. "Okay, I'll put you on Megan patrol. If you think she's a con woman, then ask Del if he's heard of her."

We kissed, and I turned out the light. A few minutes later, Jerry was asleep, but I lay awake for a long time. Outside, I could hear a soft hooting sound and hoped it was the little owls, safely back in their tree. My tired thoughts circled around to the Darkrose Coven and what sort of rituals they performed and what sort of secrets they were still hiding after all these years. Annie knew something, I knew she did. If only she would confide in me.

Chapter Eleven

Sunday morning I had a call from Tammy Price, Roger's first and current wife, who said she'd be more than glad to talk about Amanda. She agreed to meet me at Baxter's Barbecue in Parkland at noon. This was very convenient, because I wanted to talk to Olivia Decker about Kathleen Wallace's photos and check in with Renee Hedley to see if she'd found out anything useful from the Parkland chapter of Darkrose Coven.

"I have short dark curly hair, and I'll be with a fellow wearing a garish tie," I told her.

Baxter's, our favorite place to eat, was a plain little brick building you might easily overlook if it weren't for the tempting smells of barbecue and fries. The melt-in-your mouth barbecue has just the right amount of spices. The fries are always crispy, and the tea is fresh and sweet. We chose a table near the front so Jerry's yellow tie with pink doughnuts couldn't be missed. The table with its cheerful red-and-white checked plastic tablecloth and the rickety wooden chairs rocked unevenly as we ate our lunch.

Jerry passed me another napkin to catch the delicious juice from my sandwich. "I could live here. Why don't we sell the house and move into Baxter's? Maybe they'd like a short-order breakfast cook."

I checked my watch. Twelve thirty-five. "Wonder what's keeping her? She sounded eager to trash Amanda."

"Didn't you say you talked to her daughter? There might have been a crisis."

"Could be. At least I have honored my promise, and we are finally in Parkland."

A few minutes later, a slim dark-haired woman came in, scanned the lunch crowd, and came toward us.

"You must be Madeline. Hello, I'm Tammy Price."

Tammy Price was a slight, ordinary-looking woman with brown hair and brown eyes. She wore jeans and a white shirt, several gold chains, and a very large diamond ring. Jerry stood and pulled out a chair for her. She thanked him.

"This is my husband, Jerry," I said. "Thanks for meeting us."

She hung her handbag on the back of the chair. "Sorry I'm late. Roger didn't want me to come. He thinks it'll stir up trouble."

"Well, Amanda couldn't be in more trouble. She's a suspect in a murder case."

"That doesn't surprise me in the slightest."

The waitress came and took her order. When she'd gone, I asked Tammy if she wouldn't mind explaining what had happened with Amanda and Roger. She didn't mind at all.

"Amanda knew Roger was the richest man in town, so she went after him. It didn't matter one bit that he was married to me. She made a huge play for him, and he fell for it. Then once he got in, he saw what sort of money-grubbing woman she was, and he divorced her."

"Excuse me for asking an indelicate question, but why did you take him back?"

"Because I knew it was all her fault. She tricked him into marrying her. She told him all kinds of lies about me. He wasn't himself. He called me soon after they married and told me he'd made the biggest mistake of his life, and as soon as he could get a divorce, he was coming back to me, if I'd forgive him. Well, of course, I did. I still loved him." Her cell phone jangled. "Please excuse me. I promised my daughter she could call me. I'll be right back."

She left the table and went outside. As she listened to her daughter, her lips thinned and she rubbed her forehead. "You were right," I told Jerry. "Teenage crisis."

After a short while, Tammy came back and took her seat. "Sorry about that. This whole business has been very hard on my daughter. I forgave Roger, but she has yet to come to terms with what she calls his 'defection from the family.' She doesn't want to have anything to do with him, but she's thirteen and very dramatic. We're hoping she'll come around."

"Did she ever meet Amanda?"

"Oh, no. She only knows there was another woman and that Daddy made a big mistake, for which he is definitely paying. He's going to have to work a long time to win back her trust."

The waitress brought Tammy's barbecue sandwich and fries and refilled our tea glasses. Tammy ate for a few minutes and then set her sandwich down. "Who is Amanda accused of murdering?"

"Harold Stover. Did you know him?"

"Harold Stover. I believe Roger knew him. They did some business together. I don't know anyone in Celosia. Amanda had Roger build a mansion there for her, which she kept. Roger said it was worth it to get rid of her."

"So Roger's not from Celosia?"

"He grew up there, but he moved to Parkland several years ago. She came here to steal him. I've never seen anyone so determined. I would not put it past Amanda to use any means necessary to get what she wants, even witchcraft."

Jerry reached for another fry. "Odd you should mention that. We have lots of witches in Celosia."

"Are you serious?"

"I'd say the main one is more of a New Age herbs and candles kind of gal."

"Then Amanda didn't learn anything from her. She already knew that stuff."

"Herbs and candles? She doesn't seem the type."

"She isn't. She once told me her parents were hippies and nature freaks who lived in a commune and raised goats."

Jerry and I came to attention. "A commune?" I said. "By any chance was it called Peaceful Meadow?"

"I don't know what it was called, but I do know Amanda hated that lifestyle. I don't feel sorry for her, though. We all have things from our childhood to overcome, but that's no excuse for stealing someone's husband. What else can I tell you?"

"Would you mind telling me where you were Friday night from nine until ten?"

She looked amused. "No, not at all. My daughter and I went to the movies with my best friend and her daughter. The National was having a special showing of all the Pixar short films, and we're all big fans. I'll give you her number, if you like."

"That would be fine, thanks." I'd already decided that if she had her husband back, Tammy wouldn't have a motive.

After Tammy left, I called her friend and the movie theater. The National had indeed held a Pixar short film festival Friday night.

I ended the call. "Looks as if Tammy's in the clear. But how about her news? It has to be the same commune. That means Amanda and Megan both lived in Peaceful Meadow."

"So Amanda might know about the coven. I'll bet she was the head witch."

I checked the time on my phone. "Too early for the grave-yard. I'm going to see if Olivia's really the mastermind behind Kathleen's questionable photos."

Jerry tossed several bills on the table for the tip. "I'll sit this one out."

"No problem. I didn't think you wanted to deal with her."

"Why don't you drop me off at Pot Luck Alley?"

When the waitress stopped by our table to refill our tea glasses, we thanked her and had a fortifying drink before I left Jerry at Del's pawn shop and drove to Olivia Decker's place of business.

Olivia Decker was a petite blonde with green eyes, the kind of woman Jerry had been attracted to for several years before decid-ing that a tall brunette was more his style. She worked for the law firm of Provost, Collins and Best. The office was located in downtown Parkland next to the new city park. She wasn't thrilled to see me, but she's rarely thrilled about anything.

"Hello, Madeline. What brings you to the big city?"

I said the one thing guaranteed to catch her interest. "I need your help."

She paused a moment as if considering my request, but she was curious. "Have a seat."

Unlike my comfy little office, Olivia's was a grand room as cold and formal as she was: glass desk with a pencil-slim computer, hard-edged metallic chairs, and a commanding view of the park. She wore a dark suit in a rich burgundy shade and a silk scarf held in place with a brooch sparkling with red and gold. She sat behind her desk, rearranged her skirt, and looked at me expectantly.

"My client, Kathleen Wallace, is concerned about photographs that have surfaced recently. As her sorority sister, I hoped you could explain."

To my surprise, Olivia's mouth quirked in a little smile. "Oh, really?"

"Is this some sort of trick you Delta Gammas like to play on each other?"

She sat back, arms folded. "Suppose you ask her about the photographs of me."

"I can't imagine anything would embarrass you, Olivia."

"Let's just say there are a few out there that might damage my credibility."

"Would you like to hire me to find them?"

"Oh, I know where they are. Kathleen has them. Bring them here, and I'll gladly exchange them for the ones of her."

This made no sense. "Look, as much as I like being paid to do this kind of thing, why can't the two of you meet for coffee and trade pictures?"

"Oh, this feud goes way back. It's better for all concerned if there's a go-between."

"Fine, I'll do it. Anything important I should know?"

"Kathleen Wallace is not what she seems. Don't trust her."

"Are you telling me she's really into witchcraft?"

"I wouldn't put it past her."

Olivia was the least likely person to believe in anything super-natural. When she was dating Jerry she was forever fussing about his fake séances and his plans to use the Eberlin House as a psychic shop. While I didn't completely trust Olivia, I always knew where I stood with her. "These pictures of you. How bad are they?"

She leaned forward on the glass desk. "I've worked very hard to get where I am in this firm. Being blond has not been an advantage. Now I have a reputation for being intelligent and ruthless. I don't want to have that compromised by a couple of nude photos."

"Uh, oh."

"Yeah, uh, oh. Why is it that the one time I make a truly stupid judgment call, someone is there with a camera? But I never turn down a challenge, and someone dared me to pose on top of the science building. In hindsight, I should've walked away."

"I imagine everyone who works here has a secret."

"And I don't have time to ferret them out. The only secret I care about is mine."

Someone as aggressive as Olivia should have taken charge of her secret. "Why haven't you contacted Kathleen before? What's the big feud?"

Her eyes were hard as green glass. "Because I probably would've killed her. That would be quite a case for you, wouldn't it? You get those photos from Kathleen, then you'll have something I'll bet neither of us ever thought you'd have: my money and my gratitude."

"All right." As I got up to leave, I expected her to ask about Jerry, or make a snide remark about life in Celosia. But she asked about my fee, wrote me a check, and turned back to her laptop.

I pondered this curious turn of events all the way to Pot Luck Ally and the pawn shop. Before going in, I gave Kathleen Wallace a call.

"Olivia Decker tells me you have some equally unflattering pictures of her. I'll be glad to make the swap."

There was a long silence on the other end of the line. Then Kathleen said, "I don't know what she's talking about."

"She's willing to hand over the witchcraft pictures for the nude shots."

Another silence. "She said that?"

"Yes. I've dealt with her before. She'll honor her part of the bargain."

"I don't know."

"It would help me understand what's going on here if you'd give me a little background on this feud between the two of you."

Where was cheerful Dr. Wallace? Kathleen's voice was bitter. "She cheated me, Madeline. I'm keeping those pictures."

"Then I'm not sure I can get yours from her."

"You'll find a way. Excuse me, I've got patients to see."

She hung up. Well. This was not what I expected. Maybe Jerry knew enough about Olivia's past to help me out.

Bells jangled as I pushed open the door to the pawn shop. Usually, Del, a polite handsome fellow, was there to greet me. The man behind the counter talking with Jerry was large and sloppy. He had on jeans and a grubby tee-shirt that was doing its best to contain his belly. As I came to Jerry with a smile, the man's eyebrows went up.

"Do you know this lovely lady, Jerry?"

"Mac, I'd like you to meet Double-Dealing Derek, also known as the Wizard of the Double Paw. Del had some out-of-town business, so Derek's filling in. Derek, my wife, Madeline."

Derek had thinning brown hair, and his small features gathered at the center of a large fleshy face I immediately distrusted. I had a pageant flashback to the men who hung around the theater and the stage door, the large swaggering sort who believed beauty queens were dumb enough to fall for their questionable charms.

I wasn't surprised when he kissed my hand. "Delighted to meet you, Madeline."

"Derek used to do a great card act at Ali's Cavern in Charlotte."

"Still do, my boy. They've not caught on yet."

"Do I want to know what a double paw is?" I asked.

Jerry and Derek exchanged a glance that told me this was a scam they'd played together many times.

"No," they both said.

Derek motioned to the glass case filled with rings and bracelets. "Now that you are no longer in the game, Jerry, you must want to buy something for your lovely lady."

"No, the information's all I needed."

I hoped they hadn't spent all their time reliving the good old grifter days. "Did you figure out who Megan is?"

"I told Derek she calls herself a wiccan, but she knew pertinent facts about both of us, carries a nifty dragon head walking stick, and was living in an old teepee in the woods. We've already dismissed fake horoscopes, call-in lines, fake amulets, statues, and curse removal."

Derek scratched his protruding stomach. "I'm going to ask around. Megan Underwood, you said? Seems I heard that name before. Sure it's not Mucking Megan?"

"No, this woman is white with long blond curly hair."

"I'll see what I can do. And what was the other thing? Dark Coven?"

"Darkrose Coven," Jerry said.

"No problem."

After we left the shop, I stopped Jerry on the sidewalk. "Okay, I've got to know. What's a double paw?"

"Derek, as you might guess, makes a convincingly obnoxious drunk. He would come into a bar and insist on playing a card game. I'd already made friends with all the folks in the bar, and, seeing this obviously easy target of a drunk, they'd not only put up their money, they'd lend me money to play. Derek would win all the money, and I'd cool the marks—excuse me—give my pal time to get away by telling a sob story about my wife will kill me, and so forth. Later, I'd meet Derek and we'd split the money."

"And no one ever caught on?"

"We never did the same bar twice." He held the car door for me. "How is Olivia?"

"Prickly as ever." I waited until he got into the car before springing my big news. "She hired me."

"That's unexpected."

"She and Kathleen Wallace have incriminating pictures of each other, and they aren't grown up enough to meet and exchange them."

"Are they holding out for money?"

"I don't know. I've been hired by both of them to get the photos, and Kathleen's not budging."

"You are rolling in clients these days."

"And not getting anywhere with any of them." I started the car. "Let's see if I have better luck with Renee."

Jerry was delighted when Renee said she'd meet me in Parkland Memorial Cemetery.

"Finally! Maybe she's brought along the whole coven."

It wasn't the whole coven. Instead, I met another lanky young woman festooned with piercings and tattoos, including a black rose, who shook my hand and said she'd be happy to help with my investigation. She gave her name as Shadow. Despite her appearance, she was as dignified as a visiting queen with a skeptical air that radiated "I'm not sure I trust you." We sat down on curved cement benches overlooking the vast array of headstones and mausoleums that dotted the green grass of the cemetery.

"Shadow wasn't sure she wanted to meet you," Renee said, "but I told her you could help clear the coven's name."

Shadow grimaced. "You know, when there's anything even remotely paranormal in the paper, the police haul us in for questioning, and we have never committed a crime. We want to be left alone to hold our ceremonies."

"When you say ceremonies, what exactly do you mean?"

"Secret rites and rituals that are meant to enhance our spiritual powers. If you're thinking we're calling up the devil, dancing around naked, or drinking the blood of the innocent, you've got the wrong group."

"Is there a group like that in Parkland?"

She shook her head, earrings jangling. "If there were, we'd know about it."

"What do you know about Eric Levin, the man who was killed?"

"That's definitely a setup. We don't know anything about him. Whoever killed that man put those symbols on him to throw suspicion on us."

"Among other things, a symbol for money."

"Yep. We use that all the time. A setup, like I said."

"Why that symbol?"

"Because we want more money. Who doesn't?"

I looked across the wide expanse of the cemetery. The warm afternoon breeze ruffled the fresh and artificial flowers that decorated the graves and headstones. Was it possible that whoever murdered Eric Levin was trying to send a message by using that particular symbol?

Shadow twisted one of the many skull-shaped rings on her fingers. "You know, you ought to be looking in your own territory. Celosia's got its own Darkrose Coven."

"Two, actually. One from years back."

"Yeah? Well, I'm talking about the new one. You know, don't you, Renee? Girls there have something going on."

Renee rubbed her nose ring, which made me shudder. "It's just a *Pagan Desires* thing. We aren't a coven."

"What sort of something?" I asked Shadow.

"I don't know, exactly. A couple of girls from Celosia came looking for our group not long ago, wanting to know if there was a spell to get rid of a baby. I told them they were crazy and referred them to the nearest abortion clinic."

This was a horrible coincidence. "Who were these girls?"

"They didn't tell me their names."

"Do you remember what they looked like?"

"One had long dark hair because she kept pushing it out of her face. I remember that. It was dyed purple on the ends. The other one I don't remember."

"Must have been Britney Garrett," Renee said. "The other one was probably Clover. They go everywhere together."

"Did you know about this?" I asked her.

"First time I've heard of it."

"Could one of them be pregnant?"

She shrugged.

Shadow thought of something else. "Then there was that nutty woman who wanders around everywhere. She must be from that older coven. She came looking for special weeds she thought we might be hoarding."

"Long blond curly hair? Dresses like a flower child?"

"That's her. I told her we don't do weeds."

Megan Underwood.

Shadow was determined I understand her coven was above all this nonsense. "We are serious about our spiritual growth and development. We don't have time for people who are in it for their own purposes or entertainment. And we damn sure don't have to murder anybody to prove how badass we are."

I shook her hand, "I appreciate you taking the time to meet with me. I'll do what I can to clear your coven's name."

She was genuinely pleased. "Thank you."

I thanked Renee for setting up the meeting, and the two young women disappeared down one of the winding cemetery paths. Jerry and I sat for a long time on the bench, staring out at the silent graveyard. He was as disturbed as I was that a member of Celosia's new Darkrose Coven was apparently pregnant with an unwanted child. What could a desperate young woman do, especially one caught up in witchcraft? Could I keep this dark history from repeating itself?

Abruptly, Jerry tried to lighten the mood. "Did you ever think you'd be Madeline Maclin, Champion of the Coven?"

"I can't believe I'm saying this, but Parkland's Darkrose Coven appears to be the most reasonable party in all this. Certainly Shadow is fiercely protective of its reputation."

"She could be trying to deflect the blame to Celosia."

"I don't get that feeling. Why would she agree to meet me? She wanted to make sure I knew her group was innocent."

"Another innocent party? That's all we need." He stood and offered me his hand. "Who do you want to talk to first?"

I got up and brushed the back of my pants. I wasn't ready to confront Britney or any of the current Darkrose Coven. "Megan. I'm curious about these weeds she was looking for."

"If it's rhododendron, she could've found that anywhere."

"Unless she didn't know it was poisonous and was hoping the Parkland coven could tell her. Now, if I were a homeless witch, where would I go?"

"Narnia?"

"A little more real, please."

"I'd find an abandoned house. And where are abandoned houses in Celosia?"

I knew exactly. "Tinsley Acres."

Chapter Twelve

When she was playing pranks on Jerry in the hopes of luring him back into the game, Jerry's con artist friend Honor had made good use of Tinsley Acres, a failed housing development outside of town, by spending a few days inside one of the huge cathedral-like mansions no one could afford. The owners of the development and the contractors were still locked in bitter disputes. Meanwhile, what could've been palatial homes for the lucky few sat empty.

Honor had camped out in the largest fanciest house, but as we drove down the street, Jerry pointed to the last house. "I'd pick that one. It has a good view of the whole neighborhood, the bushes are up past the first-floor windows for good cover, and it's closest to the woods in case I had to decamp quickly."

"You scare me sometimes."

When Jerry led me around to the back of the last house, we recognized the row of little pots on the patio and the overly sweet strains of flower days and rainbows. Again, Megan wasn't surprised to see us.

"It's my friends from the lake, hello."

Jerry looked around. Floors had been laid in and walls painted, but all the rooms were bare and unfurnished. "Nice digs you've got here. How'd you get in?"

"The door was unlocked. Care for tea?"

"I'd love a glass."

I didn't think it wise to drink anything Megan served, but I followed Jerry's lead. "That sounds nice, Megan, thank you."

Megan had set up camp in what would have been a dining area, her meager possessions and collections of wind chimes, candles, and scarves spread about. I wondered how she could have tea without a fire or electricity, but she produced a large jar from the back stoop.

"Sun tea, courtesy of nature herself, and sweetened with honey." She found two smaller jars and emptied them of lord knows what before pouring two helpings of the tea for Jerry and me.

"Thank you." Jerry didn't drink but gestured with the jar to the room. "You know you won't be able to stay here for long."

"Quite all right. I enjoy the gypsy life."

"Me, too."

"Do you really?"

"Taking chances on the wind, finding comfort in the sheltering roots of trees, sharing the protection of a cave with the creatures of the forest." He didn't say, running from the police, hiding in trash cans, and making mad dashes for the border. Megan was entranced. I used Jerry's distraction to tip my tea into the nearest flowerpot.

"You and I are kindred souls, Jerry Fairweather."

"More than you know, Megan."

"Are you also in the play?"

"I'm writing songs for the show."

Megan rearranged two of her wind chimes. "I'm only going to stay here a few days. When I perform in the show, I'll find a place closer to the theater."

Jerry pretended to take a sip of tea. "I hate to bring bad news, but you didn't get the part."

"Who did?"

"Looks like Amanda's going to do it."

For a moment, there was an actual flash of emotion. The wind chimes clashed discordantly in her hands. "Amanda? Oh, no, I don't see that. What does she know of Emmaline's struggles? She cares only for luxury." She took a breath. "No matter. The committee will soon come to their senses and see that I am the only choice for the role. Until then, I'll perform Emmaline in my heart."

Was Megan aware of anything other than the play? "Megan, did you know Amanda's been accused of murdering Harold Stover?"

"She murdered someone?"

"I'm trying to prove she didn't. Saturday, after Jerry and I dropped you off near the park, did you go anywhere near Park Street?"

"Park Street?"

"That's where Harold Stover lived."

"No, I didn't go there. The vibrations are all wrong." She had a moment of concern. "Why are you asking me these questions?"

"I thought while you were wandering around looking for a place to stay, you might have seen someone or something suspicious."

"I can't imagine what you mean. I live in peace and harmony with all living things. I don't live with suspicion. More tea?"

"No, thank you." I handed her my empty jar.

Somehow during the conversation Jerry had managed to empty his jar, as well. "I'd like a little more, please." As she filled his jar, he said, "Megan, how did you get across the lake at Camp Lakenwood?"

"There's a bridge further down the way where the lake is narrow. I thought it would take me to Westberry, but I got turned around. Then I heard Emmaline's spirit calling."

"What did she say?"

"It wasn't words, as such, but a feeling."

"A 'Hello, come over here, stay in this old teepee' feeling?"

"I merely followed the feeling. I had promised to bring some incense to a friend." She shrugged. "Another day. Excuse me. I must water my little plants." She drifted off toward the patio.

Jerry gave me a nudge. "Check out her walking stick."

The dragon's head looked battered, and several of its teeth were missing.

"One eyeball. Told you."

"Are you thinking she used it to bash Harold?"

"We brought her back to town Saturday. Ask her where she was Friday night. I'll take a look at the plants."

I waited until Megan had finished tending her plants and wandered back to us. Jerry casually stepped back to the patio. "Megan, after auditions Friday night, where did you go?"

"Oh, around."

When she didn't offer any more information, I asked, "Where were you between nine and ten o'clock?"

She gazed off into space. I waited patiently while she gathered her thoughts. Or made up an alibi. "I was meditating."

"Any place in particular?"

"Around."

"Was anyone with you?"

"My spirit guide, of course."

"Anyone visible?"

"There may have been. I don't know. I was in my own reflection bubble. Would you care to see some crystals? I've been very pleased with the quality I find."

"Maybe later," I said. "Did you have your walking stick with you?"

"I keep it with me at all times."

"You didn't lend it to anyone?"

"Oh, no. It was carved especially for me. It only fits my hand."

The walking stick looked like anyone could hold it. Hold it and swing it.

Jerry came back from the patio. He gave me a nod.

"We may be back to talk to you, Megan, thanks."

She smiled at us, unconcerned. "Walk in peace, my friends from the lake."

"Good grief," I said as we drove from Tinsley Acres. "It's like talking to a greeting card. What'd you get?"

He took a handful of leaves from his pocket. "I took a leaf from each one. We can compare them to the bushes at home."

"Now if we only had a motive."

"If Megan's the murderer, and she used her walking stick, there might be an eyeball or some teeth left in Harold's yard—or in his head."

"I doubt the chief will let me see the autopsy report. I imagine the police have gone over the yard pretty thoroughly, but we could give it a try."

When we got to Harold's house, we found a moving van parked out front and a little lady supervising the movers as they boxed and carried out Harold's few belongings.

I parked across the street. "That must be Harold's aunt. Chief Brenner said she was coming."

Harold's aunt was a spry little woman in her late seventies with wispy white hair and blue eyes magnified behind huge glasses that took up most of her tiny face. She told us her name was Lavinia Lawrence. I introduced myself and Jerry, and said I was investigating Harold's murder.

"Well, then, young lady, we need to talk." She took my arm. "There's not anywhere to sit in the house, so let's move out to the backyard. It's much cooler out there, and I can still keep an eye on these boys."

We stood under the trees in the backyard. Lavinia tilted her head to see into the house. "Harold didn't have much, but the furniture's good. I don't want it scratched or dented."

"I'll be glad to watch out for you," Jerry said.

"Thank you, young man. That way I can give all my attention to your lovely wife."

Jerry stationed himself by the back door where he had a good view of the movers. Lavinia gave me a big-eyed stare. "So you're a detective, eh? Excuse me for saying so, but you don't look like one."

"And that comes in handy."

"I would imagine so. Any idea who might've done this?"

"I was hoping you could help me. Did Harold have any enemies?"

"None that I know of." She perched on an old upended bucket that had been left in the yard. "'Course I hadn't seen him in years. He'd call every now and then. Sometimes he'd remember to send me a card at Christmas or on my birthday. Our whole family wasn't close. I'm the only one left. That's pretty sad, isn't it? Sad business all around. From the fibers the police found in the injury and in Harold's hair they believe the murder weapon was a heavy piece of wood like a baseball bat. They've even checked the larger tree branches in the yard." She made a tsking sound. "It's a crazy world, isn't it?"

"Would you tell me what you know about Harold? Sometimes the slightest detail can be helpful."

"All right, then. He was my sister's boy, their only child. Kinda quiet and shy until he got to be about fourteen, and then he started sounding off on anything and everything. Name it, and he had an opinion about it. We decided he'd make a good lawyer, so my sister steered him in that direction, and he did right well."

"Did he grow up in Celosia?"

"No, we all lived in Knoxville. When he was thirty or so, he moved to Parkland, and last I heard of him, he'd moved here. Well, not last I heard of him. That was when the police called me. Since Harold and I were the last Stovers, we were executors of each other's wills, so I came to take care of things." She leaned over to make sure the movers weren't playing bumper cars in the hallway with Harold's bedroom suit. Jerry gave her a thumbs-up sign, which satisfied her.

"Any idea why he left Parkland?"

With the giant magnifying glasses, it was hard to tell, but Lavinia seemed to squint in thought. "Something about a woman he was going to marry. He never did, though."

"Do you recall her name?"

"Marianne, maybe? No, that was her middle name. Megan. That's it. Megan Marianna Underwood. Always thought that was a mouthful to say. Don't know what happened, but they never did get married."

I couldn't believe it. "Mrs. Lawrence, you've just given me a great lead."

"Did I? Well, good for me." She stood and dusted off her skirt. "You get out there and solve this. Harold and I might not have been as close as we should've been, but that doesn't mean I don't want justice for my nephew." Her big eyes looked uncertain. "I suppose you want payment."

"No, that's taken care of. Someone else has already hired me." People are falling over each other to hire me, I wanted to say.

"Don't want you to think I'm stingy, but paying for a murder investigation is not something you budget for."

"Don't worry, Mrs. Lawrence. If you'll give me your phone number, I'll keep you posted on my progress."

There was a muted crash from inside the house. Her head whipped around. "Oh, now what?"

Jerry hurried to check it out and returned with good news. "It's okay. One of the slats fell out of a bed frame."

"Clumsy fellows. I'd better get back in there." She gave me her phone number and thanked me. "Thank you both. This has been a very strange experience."

I'll say. I could hardly wait until Jerry and I were in the car.

"What did she tell you?" he asked. "I saw your eyes light up."

"We've got a connection. Harold was once engaged to Megan."

Jerry took a moment to process this. "Okay, I did not see that one coming."

"Maybe Megan thought Harold and Amanda were getting together, so she killed him in a jealous rage and framed Amanda all in one go."

"But everyone in town knew Harold and Amanda hated each other."

"Yes, but Megan, as we've seen, is never in town. She's always drifting about the fringes."

Jerry wasn't convinced. "I don't know. I still think all this wiccan stuff is an act, but otherwise, she seems harmless. Con men and women, con—they don't murder. If you kill all the marks, then who's left to swindle?"

◇◇◇

We couldn't find Megan. She'd already vacated the house in Tinsley Acres, and there was no sign of her in the park or any other place we thought she might be. Jerry agreed to go back across the lake and look for her tomorrow.

We were welcomed home by the roar of Austin's four-wheeler as it careened across the meadow and into our front yard. Denisha followed more sedately on her bike. I could tell from her expression she'd had about enough of Austin's new toy. Austin had added a flag, a large reflective skull, and a horn, which he beeped.

"Must be suppertime," Jerry said.

Austin hopped off the four-wheeler. "Jerry! There's a race next Saturday, and I need four sponsors. It's only twenty-five dollars, and you get your name in the program and everything. I can choose any name I like, so I thought I'd be Speed Demon. Can you and Madeline sponsor me?"

"Aren't you going to camp?" Jerry asked.

"Yes, but I can miss one day, can't I? I really want to be in this race! It's totally safe. It's kids-only, and I've got my helmet and elbow pads and all kinds of safety equipment."

"What does your mom say about this?"

"She said if I got four sponsors I could do it."

"Okay. I've got twenty-five dollars lying around the house somewhere."

"Great! Wah-hooo!" Austin jumped on his four-wheeler, revved the engine, and took off across the yard.

Denisha gave Jerry a look. "You really shouldn't enable him."

"That's a twenty-five-dollar word there, Denisha."

"I know what it means. My aunt says it all the time about her sister who eats too many sweets. She says if people keep giving her pies and cookies, they're enabling her."

"Look at this way," he said. "Austin's going to drive as fast as he can, right? He'll be safer racing on a track than on the highway, or down these twisty country roads."

"You think if he does this race, he'll get it out of his system?"

"Not completely, but he might not be as wild."

She thought about this. "It's worth a try."

I loved the way Jerry talked to the kids. He'll talk to his own kids like that. Like they had sense. Like he expected them to understand and act accordingly. Like he appreciated their intelligence. He would be a wonderful father.

Would I be a wonderful mother? I was still working on that.

I tried to get a little painting done, but up in my studio, I found myself staring blankly out the window, puzzling over more than motherhood. This Sunday had been a full day—from Roger Price's original wife, Tammy; to Double-Dealing Derek, whose icky hand-kiss I'd scrubbed away; to Renee, who believed the black rose tattoos were only for fans of *Pagan Desires*; to Shadow, who might be helpful; to Megan, still as spacey as ever. Could I make any connections? Shadow said Megan had asked for weeds. Poisonous weeds? Would Megan have reason to kill Eric Levin?

My thoughts circled back to Harold and the sad little box on the mantel. Now more than ever, I wanted in on his case. Was there any way Chief Brenner would let me assist in the investigation? Who would kill Harold in order to implicate Amanda? It didn't make sense. Why not cut to the chase and kill Amanda? I'd have a boatload of suspects then.

The biggest question was why did I agree to help Amanda? She was irritating, overbearing, antagonistic—but she'd cried, "Help me" in the most pitiful voice.

I was a soft-hearted sap.

Jerry cooked spaghetti and meatballs for supper, which met with Austin's approval. After supper, the kids went home, and Jerry and I compared the leaves he'd taken from Megan's plants with the rhododendron bushes at the side of the house. We had a match.

Jerry tossed the leaf away. "Now I'm really glad we didn't drink that tea."

Chapter Thirteen

In my office Monday morning, I made a list of what I knew so far. Friday night, between nine and ten o'clock, someone had gone to Harold's house and killed him with a blow to the head with a heavy piece of wood. Nathan had stopped by around nine-thirty, but when Harold didn't answer the door, Nathan went home. A short while later, Amanda came in to talk to Harold about the show, came into the house, and found him dead.

Tammy Price, whose husband Roger had been stolen away by Amanda, had a motive to get Amanda in trouble, but she also had an alibi. She'd been at the movies with her daughter and a friend. Plus she had Roger back.

Nathan had a motive, but it was to kill Amanda, not Harold. Unfortunately, he'd been seen at the house. I really didn't want to believe anything bad about Nathan. He had his inheritance and his camp. Why would he jeopardize all that?

Joanie Raines had a motive, but again, against Amanda, not Harold.

And Megan, well, who knew about Megan? She was the only one who might have been angry with Harold if she truly wanted to marry him and he broke off the engagement. She was also the only one with her own personal rhododendron and a large, hefty stick.

Then there was the problem of Darkrose Coven, versions one and two.

Twenty or twenty-five years ago, Joanie Raines, along with Lauren Garrett and Constance Tate had formed a secret group that met in the woods near Peaceful Meadow, the site of a commune where Amanda and Megan may have spent part of their childhood. According to Nell, one of the coven members had a baby whose body was never found, a secret only a few people knew.

Now, fast-forward to today and the new Darkrose Coven and another group of young women with poor decision-making skills and one of them pregnant. Was it Britney Garrett? Was that the real reason behind her reaction when she found me at the church? Was it her best friend, Clover, or one of the girls I hadn't been able to talk to?

Or Annie?

I felt cold just thinking about it.

My phone rang. It was Amanda in Demanding Mode. "Madeline, are you any closer to solving this?"

"I've got several good leads."

Her voice was shrill and insistent. "What are they? Who have you talked to? I expect results."

No wonder people let her have her way. It was so much easier than having to deal with her. "You have to give me time to work."

"Have you talked to Tammy? What did she say? She has Roger. She has no reason to set me up."

"She was at the movies Friday night."

"Did you check on that?"

"Yes, I did. She also said you grew up on a commune. Would that be Peaceful Meadow?"

"Good lord, did she actually drag that up? I have completely blotted that out of my life. My parents were idiots. That's all I'm going to say about that."

"I'll take that as a yes. Did you ever see anyone in the woods near Peaceful Meadow? A group of young women?"

"Are you talking about that stupid coven? Yes, I saw them. I told them to keep away or I'd call the police. You can talk to Joanie Raines or Lauren Garrett about that. They were fool enough to take part in that nonsense."

"Constance Tate was a member, too, wasn't she?"

"Yes, and a couple of other lunatics. Now what about Nathan Fenton? Why hasn't he been arrested? I hear he stopped by Harold's house right before I came."

Whew. Not my favorite client. "Amanda, you need to calm down and leave this to me."

"I can't calm down! Our first planning meeting for *Flower of the South* is tonight, and I have a thousand things to do."

It didn't surprise me that the show was the most important thing on her mind. "What about your grant? Has that come through?"

"Yes, the full one hundred thousand, safe in the Society's bank account. The city won't have to put up a dime. Now if you'd get to work and clear me of this ridiculous murder charge, I could concentrate on the show."

"Have you been charged with Harold's murder?"

"No, but the police chief told me not to leave town, and I do not appreciate that. I can sense everyone believes I killed Harold. It's unbearable."

"You can help by answering one more question. How did you convince Britney and Clover to join the Improvement Society? I thought you and Britney's Aunt Eloise were on the outs because of the silver centerpiece."

"It's part of their senior project."

"What exactly is that?"

"I thought you'd know. Every senior at Parkland High has to have a senior project or they won't graduate. Usually, it's some sort of community service or social work, a How I Can Change the World sort of thing. I told the girls this would be perfect and they'd be helping their town."

Amanda had an answer for everything. "What about Constance Tate? How did you convince her?"

"I didn't have to convince her. She's been on board since the beginning."

"Does this have anything to do with the Darkrose Coven?"

"What she did in her teens doesn't interest me."

"She doesn't have a problem doling out big amounts of cash?"

Amanda made an exasperated sound. "What else is she going to do with her money? Her husband's an invalid, and she doesn't have any children. Of course she'd want to spend her money on the arts. I don't know why you're wasting my time with these inane questions, Madeline. I think a murder charge is far more important. Get out there and clear my name and don't keep me waiting."

She hung up. "I will if I want to," I told the phone. Childish, I know, but it made me feel better.

My next phone call was from Joanie, also anxious for an update. "Madeline, what's the latest news?"

"I'm working on it."

"You have to have something by now."

Maybe Joanie would be more forthcoming about the local Witches Improvement Society. "It would help if you'd tell me what you know about Darkrose Coven."

I should have known better. There was a moment of tense silence. "I believe I told you that was none of your business."

"Was the baby yours?"

"Baby? What baby?"

"The baby that was never found. I know it's a deep dark town secret, but it's another unsolved murder, like the two we have right now."

"That's crazy," she said. "First of all, there was no baby. Second, what would this Levin guy have to do with it? And, third, everyone knows Amanda Price murdered Harold because he wouldn't go along with her demented idea for an outdoor drama. I didn't murder Harold, and you'd better prove I didn't."

Blip. Joanie hung up. Hmm, either the coven's pact was too strong, or the missing baby was Joanie's. Let's see what Lauren Garrett had to say. I called the church and was transferred to her office. "Good morning, Lauren, this is Madeline. I need to ask you about the original Darkrose Coven."

"I'm pretty sure I told you everything I know."

"You left out the baby."

Another tense silence, very similar to Joanie's. "What baby?"

"The baby whose body was never found. Isn't it time for the coven members to come clean about this?"

Her voice trembled, whether with anger or suppressed guilt, I couldn't tell. "That's a horrible story. Who told you that?"

"I heard it from a reliable source."

"I don't know where you're getting your information, but you're all wrong. We goofed around and played a few silly games, but there wasn't a baby. Why would you be interested in such a terrible rumor?"

"Because if it's true, I don't want history to repeat itself. Did you know a group of young women in town have started their own Darkrose Coven?"

"It's from the *Pagan Desires* series. That's all it is."

"I think one of those young women is pregnant."

This time the silence stretched for several minutes. "By young women, who exactly do you mean?"

"Among others, Renee Hedley, Clover Comer, Annie Vernon, and your daughter."

"How dare you suggest—" Lauren's voice cut off, and I imagined her staring at the picture of Jesus to give her patience. Sure enough, her voice was much calmer when she continued. "Madeline, I'll thank you not to spread such libelous rumors about my daughter. She would never consider being a part of a coven. You are so wrong about all of this. I don't think we have anything else to discuss."

She ended the call. Never consider being part of a coven, eh? Not even when mom was once a member? I was pretty sure that Britney had secretly decided to follow in Lauren's supernatural footsteps. But if she was pregnant with an unwanted baby, would she also decide that the Darkrose way of taking care of the problem—which involved God-knows-what sort of procedure—was the only way?

Then again, I could be wrong, and another member of the coven was struggling with ethics versus witchcraft.

I needed to talk to Annie.

◇◇◇

Breakfast was still going strong at Deely's, and the smells were too tempting to resist. I sat down at the counter, ordered a bacon biscuit and coffee from Annie, and settled in to listen. The Geezer Club was holding forth from their corner on the price of gasoline, the recent drought, and a suspicious fire that had destroyed a tobacco barn. A group of women in a booth by the door chatted about an upcoming rummage sale at the Methodist church. Two business men sat further down the counter. Both gave me a nod, and one said, "Anything on Harold's murder?"

"I've got a few leads," I said.

"That was a damn shame," the other man said.

"Do you know of anyone who had a grudge against Harold?"

"Didn't know him very well," the first man said. "It's pretty obvious Amanda Price is involved, though, isn't it?"

"That's what I'm trying to find out." When Annie came back with my order, I asked her if she had a few moments to spare.

"I suppose," she said. "What's up?"

"Let's move to a booth."

There was an empty booth back in the corner. Annie sat down, her expression wary.

"Jerry and I met Renee in Parkland yesterday. We talked with Shadow, a member of the Parkland Darkrose Coven. She said a couple of girls from Celosia had come by, asking advice about a baby."

Annie sat very still. "What did she tell them?"

"She referred them to an abortion clinic. Do you know anything about this?" She didn't answer. "Are you pregnant, Annie?"

"No."

"Were you?"

"No."

"Is Britney?"

Annie looked away, deciding how to reply. Then she looked back at me. "I can't believe she'd do something so stupid. We all agreed not to say anything."

"You made a pact."

"Yes, just like the others."

So Renee had lied when she said it was the first time she'd heard this news. "The first Darkrose Coven."

"Yes, Britney's mother was a member. When Britney found out, she thought it would be cool if we formed our own coven. We were already into the *Pagan Desires* books, so at first, we met to discuss the books. But then she said we should try casting spells. That's when I backed away."

"How did Britney find out about the first Darkrose Coven?"

"She was looking through some stuff in her attic and found this old notebook of her mom's. It had spells and chants and symbols in it. When she asked her mom, her mom told her it had been just for fun. That's where she saw the black rose. It was so much like Lissa's—you know, the heroine of *Pagan Desires*—Britney said we should all get one."

"You've seen this notebook?"

"Yeah, she brought it to a meeting once."

I took a napkin and drew the intersecting U's. "Did any of the symbols look like this?"

Annie took a look. "Yeah, I've seen that one."

"And the spells. Did any of them include recipes for making poison?"

"They did. Britney wanted to try them out, but we all said no."

"When's your next meeting?" When she hesitated, I said, "I wouldn't ask if it weren't important. This symbol and the fact that your group knew how to make poisons could very easily tie you in with Eric Levin's murder."

She looked alarmed. "We didn't have anything to do with that!"

"Can you speak for Britney? Or Clover? Or any of the others? Let me know when your next meeting is, and I'll come talk to everyone."

"I'll see."

A customer called to her, and grateful for the interruption, Annie hurried off to another booth.

Jerry came around from the kitchen, wiping his hands on his apron. "Need another biscuit?"

"They're delicious, but no thanks."

"Annie looked upset. What did you say to her?"

"That someone in her book club slash coven could've killed Eric Levin. I've shaken up everyone today. Joanie, Lauren. No one wants to talk about the missing baby. So I'm hoping Annie will tell me when their next meeting is. I do not want anyone to lose another baby."

He took Annie's place in the booth across from me. "I've got a little news. Earlier this morning, three members of the Improvement Society, including Constance Tate, came in for breakfast. The place was crowded, so they sat at the counter, and while I was refilling the juice machine, I could hear them. One was concerned that if Amanda was found guilty of Harold's murder and sent to jail, then *Flower of the South* would fall through. The other said that even with the grant the whole enterprise was way too expensive, and Constance was going to lose all the money she's already paid in."

"So Constance is bankrolling the show."

"Yep. Constance said they didn't need to concern themselves with that. Then I asked if any of them could tell me why the outdoor drama was so important to Amanda. Was this her special dream? Had she always wanted to be an actress? And none of them had an answer. One woman said she didn't think the project had caught on the way Amanda expected. I mentioned to Constance she could always withdraw her support if she didn't think the show would fly. She told me—in her frostiest voice, mind you—that that was not a problem. Then she changed the subject to Harold's murder and said it had to be Joanie."

"Any reason?"

"The other women agreed with her. They said Joanie had always been incredibly jealous of Amanda, and if she knew ahead of time Amanda was going to play Emmaline, she'd be mad enough to kill."

"But why kill Harold?"

"I asked that, too. They said he was against the show and Joanie's big chance to play Emmaline, so naturally, he had to die. They all seemed determined to pin the murder on Joanie."

"That's a pitiful reason to kill someone."

"Sounds like Amanda's got them squarely in her camp. Oh, and speaking of money, I've still got that check Constance gave me."

"She wrote that check without a word of protest. That's what makes me still think Amanda has something on her."

He got up. "Back to work. Who are you going to shake up next?"

"Megan Underwood, if I can find her."

"Let's ask the Celosia grapevine. Grapevine, get it? I'm keeping with the theme here." He raised his voice. "Has anyone seen Megan Underwood?"

A member of the Geezer Club came through with a useful answer. "I saw her out by Richardson's Goat Farm yesterday. That's over toward Westberry, about five miles from here."

"Thanks." I gave Jerry a kiss. "Keep an eye on Nathan today. I'm on my way to Richardson's Goat Farm."

Chapter Fourteen

The ride out to Westberry, like all drives in the countryside around Celosia, was along winding roads lined with fields and wildflowers, cattle farms, the occasional rusty mobile home, little grocery stores with one or two gas pumps, and dusty dirt side roads that led off into the woods with only a dented mailbox or faded sign to indicate anyone lived there.

Richardson's Goat Farm was easy to find. There were goats all over the pastures, snoozing in piles, munching on the grass, the younger ones butting each other and standing on top of whatever they could find, including the older goats. I turned down a winding gravel road and parked near a barn beside a battered white pickup truck. A man carrying a bucket waved and came over to me. He was tall and rangy, his jeans torn and frayed. Both his navy blue tee shirt and cap were decorated with a jumping goat and "Richardson's Goat Farm" in bright green.

"Morning. What can I do for you?"

"Good morning," I said. "I'm Madeline Maclin. I'm working on a case, and I'm looking for Megan Underwood. I was told she might be here."

"Well, she was. I think she's left. Come on, we'll see."

I followed him along the fence. The goats, alerted by the bucket, perked up and hurried over making all kinds of strange noises. I always thought goats made a baahing sound like sheep, and a few of these did, but there was also an array of snorts, burps, and a curious "what-what-what" from a spotted goat with one horn. The man tossed carrots over the fence. There was a mad scramble for the treats.

"She came out earlier to give 'em some crackers. They love crackers. Don't see her now, though. She must've gone."

Two billy goats fought over the last piece of carrot. Their horns clacked as they knocked heads.

"How well do you know her?"

He set the bucket down and leaned on the top rail of the fence. "Hadn't seen her in a while. She comes out here to get goat cheese to sell at the market in town. She ain't got much money, so we work out a deal with her. She tends to the goats for us, makes sure they have water, takes them up to the vet when they get sick, goes and gets more feed from the store, cleans out the pens every now and then if they need it, gets their heads out of the fence. They like to stick their heads through to get to the grass on the other side, and they get their horns stuck when they pull back." The goats gathered under him, hoping for more carrots. "Go on, now. That's all."

One fat brown goat pushed her head through the fence. I patted her head. Her weirdly slanted pupils gave her a sinister look. "Does Megan walk from town?"

"I guess. She just shows up."

Maybe I could catch her on the road. "Did you know that at one time she was engaged to Harold Stover?"

"Harold Stover. Wasn't he murdered? Seems I heard about that on the news."

"I'm investigating his murder."

"He came out here one time wanting to make sure the animals was treated properly. Nice fella. You say he and Megan used to be engaged? Can't see her settling down. She's all about free love. Told me that was the way she was raised. Like goats. That little mama goat you're petting there? Reason she's so fat is because she's pregnant. Again." He gestured to the herd. "The daddy could be any one of those billy goats out there. Free love. Only way to do it." He'd amused himself. "Saves a lot of trouble. Anything else I can do for you, ma'am?"

I gave him one of my cards. "If you see Megan, please tell her I'd like to talk to her."

"Sure thing."

A few goats followed us back to the barn and watched as I got in my car.

"Sorry," I told them. "No free goat love here."

I drove down the road to the next little town ironically called Big Pond and then all the way back to Celosia. No sign of Megan. She must have cut through the woods and fields, or perhaps ridden her broomstick home.

I went back to the house, rooted in the fridge for an apple, and sat on the porch to eat and think. Jerry called to say camp was going great, but Megan had not returned to her hideaway across the lake.

"I hope you've solved the crime because Nathan's about to drive me crazy."

"There was a Megan-sighting at Richardson's Goat Farm. That's all I've got."

Someone must have asked him a question because he said, "Sure. Be right there. Gotta go, Mac. See you later."

I went into the house for more tea, and when I returned to the porch, a strange silver car chugged up the drive. The driver parked and got out. It was Jerry's friend, Double-Dealing Derek.

"Mrs. Fairweather, hello."

I was not happy to see him. "Hello."

Instead of jeans and a tee-shirt, he had on a rumpled, sweat-stained light gray suit and a white shirt with a frayed collar. He sat down on the porch steps and fanned himself with his hat. "Whew! It's a hot one today."

"Come sit in a rocking chair."

"No, thanks. I'm fine right here."

"Want some tea?"

"If it's not too much trouble."

So I wondered what the trouble was. I brought him a glass of tea and he thanked me.

"Jerry around?"

"He'll be home at four."

"Mind if I wait?"

Actually, I did. "Not at all."

Derek took a drink and looked out across the meadow. "He's a lucky man. Nice big house. Beautiful wife."

"Thanks."

He set his glass aside. "You know, most of us have to rely on playing a character, but not Jerry. He's got one of those faces you like right away. Like and trust. Nice open, honest face. Worth a fortune. It's a shame he's quit the game, I mean, I'm sure you're glad he's gone straight. Don't suppose you'd let him have one more go?"

I knew this man was up to something. "Is that why you're here?"

"Never hurts to try."

"No. No more cons."

He grinned as if he expected that answer. "Actually, I've got a little info for him. That woman he was asking about, Megan Underwood? I think he'll be surprised by what I've found. Got something on that Darkrose Coven, too."

Did he really? "You can surprise me. It's my case."

"Think I'll hang onto it till Jerry gets home."

Oh, I could see where this was going. Whatever info Derek had, if it could help the case in any way, he wanted payment. He wanted Jerry's help with something, something that I was sure would be amazingly illegal.

I didn't want Derek sitting on my porch all afternoon, especially if the kids came over. He must have sensed my disapproval. He heaved himself up. "Why don't I check out the town and come back around four?"

"That's a good idea."

He grinned again, but his eyes were cold. "Thanks for the tea."

I watched him drive away. Jerry's friends. Good lord, where to begin? For about three years after we graduated from college, I lost track of Jerry. During that time, he was attending Big Mike's Con School and running around with all sorts of swindlers, including Rick, Del, and Honor. Del was always a gentleman, and I could handle Rick's foolishness. Honor had realized Jerry wanted to live a different life and have a family, and she agreed to leave him alone. But this man who called himself Derek—he set off all my alarms. Did he really have information? Why drive all the way to Celosia when he could've phoned Jerry with the news? Why not share it with me? What did he really want?

I was still standing on the porch, frowning, when Nell drove up in her white van.

"Who was that in the silver car?"

"Another one of Jerry's acquaintances."

She glanced at me and then squinted in the direction of the driveway. "I take it you had words."

"There's something different about this one. I'll admit I'm unsettled."

"What did he want?"

"He says he has information about Megan Underwood." I had to laugh. "Nell, I'm sure you have information about Megan Underwood. I don't know why I didn't think to ask you the other day."

"What do you want to know?"

"Anything you can tell me. Please have a seat." We sat down in the rocking chairs. "I'm really interested in her engagement to Harold Stover."

Nell took off her cap, gave her hair a swipe, and settled the cap on, pulling the little ponytail through the back. "Oh, yeah. That didn't work out. She was into all the hippie stuff even when she was in her teens. All on account of her upbringing. Now, can you see someone like Harold Stover living in a meadow? They were too different."

"Were Amanda's parents hippies, too?"

"Yeah, well, they're sisters."

I stopped rocking. What? "Megan and Amanda?"

"Yep. Oh, Amanda doesn't claim her, though. Won't have nothing to do with the family. She left as soon as she could and started working a way to get rich."

It took me a while to understand what Nell had told me. "They're sisters?"

Nell shifted in her chair. "Probably got different daddies, though. You know how it is with all that free love."

Wow. "So that's why even though Megan gave a terrific audition for the part of Emmaline Ross, Amanda dismissed her completely."

"Like I said, wants nothing to do with her."

"Would they have competed for Harold?"

"No, Amanda's always hated him."

"Would she kill him, Nell?"

Nell squinted her little blue eyes in thought. "You know, I think that would be too messy for Amanda. Most likely, she'd have somebody do it for her." She pushed herself up. "I was going to finish patching up the chimney today. Oh, and if you're worried about that guy in the silver car, get a description to Dad. He can take care of it for you."

"Thanks, I will. One other thing, Nell. I'm working a case for Kathleen Wallace. What can you tell me about her?"

"Local gal. Her dad and granddad probably delivered most of the town, so she decided to be a doctor, too. Always said she'd come back to Celosia and set up her practice here. I hadn't heard any complaints."

"You remember Olivia Decker. It seems she and Kathleen have a real problem getting along."

"Not surprising. Who gets along with Olivia?"

"This goes back to their college days. I'm thinking there was a man involved."

Nell scratched her chin. "Well, Kathleen did like a fella named Billy Sampson."

"Is he still around?"

"Yeah, works over at First Savings and Loan."

A place to start. "Thanks, Nell."

Nell had given me plenty to think about. First of all, I wanted to talk to Amanda about her sister.

I found her at the theater. She stood center stage barking orders, and three of the older members of the Improvement Society were scurrying to do her bidding.

"I'm going to need thirty-five, maybe forty chairs—no, with such a large cast, I think the supporting players can sit in the auditorium, and let's have the leads up on stage, so that's seven chairs on stage. Get the ones with the cushions. Make sure everyone has a copy of the script."

The script? She'd already written the entire outdoor drama?

Constance frowned at her. "Everyone? Even the people who don't say anything?"

"Everyone. It's important that they understand the entire concept. Make fifty copies."

"Very well."

I stopped Constance as she started up the aisle toward the office. "Is the script finished? How did Amanda get it done so fast?"

Constance looked as if she didn't want to answer. "She's had this idea for years."

An idea for a show or an idea how to hoodwink the town? I wanted to ask.

Constance brushed past me. "Excuse me."

Amanda called to another woman. "I want you to make a list of everyone's contact information, addresses, phone numbers, e-mails. Make certain we have a number for every single person. Oh, and fix a chart with all their names. If they miss three rehearsals, they're out."

This woman's voice was tinged with disbelief. "You're going to take roll every night?"

"No, that's going to be your job. Oh, hello, Madeline. Is Jerry with you? I want to go over those songs. Has he scored them for orchestra? I'm thinking we'll need at least ten musicians."

"No, he's at Camp Lakenwood. I wanted to talk to you."

She spread her arms wide to indicate the vast amount of work she had to do. "I'm incredibly busy right now. The first read-through is tonight, and there are a thousand things that have to be taken care of."

"This will only take a minute. You requested an update on the case."

Her manner changed. "Yes, of course." She came down the steps at the side of the stage and met me at the first row of seats. "It's Joanie Raines, isn't it? She's been jealous of me ever since I moved to town."

"No, it's about your sister."

She looked so blank, for a moment I wondered if Nell could possibly be mistaken. "I don't have a sister."

"Megan Underwood."

She lowered her voice to a fierce whisper. "Don't you dare let anyone hear you call that woman my sister! I will have nothing to do with her."

"But she is your sister?"

"We had the same mother, possibly the same father, who knows? Growing up in that commune was sheer chaos." She took a quick glance back at the stage as if to assure herself the Society members weren't listening in on our conversation. "My parents were all weeds and granola. I couldn't stand that. I wanted nice things, expensive things. I wanted indoor plumbing, for God's sake! I left as soon as I could. I refuse to acknowledge her in any way."

There had to be more to this than a dislike of the hippie lifestyle. "But other than being a free spirit, how has Megan harmed you?"

"Oh, she's fooled you too, hasn't she? All that spacey talk about love and peace. She ruined every relationship I ever had. Who do you think called Tammy Price and told her about me and Roger?"

I couldn't see Megan making that much effort. "If she was brought up in an atmosphere of free love, why would she care?"

"Exactly! See if you can solve that mystery. It's crazy! And then to have her show up at auditions and waltz in like a queen, expecting me to hand her the role of a lifetime? I couldn't have been more shocked."

"When was the last time you'd seen her?"

"Oh, I can't remember. Months ago. I saw her on the street somewhere."

"So she doesn't call you or try to contact you in any way?"

"No. She knows how I feel about her. At least, I think she knows. She filters everything through sunbeams."

"Tell me about her relationship with Harold."

"Oh, that. What a joke! This was several years ago, and I'm sure he was enchanted by all the fairy dust. But a man can take only so much of all that hearts and flowers, especially a buttoned-up man like Harold. He broke off the engagement."

"How did Megan take that?"

"It didn't seem to bother her. She drifted on to the next relationship."

"She wasn't angry at Harold?"

"She never gets angry about anything! It's like she's in a fog, unless—" Amanda gripped my arm. "Do you suppose she misinterpreted my relationship with Harold and killed him to keep us apart?"

"The evidence doesn't suggest that."

"Then what does the evidence suggest? I did not kill Harold!" She tightened her grip. "Quit worrying me with all this about Megan and find out who killed him. That's what I'm paying you for!"

With that, she marched back up to the stage to harass her troops. "Well? Why are you all standing around here? We have work to do!"

Chapter Fifteen

Now I needed to hear Megan's side of the story, but I couldn't find her anywhere. I decided to stop by First Savings and Loan and see if I'd have better luck locating Billy Sampson.

Billy Sampson was not hard to find. He was now William P. Sampson, bank manager, a large boisterous man with a deep voice that made the tellers and everyone in line turn in his direction.

"Ms. Maclin, welcome! What brings Celosia's most famous private eye to First Savings today?"

He reminded me of a circus ringleader. All eyes were on us, and I envisioned Sampson putting on a show for the whole bank. And in this ring, the amazing female detective and her remarkable clues! "A private matter I'd like to discuss with you."

"Of course! Glad to help." He showed me to his office and shut the door. "Please sit down." Sampson sat down in an expensive-looking leather wingback chair and rubbed his long hands together in anticipation. "I've always wanted to be part of an investigation."

I settled in another plush leather chair. "My client is Kathleen Wallace. I understand you know each other?"

"Yes, we dated for a while. Lovely woman. Excellent doctor. She's done very well for herself."

"You're still friends?"

"Well, I wouldn't say that. We had a falling out several years ago, and I don't think she's ever forgiven me."

"Would it have anything to do with Olivia Decker?"

Sampson's thick eyebrows went up. "Damn, you are good! What do you know about that?"

"The two women are at odds, and I'm trying to settle the quarrel. Did Olivia steal you away?"

He chuckled. I thought he was flattered by the idea of women fighting over him. He surprised me. "No, no. Olivia's a beautiful woman, but she's too intense for me. No, this had to do with money." His gesture took in his office and the bank lobby beyond the windows. "You see all this? My father built this bank. He was a very wealthy man, and he liked to spread his wealth around. He offered scholarships to deserving college students every year, and I'm afraid Kathleen thought I had enough influence with my dad to decide who received those scholarships."

"Oh, so when she didn't get one, she blamed you."

"Yes. No amount of explaining would convince her. She and Olivia Decker were up for the same scholarship. Olivia got it, and Kathleen believed Olivia had used her feminine wiles to enchant me and my father, but I promise you I never had any sort of relationship with Olivia, and neither did my dad. She was the best candidate, that's all."

I knew Olivia came from money. "Even though she was from a wealthy family, herself, and could easily afford to go to any college or university?"

"We didn't find that out until later. By then, it was too late and my father honored his obligation."

"I take it Kathleen's family wasn't rich."

"Not as rich as Olivia's, but they managed."

I understood now why Kathleen had said Olivia had cheated her. She thought Olivia had bent the rules by conveniently forgetting to mention her family could handle any amount of tuition.

"I don't know why Kathleen is still unhappy about all this," Sampson said. "She found a way to pay for medical school and has a thriving practice in town."

But what if she borrowed money and is in serious debt?

"I hope that answers your question, Ms. Maclin. Was there anything else?"

"No, thank you." It had occurred to me that another sorority sister might help me find the compromising photos of Olivia.

Delta Gamma would have to wait. It was almost four o'clock. Jerry would be getting home, and I had to be there when Derek arrived.

Nell's van was gone and Jerry's red Jeep was already parked in the drive when I got to the house. He greeted me at the porch just as Derek's silver car drove up. He was curious to see his former partner.

"What's Derek doing here?"

"This is his second visit. He says he has some information about Megan and the Darkrose Coven."

"He could've called me."

"That's what I thought. Do not let him talk you into anything."

Derek got out of his car and grinned. "Jerry. Got something for you."

Once again, Derek claimed a spot on the porch. He dug a wrinkled photograph out of his pocket and presented it to Jerry. "You remember that scheme in Morehead that never went down? Well, lookee here."

"Looks sort of like Megan."

"Yep. She was out on the pier with the rest of them. I think she was the bait gal, in more ways than one."

Jerry turned the picture over. The faded date on the back was from August of last year. "How did you get this?"

"Called in a favor. Now I need one."

"I'm out, you know that."

"Come on. I need your face for one night, just one. I want to catch someone who's been playing me."

"I'm sorry. I can't do it."

"Oh, but there's more. I got something on that coven, too. 'Course that stays with me until the job's done." Derek grinned another cold-eyed grin. "I'll let you and the missus thrash it out." He wandered back to his car and leaned against it, his arms folded as if satisfied.

I would have gladly wiped that smirk off his face. "I knew it. I knew he was up to something."

"What if he has information we could use?"

"What if he doesn't? What if this is all a ploy to get you involved in something really shady?"

"I've worked with Derek for years."

"Do you trust him?"

Jerry glanced at the man. "He wasn't the most reliable partner."

"Just say no." I took a closer look at the photograph. "This looks like Megan, but I can't tell for sure. What's a bait gal, anyway?"

"Someone who distracts the mark. Usually a very pretty girl."

"You've met Megan. Is that something she could handle?"

"Right now I'd say no, but we didn't know her a year ago."

"Can you get Derek to leave without getting involved in anything?"

A few months ago, Jerry would've found a way to get around my protests, but this time, he was suspicious of his old partner's motives. He walked out to Derek and handed him the photograph. They talked for a while, and I couldn't tell from either man's expression how the conversation was going. Finally, they shook hands, and Derek drove away. Jerry came back up the porch steps.

I was concerned they'd made a bargain. "What did he say?"

"He was not happy, but I told him we couldn't tell if the woman in the picture was Megan, so it wasn't very useful. As to his other information, I said that you were a very competent private investigator, and you would be able to solve this case on your own."

"Well, thank you very much. Do you still owe him anything?"

"I told him where he could find Artless Bob. He's got the kind of face Derek's looking for. Of course, now I'll owe Bob for sending Derek his way."

I hugged him. "I can't tell you how proud I am."

"That I gave up poor Bob?"

"That you didn't let Derek pull you under."

"Got to set a good example for the kids, and speaking of kids, why don't we go make some?"

"I would love to." In the distance, we heard the faint roar of Austin's four-wheeler. "But it doesn't look like that's going to happen right now."

We settled for another quick kiss before Austin arrived in a spray of gravel and dust.

"Hey! Nell says there were baby owls inside your chimney, but she let them go. Did you guys get to see them, Madeline?"

"No, but I heard them at night."

"Do you think you could catch one? A baby owl would look cool riding on my four-wheeler. What are you guys having for supper?"

Jerry made one of Austin's favorite snacks, little hot dogs rolled up in biscuits he called pigs-in-blankets. The pigs were almost done when Denisha rode up on her bike.

"Look what I made in camp today, Madeline." She proudly displayed a pink and purple lanyard. "Here's my house key, and here's a heart of an old locket my aunt gave me."

"Denisha, we missed seeing baby owls," Austin said. "Nell got them out of the chimney. I wish she'd kept them. We could each have one."

"No, thank you. I'd rather have a puppy. My aunt says if I keep my grades up next year, she might let me have one. What are you cooking, Jerry? It smells really good."

"Pigs-in-blankets!" Austin announced.

"And they are ready." Jerry scooped the biscuits off the baking sheet and onto a plate. The kids sat down at the table. Austin's hand hovered over the plate as he decided which biscuit to choose.

"Just take one," Denisha said. "They're all the same."

He made his choice. "This one's bigger."

Denisha carefully picked a biscuit from the pile. "Jerry, how do you like your job at Deely's?"

"I like it very much, thanks."

"We miss coming over here for pancakes."

"I can always fix pancakes for supper."

"True. I hadn't thought of that."

"Or pancakes at camp one morning."

Denisha turned to me. "And how is your case coming, Madeline?"

"It's at the confusing stage. I still have a lot of things to figure out."

Austin had finished one biscuit and was halfway through another. "I heard you found the witch's cottage in the woods, just like in *Hansel and Gretel*, only it wasn't made of gingerbread."

Jerry set two glasses of milk on the table and sat down. "It was actually made of cottage cheese."

Austin groaned. "That is so lame."

"It wasn't a cottage," I said. "And it's really not nice to call Ms. Underwood a witch. She was camping out in one of the old teepees on the other side of the lake. Mr. Fenton asked her to find another place."

"Doesn't she have a home?" Denisha asked.

"I don't think so, but she seems to enjoy camping. She was brought up in a commune. You know what that is?"

"Like a community center?"

"Sort of. A group of people decide to form their own community, very much like a farm. Everyone helps grow the food and tend the animals."

"So Ms. Underwood doesn't mind being outside all the time?"

"She enjoys being around nature."

This explanation satisfied Denisha, but Austin wasn't convinced. "Then how come she carries around that big old stick with a dragon's head on it? That's the kind of thing wizards and witches have."

"Maybe she likes dragons," Denisha said. "I like them."

"I still think she's a witch."

"My aunt says there used to be some people around here acting like they was witches until the police told them to stop."

The Darkrose Coven. "What else did she say, Denisha?"

She took a bite of her biscuit and set it down. "People shouldn't mess with stuff like that. God doesn't like it. That's what my aunt says."

"Has she heard about anyone doing it now?"

"No, but she knew that Levin boy's family, the one that was found in the vineyard? She said it's sad, but when you play with fire, you get burned. Only he didn't get burned, actually. It's just an expression."

"Did the police come talk to your aunt?"

"Yes, and she told them the Levin boy was wild and it was a shame the way all these girls went around batting their eyes at him. Said he should've stayed in Copeley, and then maybe he wouldn't have gotten killed."

"Does your aunt have any idea who might have been angry enough to kill him?"

Denisha wiped her hands on her napkin. "No, but she did say something about scorched women and a word I'm not supposed to say, but it starts with 'h.'"

"Hell!" Austin said enthusiastically.

She turned on him. "Austin Terrell, you are not supposed to say that word, either."

"Your aunt didn't tell *me* not to say it."

I intervened before they could get into one of their rousing arguments. "Did your aunt say, 'Hell hath no fury like a woman scorned'?"

"That's it. She said it means don't ever leave a woman, or she'll get really angry."

Austin would not let go. "As angry as hell!"

Jerry convinced Austin that hell was not a nice word to say at the dinner table. After supper, I gave Denisha a little sparkly round pin to go on her lanyard, and Jerry took a spin around the meadow on the four-wheeler. They thanked Jerry for the dinner, and then decided they'd better get home.

As we watched them ride off, I put an arm around Jerry's shoulders. "Are we sure we want kids?"

"Many, many kids."

"Let's start with one."

"Let's start right now."

"I'm afraid *Flower of the South* beckons, and I need to let you know what Olivia's been up to." We sat down in the rocking chairs, and I told Jerry about my discussion with William Sampson and how Kathleen thought she had been cheated out of a scholarship that Olivia didn't need. "Looks like I'll be paying a visit to the Delta Gamma house."

"Think the sisters will give up any secrets?"

"If I can get Olivia's photos from Kathleen and take them to her, she'll give me Kathleen's, and this whole silly affair will be over. And speaking of sisters, guess who's related? Amanda and Megan."

Jerry stopped rocking to give me a wide-eyed stare. "They're sisters? Wow, talk about taking different paths."

"Amanda doesn't claim her, big surprise."

"What about Eric Levin and the scorched woman, whoever she is?"

I was beginning to put a few pieces together. "If Eric Levin got one of the new Darkrose Coven members pregnant and wouldn't take responsibility, maybe they decided to get rid of him. What if they mixed up one of the poisons from Lauren Garrett's old notebook and left symbols on the body, hoping the Parkland coven would take the blame?"

"Or Megan, if they knew about her rhododendron plant."

I sat back in my chair. "I'd still like to know what Megan was really doing out in the woods."

Jerry checked his watch. "Okay, enough exciting news. We have exactly thirty minutes to make a baby."

Chapter Sixteen

I convinced Jerry to wait until after the read-through of *Flower of the South*. When we got there, about three rows of the auditorium were filled. The woman Amanda had put in charge of gathering contact information gave everyone an index card and a pencil. Constance passed out copies of the script. Jerry and I sat down over to one side.

Constance handed him a script. "If you'll mark where the songs go, please."

He hefted the stack of paper. "Wow, that was fast. When did Amanda write this?"

Constance stiffened and gave him the same answer she'd given me. "I believe she's been working on it for a long time."

"You know she can't have the show at Camp Lakenwood."

"I told her that was too far away. Now she's decided that Peaceful Meadow would be an ideal place."

"You'll have the same problem getting your audiences out there, won't you?"

"I'm sure Amanda has a plan."

Use Peaceful Meadow for the play? I wondered if Megan had heard this news and how she felt about it.

Amanda was on stage, rearranging the chairs and telling the leads where to sit. "You go here, and let me have Emmaline's father here. Where's Emmaline's mother?"

She turned and called out to the auditorium. "Has anyone seen Joanie Raines?"

"I doubt she took that part," I told Jerry.

"Now Amanda can play Emmaline and Mrs. Ross."

"I'll bet she would."

No one knew where Joanie was, and another woman volunteered to call her.

"Oh, here she is," someone said.

Heads swiveled as Joanie Raines came down the aisle. I thought she would be fired up and ready to tell Amanda there was no way in hell she'd play Emmaline's mother, but Joanie was smiling. It was the self-satisfied smile of someone who is going to enjoy delivering bad news.

Amanda laid on the sarcasm. "Thank you for joining us, Joanie. Please be on time in the future."

Joanie came up on stage, her voice pitched so all could hear. "Good evening, everyone. I've been on a little trip to our neighboring town of Rossboro, talking to the people at their arts council, which, by the way, is very active. They've heard rumors that Celosia was going to have an outdoor drama, and they love the idea. Only they want one of their own, and guess what? They claim Emmaline Ross."

Amanda rocked back on her heels. "What?"

Joanie was thoroughly enjoying herself. "Lots of Rosses in Rossboro. Who'd have thought it? Emmaline Ross. Rossboro. You see the theme here?"

I was prepared for a major eruption, but Amanda retreated to icy haughtiness. "They have no proof whatsoever that Emmaline Ross lived anywhere near Rossboro. You're trying to get back at me because you don't like your part. You don't have to take that part. You don't have to be in the show, at all."

Joanie got right up in Amanda's face. "I'm not going to be. I'm going to work with the Rossboro Arts Council to create my own outdoor drama. It'll be bigger and better than anything you can come up with, and we'll have a terrific Emmaline. Me. You should've chosen me when you had the chance." While Amanda spluttered for a reply, Joanie addressed the crowd. "And any of you are welcome to come be in my play. I'll make sure everyone has a speaking part, and there'll be plenty of songs and dances. You don't have to settle for Amanda's second-rate show."

With that, she sailed proudly down the aisle and out of the theater. Everyone watched her go. Everyone turned back to see what Amanda would do.

Was I mistaken, or did I read relief on Constance's face? Relief that Joanie was gone, or that Amanda's plans had been thwarted?

"Can you believe it?" Jerry said to me. "Dueling Emmalines. Stand back and watch the grapes fly."

Amanda drew herself up. "All right. You've heard what Joanie had to say. It's obvious she's upset because she didn't get the lead role, and this is her way of retaliating. Anyone who would like to leave is welcome to do so. But our show will go on, and we'll prove to Joanie and to Rossboro that Celosia can have the best outdoor drama in the state. Please turn to page one."

A few people got up and left, but the majority stayed. I figured city pride won out over theatrical ambitions. After all, there was a friendly rivalry between Celosia and Rossboro.

"I don't know why I didn't see it before," I told Jerry. "Rossboro. It makes sense they would have some claim to Emmaline."

"Which they probably didn't know they had until Joanie pointed it out."

We stayed for the entire read-through, which took two hours. Jerry played through the songs he'd written and helped choose the singers. Amanda remained calm and professional through the rest of the rehearsal, thanked everyone for coming and for staying, and told them she'd have a schedule ready tomorrow night.

Afterwards, she let loose on her committee. "I cannot believe Joanie would do such a thing! She betrayed our entire town!"

Constance tried to placate her. "Settle down. You're better off without her. If she'd taken the role of Mrs. Ross, she would've done her best to upstage the other actors."

Another member joined in. "That's exactly right. I've been in shows with her, and that's what she does. We can find someone else to play Emmaline's mother. And Jerry, don't you dare write songs for Joanie's show. Our outdoor drama has to be the best. We can't let Rossboro win."

Amanda looked gratified by their loyalty. "Thank you. We can do this. We *will* do this. Constance, make sure we get a firm commitment from all cast members. Tomorrow night, *Flower of the South* goes into production full steam ahead!"

We left the Improvement Society full of patriotic fervor and drove back home.

Joanie's defection to Rossboro and the creation of another Emmaline were twists I never expected. "Every time I think things can't get any nuttier, the people of Celosia prove me wrong. What did we do for entertainment before we moved here?"

Jerry had enjoyed all the drama. "Well, I ran cons, and you tried to keep out of pageants."

"Speaking of cons, you haven't heard anything else from Derek, have you?"

"Nope. Artless Bob must have done the job."

I still didn't believe we'd seen the last of Derek. "I didn't see Britney or Clover here tonight."

"They're still in high school aren't they? Maybe they had a pile of homework."

"Maybe they're out drawing pentagrams in the woods." There was something else I wanted to check out. "Amanda says she received the grant money for the show. I wonder if Evan knows about this."

"If it's a theater grant, the money would come directly to him, wouldn't it?"

"Would you be surprised if it came directly to Amanda? Do you suppose that's why she's been pushing so hard for this project?"

"I thought she had plenty of money."

"Then why would she need a grant?" I turned onto the road that led to our house and put the window down so we could enjoy the mild sweet-smelling night air. "She told me the money was in the Society's bank account, so I don't know how she intends to get her hands on it. I need to call Evan."

Jerry pointed ahead to a large black-and-white shape blocking our way. "Cow in the road."

I slowed to let the cow amble across. "That one gets out once a week, doesn't she?"

"We never had this much excitement in Parkland." Jerry leaned out his window and mooed. "Get along, Bessie. We've got things to do."

The cow took her time, pausing by the side of the road to pull up a mouthful of grass and weeds. I maneuvered around her and returned to our conversation. "I know you've had fun writing songs, but this whole idea has been suspect from the very beginning. Why an outdoor drama? Half the town thinks it's a silly idea. Was it just to spite Harold, her sister's old fiancé?"

"Maybe Amanda loved Harold. Maybe she's the woman scorned."

"My head is so full of all these twists and turns I don't know how I'm going to sort it all out."

"I can take your mind off that. You promised me a baby-making session, and I intend to hold you to that promise. In fact, I intend to hold you all night."

◇◇◇

Tuesday morning, I ran into Joanie at Deely's. Jerry's special today was bacon and eggs with raisin toast. I brought my plate over to her booth.

"Mind if I join you?"

"Not at all." She also had the special and added ketchup to her eggs. "I was hoping to see someone from last night. I got Amanda good, didn't I? The look on her face was priceless."

"Did you really go to Rossboro?"

"Of course! They even have a little exhibit about Emmaline in their museum."

"Do they honestly want to produce an outdoor drama?"

"Yes, they do. Even though they're bigger than Celosia, they're still a small town, too, so it's a matter of money, but they can do it. They're excited." She leaned forward. "What did Amanda say after I left? She was livid, wasn't she?"

"You didn't stop her."

"I didn't think I would. But I've got her on the run. And it's only a matter of time before she's convicted of killing Harold, so there won't be a *Flower of the South*, anyway."

"I don't believe Amanda killed Harold."

"Then who did? Or do you think I killed him?"

"I've got a few more leads to follow."

"Well, I've got a meeting in Rossboro this morning. They have a fellow there, a professional playwright, who writes plays especially for their theater group. He can't wait to write one about Emmaline. It'll be tons better than that stuff Amanda made up, and his will be historically accurate, I'm sure." She crunched into a piece of toast. "Think Jerry would write some songs for us, too?"

"He's already committed to *Flower of the South*."

"That's okay. Ours might work better as a straight drama. Sometimes songs and dances slow the action down."

I couldn't imagine what sort of action Emmaline and her slow-growing grapes would create, but I didn't mention that. "Do you have the number for the Arts Council?"

"Sure." She took out her phone and looked up the number. "Here you go."

I put the number in my phone. "Thanks."

She chopped at her scrambled egg. "Amanda had no right to dismiss me and my acting ability. Emmaline's mother! Honestly. Do I look like anyone's mother? Any old bag in town could play that part. She's going to find out what it means to be disrespected like that. What's that old saying? One wrong turn deserves another?"

"I'm not exactly sure that's the way it goes."

"That's the way I'm saying it." She pointed her fork at me. "And it's true."

"I want to forget about Amanda for the moment and talk about the Darkrose Coven."

Joanie put her fork down with a clang. "Honestly, Madeline, will you let that go? I told you it was years ago. I don't see what it has to do with anything."

"I know the original members made a pact not to talk about the baby. I think the same thing is happening to the new coven."

"Well, I don't know what the hell I could do about that."

"You could tell me whose baby it was and what really happened to it."

"I'm not going to do that. All I'm going to say is it wasn't mine. Are you happy now?"

That was more than she'd said before. "Yes, thanks. Back to Amanda. Why does everyone in the Improvement Society do what she says?"

"Because she knows where all the bodies are buried."

"Including the baby's?"

Joanie made a disgusted face. "My God!"

"Well?"

She pushed her plate away. "All right, look. Amanda used to spy on us when we had our meetings, so we kept going deeper into the woods. She says she saw everything, and what she means by that I don't know, but the other members of the coven are convinced she saw the—the problem."

"The ceremony?"

"No, no. The birth."

"What?"

"The baby was only a few weeks old. It was a miscarriage. We helped each other. We took care of everything. We gave it a proper burial and no one said anything about it. Ever. I don't think Amanda saw anything, and even if she did, I wouldn't let her lord it over me the way—" She stopped. "I'm not saying another word."

She didn't have to. Was this the sword hanging over Constance Tate?

I wasn't sure Constance would talk to me. I was right.

I went back to my office and called her. I asked if she'd mind answering a few questions about the Darkrose Coven. Her reply was quick and sharp.

"We have already been through this, Madeline, the day you stopped by Amanda's, in case you've forgotten."

"Amanda and Joanie told me you were a member."

"That has nothing to do with anything."

"A young man is dead, covered with witchcraft symbols. You don't think there's a connection?"

"No, I don't. I think you're trying to cause trouble. I think you're trying to make something out of nothing. I think you're trying to drum up business for your poky little detective agency. Stop harassing me, or I'll call Chief Brenner and register a formal complaint."

She ended the call. If nothing was wrong, why wouldn't Constance talk to me? Was she hoping I wouldn't be able to clear Amanda and her arch nemesis would be put away and out of her life forever? The last thing I wanted was the chief shutting me down, and I had no doubt Constance could follow through on her threat.

Then Lavinia Lawrence called to see if there was any progress.

I hated to let her down. "I'm sorry I don't have anything to tell you. I'm still working on it."

"I wanted you to know I appreciate all your hard work. I have a couple of things to tell you that might make a difference. In going through Harold's papers, I have found out he was much wealthier than I believed." She named a sum that made me gasp. "He left a nice amount for me, but a lot of it goes to these organizations I've never heard of like Pandas, Incorporated, and the Rustling Waters Fish and Bird Sanctuary."

"You weren't aware of Harold's charities?"

"Not that I know of, but I told you, we weren't that close. Here are a couple more: Peregrine Falcon Rescue and Rehabilitation and the Parkland Cat Shelter. Looks like each one gets a substantial amount of money. Now, I'm not a detective like you, but I've watched my share of detective TV shows, and I'm inclined to believe that if someone knew about this money and wanted it, that's a good motive for murder."

"Yes, it is," I said, "but if Harold's will stipulates that the money goes to these organizations, the murderer wouldn't get it."

"Well, what if it made them so mad, they decided to kill him? What if they wanted the money for something else, and they argued and insisted he change his will, and he wouldn't?"

Lavinia had watched plenty of TV. "I'll check on it, Lavinia."

I still had the cards Harold had given to me. I looked up each company on line, and each one had an attractive website with color photographs and grateful testimonies. I checked the "Contact Us" drop down menus and found phone numbers. All of the people I talked to said the same thing. Harold Stover was one of their most faithful contributors. The man who answered at the Parkland Cat Shelter was happy to tell me the days and times the shelter was open, how many cats were currently available for adoption, and how any donation of money or food was greatly appreciated.

"Is one of your donors Harold Stover?" I asked.

"Let me check." I heard the click of computer keys. "Yes, Mr. Stover is one of our regular donors. Did I read somewhere he is recently deceased?"

"Yes."

"Very sad news. He really supported the shelter."

In case my information was wrong, or something in Harold's will hit a snag, I decided it was Lavinia's or her lawyer's job to tell the man that his shelter was on Harold's list for a substantial donation. Then I recalled that Harold had said he helped Roger Price out of some financial difficulties. Even though Amanda was beyond cranky, I owed it to Harold to solve his murder. A visit to Amanda's ex-husband Roger was in order.

Chapter Seventeen

Roger Price had an office in one of the newer business complexes outside Parkland. His secretary informed me that Mr. Price was extremely busy.

I knew how to get his attention. "Please tell him it's about Harold Stover's murder."

She looked taken aback. She relayed the information, and in a few minutes, I was sitting in Roger's office, and Roger was all concern. He wasn't what I expected, but I should have known from the way Amanda talked about him that his wealth was the attractive part. I pictured a tall distinguished businessman in expensive clothes. Roger was of average height and build and not remarkable in any way. He wore an expensive suit, a large gold watch, and a diamond ring. He stood up to shake my hand, indicated the chair in front of his desk, then settled back in his leather swivel chair and peered at me over round gold-rimmed glasses.

"Ms. Maclin, I'm very glad you're investigating this terrible tragedy. What can you tell me?"

"I'm afraid I don't have a lot of information."

"It's fairly obvious Amanda killed him, isn't it? Didn't I read in the paper that she was found at the scene of the crime?"

"I think she was set up."

He looked surprised. "By whom?"

"That's what I'm trying to find out," I said. "You and Harold were friends, right?"

"Not what you'd call close friends, but we did a little business together. He was a fine man."

"I understand he helped you out financially after your divorce."

"Did he say that? No, I didn't need anyone's help. Amanda might have thought she got all my money, but far from it. I had assets she never knew about, I'm glad to say."

Okay, so either Harold lied about helping Roger, or Roger was too proud to admit he needed help.

"Did Harold have any other enemies in Celosia besides Amanda?" Roger asked. "They were always at odds, even when I lived there."

"One theory is someone killed Harold to get to Amanda."

"That's nonsense. Why not just kill her?" He paused and took a breath. "That did not come out right. You'll have to excuse me. If you only knew what I went through with Amanda. Thank God my wife took me back."

"Then you won't mind if I ask you where you were Friday night?"

"Not at all. I was here in my office. You can check with my secretary. We had a contract to finish, and she didn't mind staying a little later to help me get it done."

"Mr. Price, you don't strike me as someone who lets other people push them around. Why did you do what Amanda said?"

He took off his glasses and wiped them with his handkerchief. "Have you ever been in love? I mean, madly in love?"

"Yes, with my husband."

He replaced his glasses. "Then you know sometimes you do foolish things. Sometimes you forgive a lot. Sometimes you think, oh, if I hang on a little longer, things will get better. Well, I was wrong." His phone rang. "Excuse me, it's my wife."

He answered. "Hello, dear. I'm sitting here talking with Ms. Maclin about the case. Yes, I'll tell her you said hello." He listened, his pleasant expression giving way. His lips thinned, and he made an effort to control the frustration in his voice. "You're sure she doesn't want to go? I thought we had come to an agreement—yes, I realize it's going to take time, but—all right. That's fine. We'll try something else. See you soon. Love you." He hung up. "I had made plans to take my daughter to a concert this weekend. Her favorite boy band. She's decided she doesn't want to go."

Although he tried to look as if her refusal didn't matter, I could tell he was hurt. "I'm sorry. It must be tough."

He shrugged. "She's thirteen. She's still upset. We'll work it out. Was there anything else?"

"No, thank you."

He got up to escort me to the door. Up until now, I decided he wasn't a prime suspect, after all. He was angry with Amanda, of course, but so was everyone she came in contact with, and he didn't have anything against Harold.

Then I saw that Roger Price walked with a stick. Not a flimsy little walking stick, or a dinky cane, but a large beautifully carved piece of heavy dark wood with a polished handle.

"That's a nice walking stick," I said.

"Thank you." He held it at an angle so I could see the silver tip on the end. "I found this in a store up near the mountains. It's one of a kind. I broke my leg skiing several years ago, and every now and then, it acts up. Might as well look good when you're limping." He opened the door and spoke to his secretary. "Ms. Maclin would like to ask you a few questions."

The secretary confirmed that she and Roger had worked late Friday night. I went back to my car and sat down, my thoughts racing. Not only did Roger possess a potential murder weapon, he also wore little round gold glasses, exactly like Nathan's. In the dark, the neighbor who saw Nathan might have actually seen Roger.

Since I was in Parkland, I used this opportunity to stop by the Delta Gamma house on the campus of UNC-Parkland. It was one of the larger sorority houses, a brick Colonial with the Greek letters carved above the door. In college, Mother insisted I pledge her sorority, but I'd been too busy with classes and my artwork and somehow never got around to doing that. She was disappointed, but by then, I was so used to disappointing her, it didn't bother me.

The young woman who greeted me at the door was slim and dark, her eyes serious behind bright red glasses. "Welcome to Delta Gamma House. How can I help you?"

I explained that I was working on a case for a former member of the sorority and was looking for information about the class the year Kathleen Wallace and Olivia Decker had been at the college.

She invited me into the parlor and indicated the bookshelves all along the back wall. "We've got yearbooks and scrapbooks you can look through. We've also got a few of our sisters' keep-sake boxes."

The keepsake boxes were shiny pink and blue boxes with bronze trim. They looked like fat bound copies of the Classics. "What exactly are those?"

"We give one to every girl when she pledges. It's like a special personal scrapbook. They're supposed to take the boxes with them when they graduate, but, as you can see, a few have been left behind. Sometimes people drop out of college, or something tragic happens to them, or they decide they don't want to be in the sorority, but we keep their boxes as part of Delta Gamma history. What's your case about, if you don't mind me asking?"

"It involves some questionable photographs."

"Oh." She gave her red glasses a push. "Well, we warn our pledges to be very careful about what they post online. It's so crazy how fast a picture can spread."

"Is it okay if I look through the keepsake boxes?"

"Of course. Excuse me."

She hurried off to class. I found Kathleen and Olivia's year-book with all its standard pictures, but I was more interested in the keepsake boxes. I didn't expect to find Kathleen's or Olivia's, and I didn't, but now I had an idea of what I was looking for. If either of them had incriminating photos, this kind of box would be the place to hide them away.

◇◇◇

Back in Celosia, I stopped in to see the neighbor who lived across the street from Harold. Ernie Bates was a spry little man in his seventies, who was delighted at the chance to flirt with me.

"Madeline, you are the best-looking detective I've ever seen. Come in and have a drink."

I stayed on the porch. "Thanks, Ernie, but I only have a few minutes. I want you to tell me exactly what you saw Friday night."

"Always happy to cooperate with the law." Ernie had on a denim baseball cap and a red-and-white-striped shirt under faded overalls. He stuck his thumbs in the shoulder straps as if preparing for a lecture. "It was a nice evening, so I was sitting out here on the porch. I saw Nathan Fenton walking away from Harold's door round about nine-thirty or so."

"How did you know it was Nathan?"

"Well, the light caught in them funny glasses he wears. Round ones, you know. Makes him look like some kinda owl."

"So you didn't actually see his face."

"No, but I knew who it was. Who else in town's got glasses like that? Sure you can't come in for a drink?"

"No, thanks."

He indicated one of the rocking chairs. "You'll have a seat, though, won't you?"

"Just for a moment. Did you notice any strange cars?"

He inched his rocking chair a little closer to mine. "Nope."

Nathan would've had on his camp tee-shirt and shorts. "Do you remember what Nathan was wearing?"

Ernie eyed me. "Whatever it was, it didn't look half as hot as what you're wearing today."

"Concentrate, Ernie. Did he have on a Camp Lakenwood tee-shirt?"

"Kinda hard to see in the porch light. What color we talking about?"

"Bright yellow and green."

"Nah, nothing like that. My eyesight's pretty good, but at

night, I have a little trouble. I would've been able to see bright yellow, though. I sure like looking at you, girl."

Ernie's idea of a leer was such a goofy grin, I had to grin back. "Thank you."

"You ever get tired of Jerry, you know where to find me. I'll treat you right."

"I'm sure you would."

"I'm not like some people, you know, hollering and fighting and being petty like they was stupid teenagers. I know how to be a gentleman."

"What people would that be, Ernie?"

"Well, take that Amanda Price, the one who's always causing a stir, the one what probably killed Harold. Right before she and Roger divorced, they was always having these knock-down drag-out fights. Had one right down town in front of my bench. I told 'em I didn't appreciate it."

I had seen Ernie sitting on the bench in front of the drugstore. It was his regular post, and you could find him there every warm day, soaking up the sun and people-watching.

"What sort of fight?" I asked.

"Over their stuff, of course. That's the trouble with rich folks. They got too much stuff." Ernie was wound up now. "She told him if he was leaving, she wanted him to clear out all his things, and he'd better not take anything of hers. He said he would if he wanted to. They went round and round till I made 'em go away, said I was going to call the law. Amanda gave me some lip, and Roger looked at me like I was some sort of bug. I don't care how rich Roger Price is, if he hadn't of left, I was going to kick him good."

"I'm glad you didn't kick him. Doesn't he carry a big walking stick?"

"Yeah, but I coulda took him."

"Thanks for the information, Ernie."

"You come back and see me any time."

I was halfway down his walk when he called out, "I hope she's the one what killed Harold. She needs to be put away somewhere."

◇◇◇

It was almost lunchtime, so I grabbed takeout from the Chinese restaurant and ate in the car while I made a few phone calls. The folks at the Rossboro Arts Council were glad to answer my questions about grants, including the Web address of the Hunter Hardin Foundation. When I went to the site, I found it was easy to apply for grant money, as long as you were part of an organization devoted to the arts and sent in a reasonable proposal and budget. I'm not sure how Amanda worded her request, but apparently, it worked. Armed with my new info, I called Evan, who, as I suspected, wasn't aware of Amanda applying for or receiving a grant.

"I suppose it's for the best," he said. "We never could've financed such a big project."

"So the money didn't come to the theater."

"No, I guess it came right to the Improvement Society."

Of which Amanda was president.

"Anyone can fill out the forms," he said. "She can put Women's Improvement Society and describe what she needs the grant for, and if it's approved, she gets the money."

"But she can't personally get all that money, right?"

"That depends. Hunter Hardin is one of those foundations that require little or no accountability. Of course, I always create a financial report with everything listed. I don't want to get into trouble with our auditors."

"Amanda would have to have a financial report, then."

"Yes, but she could still fudge the details. For instance, on mine I have a line item titled 'Production Costs.' Anyone can see the amount that was spent—say seven thousand dollars for sets for a show—but not how it was spent or what it was spent for. Maybe a thousand went for a backdrop and another thousand for a special staircase. Those details I have in another report."

"So Amanda could say a thousand dollars is going for grape costumes when really she keeps that money for herself?"

"Unless somebody follows up on every item, yes, she could."

Then I gave a Jerry a call, but his phone went to voice mail. I didn't think much of it. He was probably teaching a craft class, or helping the campers play a game. I left him a message that I was heading out to Peaceful Meadow and would check with him later.

◇◇◇

Nell had given me directions to Peaceful Meadow. I drove out of town and down another winding country road to an old rundown barn. A sign leaned against a broken fence rail at the dirt road leading past the barn. The letters and decorations had faded, but I could read "Welcome to Peaceful Meadow" and make out a design of flowers and peace signs. My car joggled along the dirt road filled with holes and patches of grass. At the end of the drive, the land opened up to a large empty meadow. I parked and got out of the car. Grasshoppers erupted from the grass and bounced away. Birds wheeled overhead. Other than the welcome sign, there was nothing to indicate any sort of community had ever been here.

It was peaceful, though, and I imagined if you liked living outdoors and communing with nature, it could be a nice place. I also imagined young Amanda swinging a half-eaten turnip and proclaiming, "As God is my witness I'm never eating granola again!" As a child, I would've enjoyed running in the meadow, climbing trees, maybe finding a stream to play in. Normal childhood activities, unlike my upbringing, which involved standing in stiff, jewel-encrusted dresses with a pile of heavy curls on my head, and a fixed smile on my face.

That's not going to happen to my daughter, I vowed. She's going to play outside, make mud pies, ride her bike. She's going to do all the things I never got to do.

Peaceful Meadow spread down to the woods, woods that connected somewhere in the leafy depths to Nathan's property. Amanda had said she'd seen the Darkrose Coven in the woods near the commune. Hoping to find a trace of the old coven or possibly signs of the new one, I walked a little ways into the forest, keeping the meadow in sight. After a while, I realized I'd have to go deeper in than I wanted to go. This was an activity I'd better share with Jerry. And where was he, anyway? I hadn't heard back from him.

◇◇◇

I returned to the main road and stopped at the first little convenience store I found, the Speedy Spot. I finally had a little luck. The woman behind the counter, who was much older than her long curly permed hair and generous amounts of eye shadow first suggested, said she knew all about the commune.

She leaned her arms on the counter between the register and stacks of lottery cards. She popped her chewing gum. "Heck, I lived there for ten years. Lots of fun. What you wanna know?"

"Did you know Megan and Amanda Underwood?"

"Oh, yeah. Megan and I used to play together. Mandy, now, she wouldn't have anything to do with us. She was real fussy."

"Would you say the sisters didn't get along?"

"Megan wanted to, but there were plenty of other kids to play with, so after a while, we quit asking Mandy."

"She went by Mandy?"

"Yup. Hear she calls herself Amanda now. Oh, and she wasn't an Underwood. I don't know who her father was. Everybody swapped around, if you know what I mean." She paused to add another stick of gum to the wad she was chewing. "Isn't she doing some big something in town?"

"She's planning an outdoor drama."

The woman laughed. "Don't that beat all! As much as she hated being outdoors."

A man came in and bought a pack of cigarettes. I stood aside as he chatted with the woman, bringing her up to date on someone's operation and reminding her of a church picnic.

After he'd gone, I asked her if she had known about Megan's engagement to Harold Stover.

"Yeah, Megan was a flirt. I was, too. Still am. You learn a lot when you're brought up with all that swapping going on. Nothing ever came of her and Harold, though. He came out to visit all the time, but he didn't want to live in a tent."

"Was there ever anything between Harold and Amanda?"

"No, Mandy always bragged how she was going to marry the richest man in the world. Don't think Harold had that much."

Amanda would be surprised to learn how wealthy Harold became. "When did you last see Megan?"

Her answer surprised me. "Yesterday."

"Here at your store?"

"Yeah, she stops in every now and then. We talk about the good old days. She'd like to get the old place up and running again, but that ain't gonna happen."

I had to wait while she helped another customer and then asked about the coven. "Did you ever hear of the Darkrose Coven? They used to meet in the woods near the meadow."

"Saw 'em once or twice. Lot of nonsense, if you ask me. And now these young girls are fooling around out there."

"Have you seen them in the woods?"

"Nah, but they stop here on the way sometimes. Usually, one of 'em with that boy that was found in the vineyard."

"Eric Levin?"

"Yeah, I recognized him from the paper. They didn't show the body, of course, but they ran a photo of him once the police figured out who he was. He'd always have a girl with him when he came by here, always cutting up and taking pictures of themselves. You know how the kids can't breathe without their phones."

"Did you ever see him with a girl with long dark hair dyed purple on the ends?"

She thought about it, popping her gum as if it might jog her memory. "You know, usually the girls was blond, but he did have a young brunette with him last time I saw him. As I recall, she did have purple in her hair. Hard not to notice. Guess it's the style nowadays."

"When was this?"

"Couple of months ago. I remember 'cause he was so busy filming her with that phone of his, he knocked over the potato chip rack."

I was beginning to get a very good picture of my own. If Eric Levin was the player he was reputed to be, he might enjoy taking young women to the woods and filming their activities. In the heat of the moment, Britney Garrett, the pastor's daughter, might not have considered how such a little movie might ruin her future. If the convenience store owner had seen them a couple of months ago, and he hadn't bothered with a condom, that was enough time for Britney to realize a baby was on board. Not only did she have to get rid of Eric, she had to get rid of the baby, too.

The woman poked my arm. "You okay?"

I came out of my gloomy thoughts. "You've been very helpful, thank you." I gave the woman one of my cards. "The next time Megan stops in, would you please give me a call?"

"Sure thing."

I bought a soda and a bag of chips and sat in my car, munching and thinking.

If Eric made a sex tape, he could've used it to extort money from Britney. Did Britney act alone, or did she convince her coven to help her get rid of him and retrieve his phone?

More importantly, why hadn't I heard from Jerry?

Chapter Eighteen

By the time I got home, I was really concerned. When Austin and Denisha arrived, I asked if they'd seen Jerry at camp.

Austin used the edge of his camp shirt to wipe a spot of dirt off the four-wheeler's fender. "Yeah, we had relays today. Our team won. Go, Bears!"

Denisha picked up on my anxiety. "He's probably running a little late today. Maybe he stopped by the grocery store or something."

I didn't want the kids to know I was afraid old Double-Dealing Derek had made a move. "You're right. Want a snack? I can't fix anything as fancy as pigs-in-blankets, but there are cookies around here somewhere."

The kids were happy with the cookies, and since Jerry wasn't there for them to play with, they soon left for home. I could not believe how relieved I was when about ten minutes later, Jerry's red Jeep came up the driveway. He hopped out and came up the porch steps.

"Sorry I'm late. Nathan wanted me to pick up some more craft supplies."

"You'd better check your phone. I left a message."

Jerry pulled out his phone and turned it on. "Sometimes I don't get a signal in the woods. Was there something important you needed to tell me?"

I steadied myself. I wasn't going to admit I was afraid Derek might have snatched him off the street to take part in who knew what sort of highly illegal con game. "No, just keeping you up to date on the case. How's Nathan doing?"

"He's still jumpy. Amanda called again, and I'm surprised he didn't toss his phone into the lake."

I followed him into the kitchen where he plugged his phone into the charger. "I found the Peaceful Meadow commune today, or where it used to be. A woman at the local convenience store said she spent her childhood there, too. She and Megan were playmates, and they still keep in touch."

"So we've finally got a lead on Megan."

I leaned against the counter. "You know, usually I have a client I like. Someone I really want to clear. But this case! Why do I want the murderer to be Amanda? Why am I afraid it's her spacey but likeable sister?"

"Why would you think it's Megan?"

"Peaceful Meadow really is peaceful. If Megan loves it as much as I think she does, wouldn't she be angry with her half-sister for wanting to park her outdoor drama there and destroying all that peace?"

"Maybe. But I can't see Megan acting on that, even if she got angry. I'm not sure she can get angry."

"Here's something a little more disturbing. The woman at the Speedy Spot remembers Eric Levin stopping by on his way to the woods with a series of young women, the latest being Britney Garrett. Eric was making little movies of her in the store, which leads me to believe he made little movies of her in the woods doing God knows what."

"I know what, don't you?"

"Yep, and Britney was no doubt being blackmailed." I sat down at the kitchen table. Jerry fixed a glass of iced tea and handed it to me. "Thanks. I also talked with Roger Price today. Guess what he has? A big tough-looking walking stick."

"Interesting. Does he have an alibi for Friday night?"

"He says he was working late. His secretary confirmed this."

"Secretaries can lie for their employers, you know. What about a motive?"

"He says Harold didn't help him out, but I think he's too proud to admit he needed help. And Ernie Bates, the little man who lives across the street from Harold, could have seen Roger and not Nathan Friday night. Both men wear the same kind of glasses. But Ernie's eyesight isn't the best."

Jerry looked in the fridge. "There's leftover spaghetti."

"That sounds good."

He took out the plastic container. "Why would Roger visit Harold?"

"I don't know. I thought there might be a problem with the will. You should have heard Lavinia's TV-inspired theories on that. Harold's will leaves all his money to his animal charities, but Roger is a wealthy man. I can't see him killing Harold over Harold's will."

"Are the charities legit?"

"As far as I can tell. The Parkland Cat Shelter is."

Jerry heated two plates of spaghetti in the microwave and brought the plates and a container of parmesan cheese to the table. "Big Mike has loads of dummy corporations to avoid paying taxes. My favorite is Consolidated Overseas National Industries."

"CON Industries? Honestly?"

"Put it out front. Nobody blinks an eye. Oh, I liked S Oil, too. S Oil. Snake Oil, get it?"

"Big Mike is a barrel of laughs. Cheese, please." He passed me the can.

Jerry wound another wad of spaghetti onto his fork. "Didn't you say you went to the cat shelter? Why didn't you bring me some cats?"

"Austin and Denisha are enough to look after right now."

"Don't forget Hortensia. Any stirrings?"

"Not yet."

"Anything new on the Case of the Naughty Pictures?"

I pulled a stray noodle back onto my plate. "Every Delta Gamma gets a keepsake box when they pledge. I'm hoping that's where Kathleen has stored Olivia's photos."

He brightened. "Would this involve getting into Dr. Wallace's house while she's away?"

"Possibly. I'm going to look in her office first."

"You know if she turns out to be the bad guy, you'll have to look for a new doctor."

"Oh, no, I like her." I had to laugh. "Along with Amanda and Eric Levin, my doctor may also be a blackmailer."

"You said you visited Peaceful Meadow. Did you check out the woods?"

"I only went in a little way. I didn't want to get lost. I need you along to blaze the trail."

We finished supper and took our tea out to the porch. The sunset was a rich gold, the last rays touching the clouds and turning them a deep pink. A few little bats pinwheeled across the sky, making me think of Jerry's eccentric uncle.

"There go Uncle Val's pets."

Jerry gave the little creatures a salute with his glass. "I could've been a batologist, or whatever you call somebody who studies bats. I guess that wasn't my destiny."

Destiny was a peculiar thing. It was odd how Megan and Amanda had taken such opposite paths. "Do you wonder what your life would've been like if you'd gone in another direction?"

"I know what it would've been like. I would've continued in the game until my luck ran out and I got caught and sent to jail. I'd be flipping pancakes in the prison cafeteria."

"I guess I would've become Miss America."

"Or, if I'd gone in a really different direction, I would've become a flamenco dancer."

"I would've become a brain surgeon. I actually considered it for a while in fourth grade."

He leaned over to give me a kiss. "I think you turned out perfect."

Wednesday morning, I stopped by Kathleen's office and asked the receptionist if Dr. Wallace was available for a moment.

She checked a note on her desk. "I'm sorry. She had to go by the hospital and won't be back for about an hour. Did you need an appointment? I'm afraid we're really busy this morning. Allergy season, you know."

The waiting room was full of people coughing and sneezing as they stared listlessly at the TV in the corner or leafed through the ancient magazines. A young mother tried to corral her two toddlers as they enjoyed their own version of smash and grab with a stack of brochures on *Signs You're Having a Heart Attack*. I could snoop around better if Kathleen wasn't in her office, but how to get past the receptionist? Jerry would've created a diversion, but Jerry wasn't here.

The toddlers, however, as they ran and shrieked might do the trick.

"May I use the restroom?" I asked the receptionist.

She nodded, her attention on the children bouncing on the chairs. "Ma'am, if you would ask your children to sit down, please?"

The bathroom, as I remembered from previous visits, was right inside the door that separated the waiting room from the short main hallway to Kathleen's office. Up until now, I'd actually toyed with the idea of using Jerry's special skills and special keys to have a look in Kathleen's house, but now that I knew what I was looking for, I found it. Sitting among all the reference and medical text books was a fat pink and blue book with bronze trim. Kathleen's Delta Gamma keepsake box. I took it down and quickly leafed through the pages. Near the back of the box was an envelope, and in the envelope were several photographs of Olivia Decker in all her glory. I put the envelope in my purse and made certain the box was back in its right place. Then I returned to the waiting room where I thanked the receptionist.

One of the toddlers had reached his limit and was screaming furiously as his sister whacked at him with her shoe. The Dark Side of Having Kids, I reminded myself as I hurried out. Don't forget you'll have to deal with that, too.

So, now it was back to Parkland with the photos for Olivia, who thanked me and gave me the photos of Kathleen.

I hoped all this nonsense was over. "Is this all? No negatives squirreled away?"

"That's all. You have my word." She took the photos of herself and fed them into the shredder by her desk. "What did she say?"

"Nothing. I liberated those from her keepsake box."

"Well, aren't you clever."

"All this over scholarship money you didn't need."

She gave me a level gaze. "I don't care what Kathleen Wallace thinks. I earned that scholarship. She always was a sore loser. She won't thank you for stealing these pictures."

"I want this silliness done so I can concentrate on a real case."

"And what do you call a real case?"

"Murder."

The shredder finished. Olivia sat back in her chair. "That pokey little town of yours is just full of surprises, isn't it? What about that old house? Are you and Jerry still living in it?"

"It looks a lot different now."

"That's good," she said with a complete lack of interest and turned back to her laptop. "Don't let me keep you from your murder, Madeline."

◇◇◇

Since I had to run back and forth between towns, I was glad Parkland was only thirty minutes from Celosia. I met Kathleen in the parking lot as she was coming in from the hospital.

"Good news." I handed her the photos. "From Olivia. She swears these are the only copies."

Kathleen took a quick look and a relieved breath. "Thank you."

"I had to make an exchange, you know."

She paused, and I could see her thinking through what I'd said. "You found Olivia's photos? How?"

"Your keepsake box."

"You went into my office and took them out of my box?"

"Yes."

"Damn it! That was my only leverage!" She realized she was shouting and lowered her voice to a furious undertone. "Madeline, you had no right to do that! You don't know what Olivia

Decker is capable of. Those photos were my only chance to keep her in line."

"First of all, you hired me to get these pictures of you back, which I did. Second, I do know what Olivia is capable of. I also know she'll keep her word. Maybe she did get that scholarship you thought you were entitled to. Maybe you feel she cheated. But that's all in the past. You're a grown woman with a successful medical practice. You don't need Olivia Decker for anything."

Her anger faded into bewilderment. "How did you know about that scholarship?"

"Because I'm a grown woman with a successful private investigation agency."

Kathleen looked around as if the answer to her confusion was somewhere in the parking lot. "We were sorority sisters. We were supposed to look after each other. I felt so betrayed."

"Yes, but that's over."

"She didn't need the money. She took that scholarship and ran off with it, and never looked back. It's taken me years to pay off my student loans."

"But you're doing okay now, right?"

She blinked as if to clear away sudden tears. "Yes. I let it get to me. I shouldn't have."

"It was a tough break. But you survived."

She looked down at the pictures and then back up at me. "I'm sorry I yelled at you, Madeline. For a moment, I thought Olivia had won again."

This isn't a battle, I wanted to say. This was two silly young women taking stupid pictures. Nobody won. "Are you going to be okay?"

"Yes, thank you." She managed a slight grin. "I need to shred these."

When were people ever going to figure out that, thanks to the Internet and social media, anything and everything they ever did and recorded—not just pictures of what they had for dinner, or what they looked like when they were six years old—but secret pictures, sex tapes, revealing and embarrassing photos, was out in the world for all to see? If Lauren, Joanie, and Constance, the members of the original Darkrose Coven, were in their teens when they were playing witches twenty or twenty-five years ago, they were most likely in their forties, with Constance being a little older, but even at forty-five or possibly fifty years old, living in today's world, they had to know this kind of thing was possible. As for the young members of the new Darkrose Coven, they were physically attached to their devices all day long.

Megan was still AWOL. Britney would be in school until two-thirty or three. I didn't want to talk to Amanda or Joanie. Constance wouldn't talk to me, and neither, I correctly guessed, would Lauren. I needed a nature break.

◇◇◇

By the time I reached Camp Lakenwood, I was hot, tired, and hungry. Jerry sat with a group of campers listening to a wildlife expert who had brought along a rabbit, a possum, a raccoon, a big box turtle, and a black snake. He saw me and patted a seat on the bench next to him. I slid in.

"You're just in time for Nature Talk with Ranger Tom."

"I need some calm wildlife right now."

Ranger Tom lifted the snake from its cage to a chorus of little squeaks and ughs from the crowd. "Now this, campers, is a black snake. Black snakes are not poisonous. They are very helpful animals. Farmers like to have them around their barns because they eat rats and mice. People might have told you that snakes are slimy, but they are not. They feel very cool and soft and smooth. Who wants to touch it?" Several kids drew back, but many more raised their hands. "All right. Let's start over here."

With the campers' attention on the snake, I filled Jerry in on my morning activities. "All incriminating pictures have been shredded, so that should be the end of that case."

One of the campers gave a scream and jumped back from the snake. The black snake's head was up, his mouth open. The other kids laughed, and Ranger Tom said, "It's okay. He's just saying hello."

"There's one more little detail I thought of," I said to Jerry. "If Roger planned to frame Amanda for Harold's murder, how did he know that she would stop by that night? And how did he get her purse—wait!"

I didn't mean to exclaim so loudly. Ranger Tom and the campers all turned to look at me. "Sorry."

"Did you want to touch the snake?" Ranger Tom asked. "You can if you like. I assure you, he's harmless."

"Oh, um, no, that's okay. I've, uh, touched one before, thank you."

The next camper in line insisted on her turn. We moved a little further away to the nearest picnic table, and I continued with my theory.

"I think I know how he got Amanda's bag. Ernie, the neighbor, told me he'd heard Amanda and Roger arguing. She wanted him to get all of his things out of the house, but said he'd better not take anything of hers. Roger said he would if he wanted to. When Amanda asked me to find her missing Louis Vuitton, she had no idea where it was. What if Roger took it and her credit card to spite her, and then saw an opportunity to make it look as if she'd been in Harold's house?"

"Sounds like a cunning plan, but how are you going to prove it?"

"I'm too hungry to prove anything right now. What have you got in the way of camp chow?"

"You're in luck. After Ranger Tom's talk, it's snack time."

Ranger Tom finished traumatizing the more timid campers, packed up his menagerie, and waved good-bye. I had a vague notion that camp snacks involved marshmallows and graham crackers, but Jerry had apples and boxes of raisins for everyone.

Nathan sent the campers to get their snacks and came to me. "What's up with the case, Madeline? I hope you're close to solving it."

"Tell me again why you went to Harold's Friday night."

"I knew he'd been having trouble with Amanda, and I thought he could help me deal with her."

"Why didn't you call?"

"I don't know. I told you I don't often lose my temper. I guess I wasn't thinking straight. A phone call would've made more sense, I suppose."

"I know you were in an emotional state, but I want you to think back and see if you remember anything. A car, a strange noise, a shadow, anything."

Nathan squeezed his eyes shut to think. Jerry and I stopped crunching our apples so we wouldn't interrupt the process. After a few moments, Nathan opened his eyes.

"Nothing, sorry. I went up to the door. I knocked. I listened. I didn't hear anything, so I went home."

"No strange cars parked outside that you recall?"

"I wasn't noticing cars. Besides, I don't know everyone who lives on that street much less the cars they drive." A counselor called to him, and he hurried off to supervise another activity.

Jerry finished his apple and tossed the core into a nearby trash can. "You want to search the woods today?"

"Yes, after I talk with Britney. Meet you back at the house?"

He gave me a kiss. "See you there."

Chapter Nineteen

I went back into town and did some work in my office until two-thirty. Then I drove to the high school and parked near Britney's white convertible. I waited, leaning against my car. When the bell rang, she and Clover came out, carrying their books, their purses swinging on their shoulders, looking as if they hadn't a care in the world, just two ordinary high school girls on the way home.

When Britney saw me, she stopped. Clover bumped into her. "What's wrong?" Then she saw me, too.

I kept my eyes on Britney. "Got a minute? It's about Eric."

They exchanged a nervous glance. "Go ahead," Britney told her friend. "I'll text you later."

Clover got into a red Mini Cooper, gave Britney one more scared look, and drove away.

Britney's chin went up defiantly. "I don't want to talk to you."

"I might be able to help you."

"What makes you think I need your help?"

"I know you went to Parkland to see a young woman named Shadow about a very personal matter."

Her expression changed. Now she looked young and scared. "I don't want to talk out here in the middle of the parking lot."

"Then why don't we sit in my car?"

She reluctantly agreed. Once inside, I said, "I'm not going to run to your mother. I don't want to get you in any more trouble than you already are. I want to hear your side of this story."

She made one more try to brazen it out. "What story would that be?"

"The woman at the Speedy Stop remembers seeing you and Eric a couple of months ago, right before you went into the woods and he made a video of you. Was he blackmailing you? Is that why you had to get rid of him?"

Abruptly she lost control. "I didn't kill him!" She took a shuddering breath and clenched her fists. "Believe me, I wanted to. I thought he loved me, but he just wanted money! He said if I told anyone, he'd post the video all over Facebook. And now I'm pregnant, and I know the baby is his, and I can't wait to get rid of it!" She burst into tears. "If my mother finds out, she'll kill me!"

I handed her a tissue and let her cry until she managed to stop. "So Eric extorted money from you for a couple of months?" She nodded. "And he's the only one you've had sex with?" Another nod. No wonder she finally broke down and talked to me. This was a heavy secret to carry that long.

She gripped my hand. "Madeline, swear to me you won't say anything about this to my mother."

"I promise. But eventually you'll have to tell her."

She pulled away. "No."

I let that pass for now. "What about the video? Don't the police have Eric's phone?"

"I don't know where it is."

"Aren't you afraid whoever killed Eric might decide to post it?"

"They would've done that by now, wouldn't they? Or approached me for more money?"

Someone else liked to have power over people. "Britney, does Amanda know about this video? Is that why you joined the Improvement Society, so she wouldn't tell?"

Britney had been tearing up for another round of sobs, but at this, her expression darkened with anger. "That horrible old bitch wants money, too."

I stared at her in surprise. "Money?"

Now that I'd promised not to rat on her, Britney was more than ready to expose Amanda. "She's broke, did you know that?

I came by her house one day with my weekly payment, which was my allowance, can you believe it? I heard her talking on the phone to what must have been her bank. She's got the house, and that's it. Why do you think she wanted you to stand guard during her party? She needs that silver service and that centerpiece to sell. She has no source of income, except for me and whatever member of the Society she's got dirt on."

"She didn't get anything from her divorce?" North Carolina was an equitable distribution state, which meant both parties not necessarily received an equal share of property but whatever the couple or the court decided was a fair share.

"All she wanted was that house. I guess she thought she could sell it for more than it was worth, or maybe dupe another stupid rich man into marrying her. But taking money from a high-school girl? I mean, come on! That has to be the lowest trick ever. I even had to borrow money from Clover several times to have enough."

"Then why was she pushing so hard for an outdoor drama?"

"Duh! For the grant money. I heard her talking about that, too."

Just as I suspected. CON Industries had nothing on Amanda. "How did she find out about you and Eric?"

"I don't know."

"Does Clover know? Does Annie?"

"Why would they tell Amanda? I can't believe they'd betray me." She dug into her purse for her compact and repaired her tear-stained face. "If only I had his phone. I could make all of this go away."

I didn't mention Eric could've made copies or forwarded the video to someone else for safekeeping. Britney had probably already thought of this. "Are you sure you want to make the baby go away, too?"

"Yes."

"Promise me you won't do anything crazy."

She snapped her compact shut. "I don't want it."

"Someone else might."

"I don't care."

"Do you have any idea who might have killed him?"

"Maybe another girl he was blackmailing, and she had the guts to do something."

"Where were you that night?"

"At Annie's. She's so lucky she has her own place. She doesn't have to answer to anyone. She isn't constantly watched and questioned." Abruptly, she broke off. "I've got to get home." She gathered her books and swung her purse onto her shoulder. She got out of the car, paused as if she wanted to say something else, then shut the door.

I watched Britney get into her convertible and drive away, my heart aching for the troubled young woman and the decisions she'd been forced to make. When the truth came out, and it would, she might have a hard time dealing with her mother, but surely Lauren would forgive her and help her. As for Amanda, she'd reached new lows in the despicable department. I wanted to stand in the town square and announce her financial situation to the world—she's a fraud, a penniless fraud!—but she was my client, damn it. Now more than ever I wanted to solve Harold's murder.

◇◇◇

When I got home and saw the silver car parked next to Jerry's red Jeep and Austin's four-wheeler, I forgot about Britney and Amanda and everything else. Derek sat on the porch, looking as smug as Joanie Raines.

"Good afternoon, Mrs. Fairweather."

"Derek."

"Hope you don't mind me stopping by to let Jerry know how things went."

There were no words to describe how much I minded. "Where is he?"

"Oh, he and those two kids are in the kitchen making cookies or something. Cute kids."

The cold look in his eyes gave me the chills. I didn't want him anywhere near Austin and Denisha. "Well, I'll go see how they're getting along."

Jerry had rolled out the dough, and Austin and Denisha were cutting cookies into animal shapes. Jerry glanced up, and even though he kept his tone light, his expression said something was very wrong

"We decided to make sugar cookies. Choose your animal."

Denisha pressed her cookie cutter into the dough. "I'm making cats."

Austin was rolling dough between his hands. "Snakes for me. They're going to have chocolate chip eyes."

I took a bird-shaped cookie cutter from the collection on the table. "Looks like fun. Are you staying for supper?"

"Jerry said he was taking you out tonight, but he's going to grill hamburgers tomorrow."

"Oh, that's nice," I made a couple of bird cookies and handed Jerry the cutter. "Where are we going?"

"Parkland. For a couple of hours, maybe."

"I thought we weren't going to go."

"There's a special tonight."

"Wasn't your friend Artless Bob taking care of that?"

"Bob can't come."

My heart sank. "Did he give a reason?"

"He had an accident."

An accident. My heart skipped a beat.

"Look, Madeline! I gave him some fangs."

I admired Austin's cookie dough snake. "That's great."

Denisha wiped her hands on a dishcloth. "Mine are all ready, Jerry."

Jerry put Austin's snakes and Denisha's cats, dogs, and pigs onto the cookie sheet and put it in the oven. "Ten minutes. Set the timer, Denisha."

Austin started out. "I'm going to see how many laps I can do in ten minutes."

"Go out the back door," Jerry said. "It's closer."

Austin dashed out the back, and in a few moments we heard the roar of his four-wheeler.

"Do you think your friend would like a drink?" Denisha asked.

"That's okay. Mac can ask him. Would you do me a favor and go upstairs and see if I left my cookbook in the bedroom? I was reading it last night."

Denisha skipped out of the kitchen.

The minute she was gone, Jerry explained why Derek was parked on our porch. "Here's the deal. Derek owes a lot of money to a really bad character, and if I don't go along tonight and help him, I'm a little worried about what he'll do."

"Derek or the bad character?"

"Both of them."

"Are the kids in danger?"

I'd never seen Jerry look so serious. "I told Derek I would kill him if he even looked at them wrong."

I had to get rid of Derek once and for all. "Where are you going?"

"Talley's. It's a sports bar in Parkland."

I thought a moment. "All right. Nell told me if I needed help to call her dad. He'd know someone in the Parkland Police Department, wouldn't he?"

"Mac, you can't call the police. If they catch and arrest Derek, they'll probably catch and arrest me. I sure don't want to spend time in jail with Derek and his pals, especially if they know my wife blew the whistle."

"What do you want me to do?"

"Hope this con goes over without a hitch."

That settled it. I was going to take care of Derek myself, and I knew how.

The kids came back, the cookies came out, and the rest of the afternoon rolled along as if nothing was wrong. Austin and Denisha went home. Derek and Jerry talked on the porch. And I called Big Mike.

Chapter Twenty

During my last case Big Mike gave me a phone number to call if I ever needed his help. Upstairs in my studio, I punched in the number. For a moment, I wondered if it was a real number. Jerry had told me Big Mike was very elusive and never stayed too long in one place. What if he'd moved? What if he wasn't able to help? I would have to call Chief Brenner and arrange a raid on Talley's sports bar and pray that Jerry could get out without being arrested.

The deep cheerful voice that answered immediately calmed my fears. "Madeline, my dear! Wonderful to hear from you! How's our chef?"

"That part of his life is going very well, thanks," I said, "but a fellow named Double-Dealing Derek is forcing him to take part in a con tonight to pay back someone Derek owes."

There was a long thoughtful "Ah." "And where is this happening?"

"Talley's in Parkland."

"I know Derek and I know the place. Leave it to me."

"Thank you."

"However…"

Uh, oh.

"If I do this for you, Madeline, you will owe me a favor."

I'd almost forgotten who I was dealing with. "As long as it doesn't involve anything illegal."

"I can't guarantee that. There will come a time when I need a favor, and you will say yes. Otherwise, no deal."

When Big Mike had visited, he'd been extremely polite and jolly, but I'd sensed something about him I never wanted to rile. If honoring this favor was the only way I could rescue Jerry and make Derek disappear, I would have to say yes.

"You won't kill anyone, will you?"

"I'll make certain Derek doesn't bother you or Jerry again."

Wondering what in the world I was getting myself into, I agreed.

"A pleasure doing business with you, Madeline. By the way, this number was only good for one call. Good evening."

I put my phone away. What have I done? Made a deal with the king of the con men. Now I owe him a favor. All I could think of were those fairy tales where the princess has to give up her firstborn child. Well, since I couldn't get pregnant, that wasn't a problem. But what could someone like Big Mike need? Had I made an amazingly foolish decision?

Then Jerry called up the stairs. "Mac? We're leaving now."

"Just a minute."

We met at the foot of the stairs. Due to the seriousness of this venture, Jerry wore his plainest gray tie. The minute I saw him, I knew I'd made the right decision. I'd do anything to protect him. I gave him a fierce hug.

He returned the favor. "It's probably better if you stay here."

"No, I'm coming, too. I'll bring my car and wait outside."

"If anything goes wrong—"

"It won't. I promise."

He couldn't keep me from joining this little adventure. "All right. But at the first sign of trouble, you need to get away."

Whether Big Mike comes through or not, I'm not getting away without you, I wanted to tell him.

I expected a dark, grubby bar located down a side alley, but Talley's was on one of Parkland's main streets. Warm light spilled out its windows, along with lively conversation and the sounds of cheering as various teams scored. I didn't see Derek's silver car, but figured he didn't want to be that obvious. I sat in my car across the street, ready to bolt if I heard sirens and Jerry came running.

Nothing.

People went in and out, mostly men, but several couples. Which man was the mysterious bad character and how much did Derek owe him? How dangerous was he? Was he likely to cause trouble? I was also on the lookout for Big Mike's black Hummer. No, he wouldn't be that obvious, either.

This is what it's come to. Here I am, poised to drive the getaway car, an accessory to whatever nefarious scheme Derek was playing. And Jerry had been trying so hard to stop. Well, if I ever got sucked back into the pageant world, I was sure he'd do his best to get me out.

The longer I sat, the more my worries grew. Jerry could protest all he liked, but if we ever got out of this situation, I would never let another one of his friends come near him, no matter how creepy or innocent they appeared. We wouldn't be in this fix if I'd kicked Derek's big fat rear off my porch.

An hour went by, then another. I wanted to scream with impatience. How much time did this con take? Suppose things went really wrong, the game was discovered, and that happy crowd in the bar turned into an angry mob? What if Double-Dealing Derek lived up to his name and double crossed Jerry, leaving him to take all the blame? Or what if the con was a success, but Derek pulled a gun on Jerry or stabbed him and took all the money?

Okay, that was it. I had to go in. As I reached for the door handle, a face at my window made me jump. A young woman all in black with a long blond braid under a black baseball cap gazed at me with wide eyes. She looked so youthful, I thought at first she was a child. I kept a firm grip on the handle and with my other hand, reached for the keys in the ignition, ready to drive off if she attacked. What was she doing out here? What did she want? Was she homeless and looking for a handout? A thief? A car-jacker? Then she smiled a very knowing, very adult smile.

"Mrs. Fairweather? Big Mike says to tell you everything's taken care of. If you'll drive up to the corner, Jerry will be waiting."

Before I could thank her, she slipped away into the shadows. Good lord, I'd fallen into *Oliver Twist*, and Fagan had sent one of his minions with the message. Everything's taken care of? Did I even want to know what that meant? Shaky with relief, I took a moment to calm my nerves and drove to the corner.

Jerry was indeed waiting, a messenger bag slung over one shoulder. He got into the car. He looked as puzzled as I felt.

"Are you okay?" I asked. "How'd it go?"

"Fine, I think. We did the Paw. I gave Derek time to get away. He was supposed to meet me here to finalize the deal and make sure he had enough to pay off that guy, so where is he?"

"That's good, isn't it? We don't want to see him anymore."

Jerry indicated the bag. "But he needs this money. That was the whole point of this job. What do I do with it?"

"Here's a wild idea. You could return it to its rightful owners."

"I can't do that. I'll be right back where I started. He'll come looking for it, and he won't be happy."

"No." I turned the car around. "We're going back to Talley's."

Jerry looked alarmed. "Mac, what are you doing? You never go back! You'll give the whole game away."

"I know how to fix this. Just play along."

Jerry was so stunned, he didn't say anything during the short ride back to Talley's. When we went inside, everything stopped, exactly like an old Western movie when the new sheriff steps into the saloon. Everyone stared at Jerry and not in a friendly way. Several men got up from their seats, and instead of six-shooters, reached for their cell phones.

One man approached us ready for a fight. "What the hell is going on? Where's our money? You've got two seconds to explain, or I'm calling the police."

I took out my private investigator's license. "If I could have your attention, please. My name is Madeline Maclin, and this is my partner, Jerry Fairweather." Jerry winced at the mention of his real name. "I'm a private investigator, and we've been tracking a swindler named Double-Dealing Derek for months now. With your help, we caught him. The police have him in custody. We're here to return your money."

That was the magic word. Jerry plopped the wad of cash on the bar. Expressions changed from hostile to relieved. The men laughed and patted Jerry on the back.

"Man, you were convincing!"

"So the big guy was a con man? Hope he gets what's coming."

They insisted on buying us drinks, and Jerry, recovering quickly, regaled them with stories of our other "cases," stories of his own escapades modified to include me as the crusading detective. We finally got away from our new friends and got into my car.

Jerry grabbed me and kissed me. "My God, Mac, you were fantastic."

"Let's hope I never have to do anything like that again."

He became serious. "But I've got to find Derek. I've got to explain. He's going to be furious, but I can't have him showing up like some moldy mushroom every time he needs cash. What happens when we have kids? He'll have even more leverage."

"Jerry."

"You've tried to tell me that my friends are dangerous, and up to now they've only been annoying. But Derek *is* dangerous, and I want him out of the picture forever. You won't like it, but I've got to call Big Mike."

"That won't be necessary."

He looked at me blankly. "Why not?"

I took my time adjusting my seat belt. If Jerry had been amazed by my act in the bar, this was going to completely blow his mind. I needed to be strapped in. "I made a deal."

"With Derek?"

"With Big Mike."

For the second time that night, Jerry was speechless. Then he stammered. "How?"

"He gave me his number."

"You made a deal with Big Mike?"

"Yes. Don't say that like it's the end of the world."

"And he took care of Derek."

"That's what his henchwomen told me."

"What??"

"Let's go home, and I'll explain everything."

"Oh, no. You're going to explain everything now."

I told him to take a deep breath and settle down. I took a deep breath, too, not certain how he'd react to the full story. "When Big Mike came to lunch and we talked about your future as a chef, he gave me his number so I could give him a progress report."

"He never gives anyone his number."

"In this case, I'm glad he made an exception. I called and told him about Derek. He said he'd take care of the problem."

Jerry was quiet for so long, I wondered if I'd made a major mistake. "Did he say anything about a favor?"

"Yes. I hope it's a simple request, like pick up my dry cleaning, or make dinner reservations at Chez Paris." Jerry's strange calmness was making me uneasy. "About this favor. Am I in big trouble here?"

"No. Everything's fine. You did what you always do, which is save the day. Thank you."

"So you don't think Big Mike will call in this favor?"

"Oh, he will. But if he gave you his number and came when you called, I'd say he likes you. He won't make you do anything you don't want to do. Now please explain the henchwoman."

"Big Mike sent a young woman to tell me Derek was out of the picture and you were waiting on the corner. Then she slipped away into the night. I wondered if Big Mike would crash his Hummer into the bar and into Derek, but that would create more attention than he'd want. What about the man Derek owed? Do we have to worry about him, too?"

"If Big Mike took care of Derek, that's no longer an issue."

As relieved as I was this ordeal was over, I sensed Jerry wasn't telling me everything.

There was no singing in the shower Thursday morning. The water cut off. I heard drying and dressing sounds and then Jerry's footsteps as he went down the stairs. No grape duets, no cheerful strains of *Hansel and Gretel*. This was curious enough to make me get up. I came in the kitchen, accepted a cup of coffee, and sat down at the table.

"You okay?"

He stirred egg and milk in a bowl. "Sure."

"I missed the morning concert."

He reached for the loaf of bread. "How 'bout if I make you some French toast?"

"That would be very nice." He sopped up the egg mixture with bread and placed the slices in the frying pan. "You want to tell me what's bothering you?"

He waited until the toast was done. "Yesterday scared the hell out of me."

"It wasn't the best situation, that's true."

Jerry gave me my plate and sat down. "Just the thought of Derek coming anywhere near the kids—" He swallowed hard. "He probably would've continued to use Austin and Denisha to make sure I went along with his plans. Thank God you had Big Mike's number." He grinned a wry grin. "Giving all that money back was tough, too."

"You should feel light and happy you did the right thing."

"I did the right thing when I married you, Miss Parkland."

Jerry's the only one who can call me that. "Never realizing you would change a beauty queen into a con artist."

"You did an excellent job."

"That's because most of what I told those people was the truth."

"That's all you need. Mostly truth." He refilled my coffee cup. "Now that Derek's out of the way, you can concentrate on your real cases. How's your investigation coming along?"

"I finally got Britney to talk to me. Eric made an embarrassing video of her and threatened to post it unless she gave him money. He's also the father of her baby. As bad as that is, here's more news that probably won't surprise you. Somehow Amanda found out about this video and was also blackmailing poor Britney, even taking the girl's allowance."

He grimaced. "I think we've found our real witch."

"And get this, Amanda is actually broke, but since she hired me, I can't tell anyone except you."

"*I* can tell."

"Hold off on that. I want Amanda to think she's got the upper hand. I also want to find out why Megan was in the woods the other day. She told us she took a wrong turn, but maybe she lied to us and was on her way to the site of the coven. She could've been there many times. Maybe she saw Eric and Britney that night."

"Would she run to tell Amanda?"

"If I could ever find her, I'd ask her. The French toast was delicious, thanks. Are you at camp today?"

"No, Nathan only needed me for a few days to help get things up and running. After breakfast at Deely's I can help you search for Megan."

Another frantic phone call from Amanda interrupted our morning.

"Madeline, you need to come to the theater right now!"

"What's the matter?"

"Chief Brenner is here, and I'm not saying another word until you get here."

"What now?" Jerry asked me.

I took a last quick drink of coffee. I was going to need the caffeine. "Sounds like Amanda's been accused of another crime."

Chapter Twenty-one

On the stage of the theater, the members of the Improvement Committee stood in silence. Chief Brenner and Amanda faced each other, both with arms folded and expressions grim.

"There you are, Madeline. May I proceed, Ms. Price?"

"Yes. I want her to hear all this."

"What's going on?" I asked.

I'd never seen the chief look so annoyed. "Got a call from one of Joanie Raines' neighbors a short while ago. Said he heard groaning from inside the house, so we went in and found Ms. Raines on the floor. She'd been hit over the head with a blunt object. I'd like to know where Amanda Price has been this morning, but she refused to tell me anything until you arrived. Believe me, I want to arrest her for obstructing justice."

"Is Joanie all right?"

He spared me one more brief glance before turning his stare back to Amanda. "Doctors say it's a concussion. She'll be okay."

Amanda puffed up with indignation. "I've been right here. You can ask any of these women. We came in early to get some work done."

"I understand there's been a lot of ill will between you and Ms. Raines lately," the chief said.

"I certainly wouldn't sneak into her house and hit her! I plan to crush her dreams of playing Emmaline Ross by having the far better production."

"I see. Can you ladies vouch for Ms. Price? Has she been here all morning?"

The committee members assured him Amanda had been with them. She smiled a tight, satisfied smile.

"You see? Don't you have better things to do than harass me?"

"I'm doing my job, Ms. Price. Thank you for your cooperation."

Ignoring the chief's sarcasm, Amanda turned to her committee with a flurry of orders.

I followed Chief Brenner out. "Was this a robbery?"

"Nope. Not a frill out of place. Somebody meant to give Joanie a smack on the head, and whoever it was, he or she succeeded." He looked back at Amanda. "Wouldn't put it past her to put out a hit on the woman."

I knew better than to ask if I could have a look in Joanie's house.

I called the hospital, but Joanie wasn't able to have visitors or talk to anyone on the phone yet. Hit over the head with a blunt object, like Harold. Would Megan have had time to get to town and attack Joanie? Would she have been that upset over Rossboro horning in on the Emmaline story? Just where was Megan, anyway?

◇◇◇

I considered going back to Peaceful Meadow, but I was sidetracked by a phone call from Dr. Wallace's office. Test results had come in, and the doctor wanted to talk to me. Seized with a strange dread that went from my toes to my throat, I said I could come right now.

My dread was replaced with extreme surprise when I found Megan Underwood sitting in the waiting room, rooting through her oversized fringed bag.

"Why, hello, Megan. What brings you here? Nothing serious, I hope."

She looked up and smiled her little half-smile. "My friend from the forest. So nice to see you again. I appreciate your concern, but I'm merely here to leave some medicinal herbs. You're not ill, I trust?"

"Checking on test results." I gave her a critical look, but there were no incriminating blood stains on her blouse to prove she'd whacked poor Joanie on the head, and no dragon's head walking stick, which I found suspicious. "Actually, I want to talk to you. Did you know Joanie Raines had been attacked in her home?"

She looked genuinely appalled. "My goodness. Such a sad world we live in today. Is she going to be all right?"

"I think so. Do you need a ride somewhere?"

"That's very kind, but I have the truck."

"The truck?"

"From the goat farm. I'm picking up feed today."

So that's how she got around. "Do you often run errands for the farm?"

"Whenever I can. Those dear little animals depend on me." She stood, gathering her skirt and shawl and numerous scarves around her. "I'd better take care of that right away. I hope Joanie Raines has a speedy recovery."

I watched her from the window of the doctor's office. She got into the dented dirty white pickup and drove away. The walking stick was probably in the truck. If I'd known, I could've had a look at it before I came in. I turned to go and saw that Megan had left her shoulder bag under her chair.

Time for a quick peek inside.

Besides little bags of what I hoped were only herbs, there were rocks, feathers, beads, an old spiral notebook, dog-eared and tattered with age, and a brand new pink baby rattle. This was so incongruous, I took it out and stared at it and was still staring when Megan hurried back in.

"Oh, good, you found my bag. I'm always leaving it behind. Thank you, Madeline."

I handed her the bag and the baby rattle. "This fell out."

She took both items with her customary unconcern. "It's pretty, isn't it?"

"Is there a baby girl in your family?"

I expected her to say, "No, I use this to frighten away evil spirits," but she smiled. "This is for the baby in the woods."

Oh, my God. "What baby, Megan?"

"The poor little baby from long ago. I'm going to put this on its grave as soon as I find it, but it was so long ago."

"You don't remember where the women met?"

"No, I didn't like to go where they were. Mandy said they were evil. She said one of them had a baby, but it was dead, and they buried it in the woods. I've been trying to find its grave so I can make sure its little spirit is at peace."

When at night I go to sleep,
Fourteen angels watch do keep.

I was glad we were the only ones in the waiting room and the receptionist was on the phone. Megan's story brought tears to my eyes. "That's very thoughtful of you."

"I'm sure I'll find it someday. I'll keep looking."

"Is that why you were in the woods near Nathan's camp?"

"Yes, but I didn't find anything there."

"When you were searching for the gravesite, did you ever see young women from town? There could've been a young man with them."

"No. Are there more evil women? I hope there's not another baby."

I was spared from explaining this by the nurse calling my name.

Megan looked around. "I didn't leave my walking stick here, too, did I?"

"Is it missing?"

"No matter. It will come back to me. It always does." With that, she drifted out.

◇◇◇

Kathleen assured me that the results showed a slight decrease in my estrogen levels, and she suggested I take another supplement.

"We'll see if this helps."

"You know I'm willing to try most anything."

"We won't go crazy with pills, trust me." She was back to her cheerful self.

"Thanks. You look relaxed, Kathleen. Everything's okay?"

"Yes, thank you. I've had time to think about what you said. I have made my own way, and I should be proud of myself instead of holding a grudge against Olivia. Would you say she's happy and successful?"

"Successful, yes. I'm not sure about happy."

"I'm not going to worry about her anymore."

"Good. Now let me ask you a question or two about Megan Underwood. Does she often bring you herbs?"

"You mean this?" She reached to the shelf behind her and handed me a large Mason jar filled with weeds. "She claims this has medicinal properties, but it's just grass and daisies. I always take what she brings me and thank her, but it's nothing I would ever use."

Thinking of the rhododendron leaves, I was glad Kathleen was cautious. "Did she ever see the photo of you in your wiccan outfit?"

"Do you mean does she think I'm one of her people? Even if she did see the picture, and I can't imagine where, she's never mentioned it. I hate to admit it, but whenever she comes around, I take the jar so she'll leave."

"Does she ask for payment?"

"No. She says she wants to help."

I set the jar on the desk. "In your opinion, as a doctor, is she a threat to herself or others?"

"I'm not a psychiatrist. I think she's slightly delusional, but she's happy, and she believes she's doing the right thing."

I called Jerry and asked him to meet me at Joanie's house. On the way, I thought about Megan's missing stick. Anyone could have picked it up. But she'd said, "It always comes back to me." Didn't that sound like the murderer took it whenever he or she needed it and then returned it so Megan could "find" it again?

I tried out this theory on Jerry. I also told him about the baby rattle and how Megan was searching for the baby's last resting place.

"That's why we found her wandering in the woods."

"Did she know whose baby it was?" Jerry asked.

"No, but I'm almost convinced it belonged to Constance."

This time, Jerry found a side window that was open, and soon we were in Joanie's living room.

"What are we looking for that the police could've overlooked?" he asked. "Although a better question is, how do we get past all these ruffles?"

"Megan isn't the culprit. Someone used her walking stick, so look for something that might have fallen out of a dragon."

"A tooth, maybe?"

"That would be ideal."

Jerry got down on his hands and knees and looked under furniture while I checked the tops of the chairs, tables, and all the plates and spoons, being careful not to dislodge any rabbits.

"I don't see how she moves in here."

Jerry's voice was muffled under the sofa. "Was there even room for Megan to bean her? And how did Joanie manage to miss everything when she fell?"

"You're right. Maybe she was attacked somewhere else and stumbled and fell in here."

A short hallway led to Joanie's back door. "Jerry, look at these pictures."

The row of framed photographs along one side of the hallway was perfectly straight, but the row on the other side was slightly askew.

"Do you suppose the EMTs dislodged them coming in to help Joanie?"

"Or her attacker came along here."

The back door opened onto a stoop. "Joanie sees Megan at the door and has no reason not to open it. Megan takes a swing at her. Joanie stumbles back, tries to run, and gets hit. She makes it as far as the living room and falls."

On the stoop was a vase with a ruffled cover. The vase was filled with shiny little stones, the kind people use for decoration and to hold up flower arrangements. I dumped out the vase, and we searched through the stones.

Jerry found the odd-shaped piece. "Here it is."

It was a tooth exactly like the teeth we'd seen in the dragon's mouth in Megan's stick.

"Lost it on that first swing," Jerry said.

I examined the tooth. Something wasn't right about this whole thing. "This seems awfully convenient."

"Not awfully lucky?"

"Chief Brenner's no slouch, and neither are his officers. They know about Megan and her walking stick. I don't see how they could've overlooked this."

"Are you saying someone planted it after the police had gone? That would suggest they wanted another person to find the clue."

"Yes, me. Everyone knows I'm on the case. Amanda's been griping about my technique ever since she hired me."

"You think someone put the tooth here to incriminate Megan?"

I put the tooth in my pocket. "Let's find out."

The dented white pickup was parked next to Amanda's car in the theater parking lot. The stage door was unlocked. When we stepped into the cool darkness of backstage, we heard two voices, Megan's and Amanda's. Megan sounded calm.

"I won't let you destroy our home, Mandy."

"Oh, for God's sake, wake up and face reality! This is the only way to make you get out into the real world and be something other than a weird flakey tree-hugger!"

"I'll find another way in," Jerry said. "We might need a diversion."

I kept in the shadows of the curtains. The sisters were on stage near the edge of the orchestra pit. Megan held her walking stick to her side, her hand resting on the now considerably battered dragon's head.

"Peaceful Meadow is our home," she said.

Amanda gave a short mirthless laugh. "Home! Maybe it seemed like home to you, but I hated it."

"You didn't have to live there. But you are going to leave it alone."

"No, I'm not. I need it."

Megan smiled a peaceful little smile. "Well, it's mine, and I would do anything to protect it."

Amanda gasped. "Did you kill Harold? Did you kill him and leave my purse there so the police would arrest me?"

"How would I get your purse, Mandy? I've never been in your house."

"Stop calling me Mandy!"

How would Megan get Amanda's purse? Aside from the people at her fundraiser, the only other person I'd ever seen at Amanda's was Constance Tate. Would Constance set the sisters against each other?

"It doesn't matter." Megan raised her walking stick. "I wouldn't hurt Harold or Joanie, but you have to go."

I stepped forward. "Megan."

She turned. "Hello."

"Megan, that's not a good idea."

Amanda pointed a shaking finger at her half-sister. "She's crazy. I've always known it. She's completely out of her mind."

"I'm not so sure about that. I think someone's been taking advantage of her spacey reputation." As long as Megan was talking, she wasn't swinging that stick. "Amanda, why don't you walk over here?"

Amanda cautiously edged her way around to me. I countered so that I was between Amanda and Megan. "Megan, did you hit Joanie?"

"I didn't hit Joanie. I didn't like her, though. She thought she could be Emmaline Ross. I am Emmaline Ross. She fought for her land, just as I fight for Peaceful Meadow."

"But your commune was all about love and peace."

Amanda's patience was gone. "Why are you arguing with her? She's insane."

"No, I'm not," Megan took a sudden swing. Amanda and I ducked as the stick whistled past our heads. "I must have Peaceful Meadow."

I shoved Amanda toward the stage door. "Get out of here."

As she ran for the door, I saw Jerry slowly making his way down the aisle. I countered again so that Megan's back was to the auditorium.

"Megan, tell me your plans for Peaceful Meadow. Tell me what you want to do."

Jerry reached the orchestra pit, climbed over the edge, and quietly dropped in. Megan must have sensed something because she turned her head, but he'd already hunkered down in the shadows. While she was distracted, I made a grab for the walking stick, but she was too quick. I ducked her next swing.

"Megan, calm down. We can work this out."

"You don't understand. You're like all the others."

"I want to understand. Did you go to Joanie's house? Did you go to Harold's?"

"I would never hurt Joanie or Harold."

I moved to one side, maneuvering so she was closer to the edge of the pit. "I think someone's using you, Megan. Someone wants you to take the blame."

As Megan took another swing, Jerry reached up and grabbed her ankles. She struggled to regain her balance, but I gave her a push and toppled her into the pit. There was a cry and a crunch.

"Oops," Jerry said. "I forgot about the drum."

I looked over the edge. Megan was sprawled on top of the remains of a snare drum, her walking stick cracked in two. She groaned and opened her eyes.

"I want things to be like they were."

Behind me, I heard footsteps and Amanda's shrill voice.

"Constance! Thank goodness you're here! Do you know what this crazy woman tried to do to me?"

As she proceeded to fill Constance's ear, I watched the other woman's face. Was there disappointment in her otherwise impassive face? Had she arrived hoping to find Amanda dead?

Amanda being Amanda, she was completely unsympathetic about her sister's physical and mental state. While she railed at Megan from the edge of the pit, I called nine-one-one. Within a few moments, we could hear sirens.

Amanda smirked with triumph. "That's it for you, Megan. You see where all that peace and love crap gets you? Now you can sit in Peaceful Penitentiary! Not much sunshine there, though."

I really wanted to push Amanda into the pit, too. "Amanda, I think your sister's been through enough."

"She's a murderer. She doesn't deserve anything."

"I'm not so sure about that."

With Jerry's help, Megan was able to sit up. She clutched his hand. "My arm hurts."

"We'll get you to the hospital," he said.

"You can share a room with Joanie Ralnes," Amanda called down. "I'm sure the two of you will have plenty to talk about."

While the EMS team examined Megan, I told Chief Brenner what had happened, interrupted constantly by Amanda. Constance stood off to one side, still expressionless.

"We'll take care of things from here," the chief told Amanda.

"I'm going to press charges. You make certain she's prosecuted to the full extent of the law."

"Let us handle this right now."

Megan was put on a stretcher and lifted from the pit. Amanda berated her sister all the way to the stage door and then abruptly turned and went back inside. Jerry and I followed the EMS team and the chief out to the ambulance.

I handed him the tooth Jerry and I had found at Joanie's. "This is from her walking stick. We found it on Joanie's back porch."

His little eyes narrowed. "We went over every inch of that porch."

"I think someone came along after you left."

"Any idea who?"

I had absolutely no proof that Constance had anything to do with any of the crimes, just a strange gut feeling and the lack of emotion in her eyes. "No, unfortunately not. But jail's not the place for Megan. She needs psychiatric help."

"I know," he said. "I'll do my best to see she gets it."

"There isn't any way to blame this on Amanda, is there?" Jerry asked.

"As much as I'd like to, I'm afraid I can't arrest people for being mean-spirited."

Jerry and I watched the ambulance and patrol car drive away.

"I'm not going back into the auditorium," I said. "I don't care if she is my client, I can't take anymore of Amanda right now."

"She's probably in there crying her eyes out."

I gave him a look. He grinned.

"Or not. Probably pissed about the drum, though."

I indicated Constance's dark red Cadillac. "I'm wondering if it's only a coincidence Constance came by at this particular time."

"Are you thinking she had something to do with all this? Proper, socially conscious Constance?"

"If Constance did have something to do with this particular incident with Megan attacking Amanda on stage, she didn't get what she wanted, which was to have Amanda out of the picture."

"She might be in there killing her right now."

I heaved a sigh. "Then we'd better go in."

Amanda was still ranting about Megan's attack, waving her arms and striding back and forth on the stage as if performing *My Narrow Escape* for a packed house. Constance, as always, stood to one side, tall and quiet, arms folded, expression neutral.

I'd seen her standing exactly like that many times. At the fundraiser, when Harold arrived to confront Amanda. In Amanda's kitchen, when I asked about Amanda's potential enemies. At the theater when Megan auditioned for Emmaline and when Joanie announced her plans for a rival production. She knew what was happening every step of the way and easily deflected attention away from herself.

I imagined Constance casually picking up Amanda's purse and a credit card to plant in Harold's house, or taking Megan's walking stick out of the white pickup. Was Constance capable of murder? If so, how was I going to prove it?

Constance turned her head and regarded me calmly. "How's Megan?"

"Confused but not badly hurt."

"Poor thing. It was only a matter of time before she snapped."

Amanda jumped on this. "Don't call her a poor thing! She knew exactly what she was doing."

"Of course. You're right." Constance's tone was even, but if Amanda hadn't been so self absorbed, she would've seen what I did, a dangerous glint in Constance's eyes. "If you'll excuse me, I need to speak with Evan."

I gave Jerry a little tilt of my head toward Amanda, and he picked up on my cue. "Amanda, are you sure you're okay? I didn't get to hear everything that happened."

Leaving Jerry to take one for the team, I followed Constance down the aisle toward Evan's office. "Was there a meeting of the Improvement Society today? Since you and Amanda have issues, I was wondering why you came by the theater."

Constance remained calm. "I may have issues with Amanda and her methods, but I really want *Flower of the South* to succeed. I wanted to check with Evan about using some of the theater's costumes. I never thought I'd walk in on more drama. What were you and Jerry doing here?"

We pushed the doors open into the lobby and went up the stairs to Evan's office. "We'd been in Joanie's house, looking for clues, and we found a tooth off of Megan's walking stick."

"Good thinking."

"The only problem is, the police had gone over the house very thoroughly, so I don't see how they could've missed the tooth."

Constance seemed to have forgotten her pointed comments about me and my agency. "That's why your business is so successful, Madeline. You find things everyone else overlooks."

Does that include you? I wanted to ask.

A sign on Evan's office door informed us that he was at home with a cold and to call if anything was needed.

Constance's lips thinned with disapproval. "Home with a cold, indeed. He doesn't want to deal with Amanda." Even through closed doors, we could hear Amanda's voice. "I'll give him a call. Glad you were here, Madeline. We certainly wouldn't want anything to happen to Amanda."

She said this without a trace of irony. Was she willing to kill Harold and attack Joanie and manipulate Megan, all to get rid of Amanda?

Back on stage, Amanda showed no signs of stopping. Jerry listened, occasionally saying, "Really?" and "I can't believe it," and other remarks of false concern.

When she paused for breath, I said, "Amanda, you've had a horrible experience. You need to go home and rest."

To my surprise, she agreed with me. "Yes, I can't let people see me in such a state. Will you follow me home? I'm so shaken up, I'm not sure I can drive."

"Why don't I drive you home?" Jerry said. "Mac can follow, and we'll make certain you're safe."

Amanda thought this was a wonderful idea. Jerry and I saw her safely to her mansion, and then Jerry hopped into my car. "You owe me big-time."

"I know. I'm sorry."

"Learn anything from Constance?"

"All this time, I've been concentrating so hard on Megan, and now I think Constance might be the murderer."

"Kill Harold to frame Amanda? That's a little extreme."

"To use a theater metaphor, Constance has been standing in the wings, waiting for the star to break a leg for real. She's often at Amanda's house. It would've been very easy for her to take Amanda's pocketbook and slip one of her credit cards inside."

"What about the tooth?"

"You've seen how beat up that walking stick is. I'll bet Megan left teeth everywhere she went."

"Including the theater."

"Yes. Constance was genuinely upset about Joanie's plan to launch another Emmaline show. I can see her smacking Joanie on the head."

"There's a small flaw," Jerry said. "Constance drives a conspicuously big, old red Cadillac. Wouldn't someone have seen her car at Harold's and at Joanie's? Unless she parked around the corner or hired a getaway car."

This was true. "Maybe I need to rethink my theory."

Chapter Twenty-two

Friday morning, I took my second cup of coffee to the porch. Friday, already. Had it been only a week since *Flower of the South* auditions and Harold's murder? During that week, I'd retrieved unflattering photos, uncovered not one but two Darkrose covens, and routed a disreputable con man. But there were still two unsolved murders.

Even though I suspected he would refuse, I called Chief Brenner to see if he'd allow me some time with Megan.

"Sorry, Madeline, that's not possible. She's been taken to Regional Hospital for evaluation and safekeeping. We don't want her wandering off hurting herself or anyone else."

"I don't think she's a murderer."

"She did attack her sister, and we consider her a flight risk."

"Could she be prosecuted for attacking Amanda? She's not really mentally stable."

"We'll take care of her for now."

I heard the dismissal in his voice, so I thanked him and hung up. Jerry came out on his way to Deely's. "I can't talk to Megan, but I might be able to see Joanie today."

"Anything I can do?"

"Listen for news at Deely's. People will be talking about what happened at the theater. You never know what might be useful. I'm going to talk to the other members of the Improvement Society. Somebody might have insight into Constance versus Amanda."

"They were hanging around Peaceful Meadow at the same time, weren't they? Maybe Constance and Amanda are sisters, too."

Something else occurred to me. "Jerry, I know Megan had her walking stick with her because she was swinging it at me, but what about her bag? Did she have that at the theater?"

"I don't remember seeing it."

"Besides the baby rattle, there was an old spiral notebook. There may be something in that notebook that would give me a clue."

"Wouldn't the police have found it?"

"Maybe, or it could still be at the theater somewhere." I glanced at my phone for the time. "The theater's not open yet. I'm going to visit Joanie and then go over there."

"I'll meet you after the breakfast shift."

Joanie was awake and glad to see me. She was dressed in a ruffled gown and looked like a queen on a throne of pillows. "I hope you're on the case, too, Madeline. I want to know who had the nerve to attack me in my own home."

I pulled up a chair. "Do you remember anything?"

"The back doorbell rang. I went to answer, and there was a figure all in black. Before I could say or do anything, this person hit me on the head. I fell and hit my head again, so I'm useless as a witness."

"Are you going to be all right?"

"The doctor says I can go home tomorrow."

"This figure. Was it short? Tall? Did it say anything?"

"Everything's a blur. You don't expect to find something like that on your doorstep, now do you?" She leaned forward eagerly. "What's this I hear about Megan and Amanda getting into a fight? Did Megan really take a swing at Amanda?"

"Yes, she was very upset about Amanda's plans to have *Flower of the South* in Peaceful Meadow."

Joanie leaned back on the pillows and took a sip from a paper cup on the table near the bed. "So maybe she's the one who hit me."

"Someone would like to make us think so. Jerry and I found a tooth from Megan's walking stick on your back porch, but the police had done a complete search before. Megan might have been set up."

Joanie set the cup aside. "Oh, it was probably Megan. She has to be angry at me for stealing the part of Emmaline out from under her. And if Amanda Price thinks any of this is going to keep me from stopping the Rossboro production, then she's got another think coming." She paused to take another sip of water and held up the cup as if making a toast to herself. "I'm going to be the best Emmaline anyone's ever seen."

"I'm sure you'll be terrific. Let me ask you about the Women's Improvement Society. I'd like to know more about the members."

"You think one of them is jealous enough to attack me?"

Joanie's ego was big enough for the entire town. "That's very possible."

She settled back into her ruffles. "The main thing about them is they're all rich. They all belong to the country club and sit around the pool all summer gossiping." Joanie held forth on the rest of the Society members, telling me all their various faults and remarking on their lack of artistic talent. "Which is why they can't understand me, or realize why I would be the ideal choice for their show. Then there's Eloise Michaels, who never worked a day in her life and thinks she can sing. I've heard her sing. Talk about pitiful! A mouse with its tail caught in a trap sounds better."

Eloise Michaels was the same Eloise who wanted Amanda's silver centerpiece, the same Eloise who was Britney's aunt. I'd met her at the fundraiser when I'd bravely defended the centerpiece from her advances. Why hadn't she been at the theater all this time?

"Eloise wasn't at auditions," I said. "Is she involved with the show at all?"

"You'll have to ask her. She's odd. She's the only one of those women who doesn't live up in the Sunnyside Lane neighborhood. Lives on Tasmin in one of the older sections of Celosia."

I thanked Joanie for her information, skewed as it was, went back to my car and looked up Eloise Michael's address. Tasmin Avenue was two streets over from Harold's street.

Eloise Michaels blinked at me through her screen door. "Oh, hello, Madeline."

Until Joanie had compared Eloise to a mouse, I hadn't seen the resemblance, but the small woman's light brown hair, sharp little nose, and furtive air did give her a mouse-like appearance. "May I ask you a few questions about the Improvement Society?"

She crossed her arms. "I don't know that I have anything to say about that."

"Are you still a member?"

She sniffed as if getting a whiff of rotten cheese. "Well, *some* people don't think so."

"Amanda Price?"

"We were getting along just fine until she made herself our fearless leader. I don't live in her hotsy-totsy neighborhood. I don't wear clothes from big snooty stores, and I certainly don't go around town declaring myself the best thing since striped toothpaste."

I'd never heard anyone actually use "hotsy-totsy" in a sentence. "But you came to her party."

"Yes. I wanted to see that silver centerpiece."

"You know Amanda hired me to keep an eye on her things."

Her little nose quivered. "I wasn't going to steal it, for goodness sake! When Delaney's Antiques held their annual auction last month, that centerpiece was the only thing I truly wanted, but Amanda knew that and purposely outbid me. I wanted to see for myself that she actually bought it and took it home and didn't buy it only because I wanted it. I wouldn't take it now if you paid me, not when she's had her grubby hands all over it."

It was a wonder Amanda was still alive. "You said Amanda came along and made herself leader of the Society. Who was your leader before?"

"I should have said president. Beverly McAdams was our president, but she retired, and quite frankly, no one wanted the job. That's when Amanda stepped up. Everyone was pleased at first. We had no idea how pushy she was."

"Constance is vice president?"

"Yes, and I was the treasurer. I don't know who took that position. Probably Amanda."

"So you haven't come to any meetings at the theater?"

"No, but I've heard more than I want to about *Flower of the South.* I think that's a crazy idea, so I'm staying out. I told Constance it wouldn't work."

"When did you last talk to Constance?"

"You know, she's the only one who'll stop by and visit. Such a fine lady. Real class. Amanda Price could take lessons on how to behave from her. Constance has kept me up-to-date on the Society, and if Amanda ever leaves, I'll be happy to come back."

"Did Constance visit you last Friday?"

There were more mouse-like wrinklings of Eloise's face and nose. "Last Friday. I think so."

"It would've been audition night when Megan Underwood and Joanie Raines showed up."

"Oh, yes, now I remember. Constance came by to tell me about the witch woman and what a surprisingly good job she did, and of course, Joanie Raines tries out for everything, especially the parts she's so wrong for. We had a good laugh about that. I was glad to see she'd cheered up. Harold's phone call upset her, but I told her not to worry. He called me, too."

"When was this?"

"As soon as he heard about Amanda's plan, he called every member of the Improvement Society to try to convince us not to go along with it. What are you getting at, Madeline?"

I still wasn't sure about motive, but I was getting at a really good opportunity. "I wanted to know more about the Improvement Society, thanks."

"I'm not going back until Amanda Price is gone, you can tell them that."

"Not even with your niece involved?"

She gave a short laugh. "Hah! I spent months trying to get Britney to join. I thought it would be a good opportunity for her senior project. She turned me down every time. Then along comes Amanda, who asks her one time, and she jumps right in, and her best friend Clover, too."

I would leave it to Britney to explain why that happened.

I thanked her again and walked back to my car. Tamsin Avenue was a typical middle-class neighborhood with older houses and large trees. If Constance came to visit Eloise often, no one would think anything of her red Cadillac parked on the street. It would've been very easy for her to leave her car out front, or move it down so Eloise would think she was gone, and then travel on foot over to Harold's.

In fact, I was going to do that now.

This might have been more difficult in a wealthier neighborhood—excuse me, a hotsy-totsy neighborhood—where everyone had gates and fences and security systems, but walking down Tamsin and around the block to Miller was a breeze. Harold's street was the next one, and his house was in the middle. I decided to walk down Miller to see if there was a place to cut through to his backyard. I noticed an empty house with a For Sale sign about halfway down the street. No one questioned me or set off any alarm as I walked down the driveway of the empty house. I appeared to be interested in the house and strolled around to the back. The backyard of this house ran right into Harold's backyard with only a line of trees separating the two lots. At night, with no lights on in the empty house and no one watching, it would've been easy for Constance to get to Harold's back door without being seen.

Now I knew how Constance had gotten in. I still didn't know why, but it might have had something to do with Harold's phone call.

I drove to Joanie's neighborhood and tried the same thing. It was a little scary how easily people could prowl around. In most Parkland developments, there were fences and barriers and neighborhood watch patrols. Here in Celosia, one yard ran into another, and there was an open-door policy in most of the smaller neighborhoods, where friends and neighbors could come and go into each other's houses to visit. A great thing if you were friends, but also a great thing for your enemies.

The streets in Joanie's neighborhood were narrow with big piles of branches stacked along the curbs where work crews had trimmed the trees from power lines, making parking more of a challenge. If Constance had parked a few streets over, as I imagined she did in Harold's neighborhood, her choices would've been limited with few Cadillac-sized spots. But I found a likely place one street over with a straight shot to Joanie's back door. Constance would've been in a hurry to plant the tooth. How had she managed to race through the bushes and back to her car without being seen? I decided to try it.

I parked my car where I guessed Constance would've parked, got out and ran to Joanie's back door, zigzagging around hedges, past clotheslines, swing sets, garden sheds, and garages. No one called out or demanded to know what I was doing. I pretended to toss a tooth into the jar on Joanie's back stoop and ran back. Okay. It wasn't impossible. What was impossible was imaging a prim and proper woman like Constance, who was always dressed in beautiful expensive-looking clothes and jewelry and always looked perfectly put together, making a mad dash through the hedges.

Or maybe she didn't dash. Maybe she put on jeans and a tee-shirt and took her time as if out for a casual stroll.

Maybe I was wrong about this whole thing.

By now, the theater was open. Evan turned on the house lights so Jerry and I could look around. Since we weren't sure how Megan had entered the auditorium, we started in the back and went up and down each row. While we searched, I told Jerry about my findings. "Even Eloise could be a suspect. She's furious with Amanda for buying a silver centerpiece she wanted."

"Amanda's the gift that keeps on giving, isn't she?"

"The champion at riling people, that's for sure."

"Eloise told me Harold called all the women in the Improvement Society to complain about Amanda's plan. I'm wondering what he told Constance. If he dated Megan, then he was visiting the commune. Maybe he knew about Constance's involvement with the coven. Oh, is that the bag over there?"

False alarm. What looked like Megan's bag was a pile of skirts someone had pulled from the costume shop.

Then Jerry tugged something from under a back curtain. "Found it." He handed me Megan's rumpled shoulder bag. "She must have flung it off in her rage."

We sat down on the stage, and I dumped the contents out. "I'm looking for a notebook." There it was, in a shower of flowers, nuts, rocks, loose change, feathers, receipts for goat chow from the feed store, and the pink rattle, which rolled out and came to a stop. My emotions rolled with it, a wave of sadness for a lost life. Megan never got to place it on the baby's grave.

Jerry brushed the loose petals off the notebook. "Is this her book of spells?"

The first few pages were covered with scribbles and drawings of flowers and weeds. There were recipes for dandelion jelly, corn pudding, and sun tea. But near the back, in a different handwriting, was a play.

A play about Emmaline Ross.

"I don't believe it," Jerry said.

I turned more pages, examining the faded paper and ink. It was only the first few scenes, but it was excellent. "This looks like it was written several years ago."

"By Megan? She thought she was Emmaline."

"No, this is a different handwriting from the recipes. I've seen this handwriting, but I can't remember where." I read more. "This is very good. This is much better than Amanda's version." I paused. Now I knew why the handwriting looked familiar. I'd seen it on neat lists of cast members and outdoor drama expenses. "Jerry, this is Constance's handwriting. Constance wrote this play."

"What's it doing in Megan's bag?"

"I don't know. Apparently Megan picks up everything." I read a few more pages. "This is actually good."

"But Amanda has steamrolled her version into Celosia."

We put everything back into Megan's bag and stopped by Evan's office to thank him for letting us look. We stowed the bag in the trunk of my car.

Jerry shut the trunk. "What do you want to do now?"

"I need proof that Constance was in Harold's neighborhood and in Joanie's. Come help me look."

Jerry followed me in his jeep to Harold's neighborhood, and I showed him how I imagined Constance had used the empty house as good cover to get into Harold's backyard. I'd looked for clues before and hoped with two pairs of eyes we might find something I'd overlooked, but there were no clues. Next, we drove to Joanie's neighborhood, and I retraced my steps. No scrap of expensive cloth dangled from a rosebush. No footprint dented the grass in Joanie's backyard. No missing earring. No crumpled piece of paper with "I did it!" in big black letters.

We went back to our cars and leaned against the jeep. "Constance has all the motive in the world," I said. "Plus plenty of opportunity, but I'll need proof before I confront her."

"You could always *say* you have proof, and see if she cracks."

"She's too in control to crack. She'll ask to see it."

"There's her play."

"Yes, I'm interested to see how she reacts to that. Then again, she could say, 'Oh, yes, I wrote that. Thanks for finding it.'" I straightened. "Okay, it's worth a try."

Jerry pointed to the pile of branches behind our cars. "Be careful backing out. I caught a good scrape on the side coming in."

I stopped. "Say that again."

"Be careful backing out."

"No, the other part."

"I caught a good scrape on—oh, I get it! Constance's Cadillac."

"Which is much bigger than your jeep or my Mazda." Was it possible there was an incriminating scratch on the dark red finish?

Jerry thought the same thing. "She may have fixed that by now."

"Or she may not have noticed."

"Then we'd better hurry and find her car."

Chapter Twenty-three

I tried to think of where Constance would go. "Jerry, this might be a long shot, but Constance said she had her hair done every Friday by someone named Delores, who is also Amanda's hairdresser. I'm going to call Amanda for the address."

Amanda told me the salon was called Hair Apparent, located on Brisbane Avenue, one street over from Main. Constance's Cadillac Sedan deVille was parked between a white Camry and black Ford 150 truck. Fortunately, the truck blocked the view from the salon's front windows, so Jerry and I could have a private look at the Cadillac. The back of the car was smooth and unmarked, but when we took a closer look at the front, we found scratches in the dark red paint and many little twigs and branches wedged in the imposing grill.

I didn't want to confront Constance in the beauty salon. "I'll invite her to my office and see what she says."

"I can hide in the closet in case she makes a move."

"I'll take you up on that."

"And it wouldn't hurt to have a policeman parked across the street."

During my short private investigator career, I've been threatened by a deranged beauty queen with a gun, leaped upon by an angry librarian, attacked by a delusional woman with a hypodermic needle, and assaulted by a vengeful artist with a brick, so it was unnerving to have Constance so calm. She sat in the beige and green client chair and gave her newly treated hair a little pat.

"What's all this about Amanda, Madeline?"

I didn't think she'd come to my office, but when I called, I told her there was a breakthrough in the case and things didn't look good for Amanda. As I'd hoped, she was eager to hear this. She apologized for being so short with me before and agreed to hear me out.

"I have a theory," I said. "I think I know why Amanda was blackmailing you."

"I'm not sure what you mean by that."

"She grew up in Peaceful Meadow. She knew about the Dark-rose Coven. I believe she knew about the baby, too."

Constance paled but said nothing.

"I also think Harold was blackmailing you. He called all the members of the Improvement Society in an effort to stop them from following Amanda, and he had the perfect weapon to use against you. When he was courting Megan, he was often at Peaceful Meadow, and he'd seen you there. He called to tell you if you endorsed Amanda's plan for the outdoor drama, he'd let everyone in town know about your baby. You had to get rid of both of them. Since it was common knowledge Amanda and Harold were at odds, and everyone heard them argue at Amanda's party, it was easy to set Amanda up as a murderer. You had access to her house and her things, so you left one of her purses at the scene, and to make certain no one saw your car, you left it on Tasmin Avenue after you visited Eloise Michaels and walked through the backyard of an empty house on the next street which has access to Harold's house. I'm guessing you used a baseball bat and then took the bat home and burned it."

Constance's face was expressionless. "This is a very interesting story."

"Megan was also at Peaceful Meadow when the coven was meeting near there, but she's rarely in town, and when she is, no one pays any attention to what she says. Then she shows up for auditions, and suddenly there's a chance she might remember you and make a scene. You had to get rid of her, too. You also attacked Joanie and left a tooth from Megan's walking stick."

"Which should prove Megan is the culprit."

"Except Jerry and I found the tooth after the police had been all over Joanie's house and yard. I think you forgot to leave it, so you came back and planted that little piece of evidence later."

"Again, no proof."

"You did the same thing in Joanie's neighborhood that you did in Harold's. You parked a few streets over and went through backyards. But in Joanie's neighborhood, there's not a lot of parking available and what's there is hampered by piles of branches the work crews left behind. You managed to squeeze the Cadillac in. After all, you were only going to be there a few minutes, once to attack Joanie, and then later to leave the tooth. There are some pretty good scratches on your car from those branches."

"Scratches that could be from anywhere."

"Not from your upper-class neighborhood. Not from driving around town. Where else do you go? The forest?"

"A careless driver could've scratched my car."

"Yes, but then there's this." I put the little piece of branch I'd pulled from the Cadillac's grill on top of the notebook. "It's from the front grill of your car. See where these twigs are broken off? There's a pile of branches one street over from Joanie's, the spot where there's a clear path to her back porch."

Nothing disturbed her icy calm. "Are you looking for matching twigs, Madeline? How quaint. You should write all this down. It would make a fascinating novel."

"It's interesting that you should mention writing. I happened to find this." I put the faded spiral notebook on my desk. "It was in Megan's bag. Most of it is recipes and pictures of flowers, but in the back, there are several pages of a play, a play about Emmaline Ross."

"Even more fascinating. I wouldn't believe Megan could write a play."

"But I believe you could. I recognized your very neat handwriting. When Jerry asked how Amanda could've written a play so quickly, you told him the same thing you told me, 'I believe she's been working on it for a long time.' I believe *you* wrote a play about Emmaline Ross and it was always your dream to have it produced. Then Amanda comes along with her idea about an outdoor drama, and because she threatened you with your past life, you had to sit back and let her version take over."

"If what you say is true, how did the notebook get in Megan's bag?"

"Megan's bag was full of little mementos she picked up. You were probably working on the play out in the woods where it was nice and calm. You probably forgot about this notebook, but I'll bet you have other copies of your play at your house." I turned the pages in the notebook. "It's amazing how popular Emmaline is. It's only a few scenes, but your version's pretty good. Oh, and Megan had this, too." I took out the rattle and placed it on my desk.

Up till now, Constance had been the Ice Queen, but when she saw the rattle, her mouth trembled before she got it under control.

"Megan's been out in the woods trying to find where your baby is buried. She wanted to leave this on its grave."

She reached out and touched the rattle. The beads inside shifted, sounding like a sad little sigh.

I realized something in my earlier theory wasn't right. If Harold called Constance to threaten her with her past indiscretions, why would he be so concerned? Why would he think he had something on her no one else had, something guaranteed to frighten her?

"Was Harold the father, Constance?"

She flinched and sat back.

"There was a lot of free love floating around back then, wasn't there? Harold was seeing Megan, so he was often at the commune. He told me he knew about the coven. 'Some girls playing like they were witches,' is how he put it. But maybe that's not all you were playing. You didn't want him to know the baby was his. And then you lost it. He didn't call you to complain about *Flower of the South*. He'd found out about the baby. I'll bet Amanda was the one who told him."

Constance's voice was still calm, but a calm of suppressed rage. "She took everything."

"Why did you let her?"

"I didn't want everyone to know about my past lifestyle. I went to college, married, established myself in town. I had social standing. Do you think I wanted the sordid details of my old life dragged out all over town? You know how people talk! And my husband would never have understood or accepted any of that. He's very ill. He's housebound. I would never want him to know any of this. Witchcraft! A miscarried illegitimate child! My God."

"Amanda said she would tell if you didn't finance her show."

"That was her twisted little way of keeping me in line, yes. She knew how much *Flower of the South* meant to me."

"Then why not kill Amanda?"

"Everyone knew how much I hated her. It was easier to set her up for a murder charge."

Amanda wasn't the only one with twisted ideas. "Did you hate Harold so much?"

"He never admitted the child was his, but it was and we both knew it. Oh, he knew it. He only brought it up because of Amanda's plans. He said if I didn't stop Amanda, he would tell my husband exactly what went on in the woods that night." Constance regained her rock-like composure. "So what now, Madeline? You have an old notebook, a baby rattle, and a few twigs. I don't think that's enough."

"You're right," I said. "That's why I also have Jerry in the closet."

She whirled around in her chair. Jerry opened the closet door and gave her a friendly wave of his cell phone. He'd recorded our conversation. Constance stood up so suddenly, her chair rocked back. I was surprised by how fast she ran out.

Jerry paused at the door. "Think the officer will catch her?"

I took out my phone. "If her husband's an invalid, she won't leave Celosia. Chief Brenner might not be happy about this, but I think I've solved the case."

◇◇◇

The chief called later to report Constance broke down at the station, confessing that between her fears that someone might expose her and Amanda mangling the wonderful story of Emmaline for her own greedy purposes, she'd simply had enough.

After ending the call, I told Jerry what he'd said.

He was sitting on the porch rail and raised his glass of tea in a salute. "Did he thank you for your excellent detective work?"

"Not exactly in those words."

From the music room came the cheerful sounds of *Hansel and Gretel*, of children's voices singing.

Children, here's a lesson taught!
How the witch herself was caught,
Unaware, in the snare
Laid for you with cunning rare!

"That's perfect, isn't it?" Jerry said.

"Except I haven't figured out if Eric Levin was killed by witch wannabes. Then there's poor Megan. I hope she won't be locked up indoors somewhere."

"We could always put in a good word for her. The only one she was angry with was her sister. And we're all angry at Amanda."

My phone rang again. "Speaking of the devil." It was Amanda, full of righteous fury. "Madeline, I just heard that Constance Tate was behind all this! I can't believe it! When I think of how I took her under my wing and showed her everything about the theater, not to mention letting her in my home and trusting her with my plans and dreams. I feel utterly betrayed."

I started to say, you are not the one who was betrayed, but Amanda charged on.

"I was harboring a murderer, Madeline. She could've attacked me at any time. Why in the world did it take you so long to figure this out? I am simply speechless. First Megan going crazy at the theater, and now to learn about this horrible plot that Constance cooked up. And it wasn't only me who was in danger, what about *Flower of the South*? It could've been ruined. Celosia might not have had an outdoor drama. Do you know what a tragedy that would've been? It takes my breath away!"

I jumped in. "I'm glad you and the show are okay. If you'd like to come by my office later today, I can give you all the details."

"I'm far too busy for that! There are a thousand things to be done with the play, and since Constance is no longer here, I have to delegate all of her duties to the other members of the Society. I'll talk to you another time."

I'd had enough, too. "No, Amanda, you'll talk to me now. How did you find out about the video that Eric Levin made of Britney Garrett, and why the hell did you think it was all right to blackmail a high-school girl?"

She sputtered for a while but didn't hang up. "The very idea!"

"That's what I say. You can explain it to me or to the police."

"Is it my fault these girls put themselves all over the Internet?"

"I've got Chief Brenner on speed dial."

Another round of huffing. "I picked up her phone by mistake. You know I'm always misplacing mine. It was at one of our meetings."

"A couple of months ago?"

"Yes, around March. Britney must have been admiring herself because the video came right up. That's when I realized it wasn't my phone. I left the phone where I'd found it, and she came running in not long after looking for it. I knew her mother was an extremely inflexible parent. That's when we made our little arrangement."

I still couldn't believe Amanda saw nothing wrong in this. "And at no point did you think, this is not right? Are you that desperate for money?"

"My finances are none of your concern."

"You're broke, Amanda, and I'm going to make sure everyone in town knows it."

She gasped. "You can't do that! I'm your client!"

"Not anymore. I solved your case. I'm clicking on social media right now."

"Wait!" There was a long pause and I imagined Amanda weighing her options, which were very few. "What do you want?"

"How much money do you have?"

"Oh, so you're going to blackmail me now?"

"Stop sneering and listen. Pay back everything you took from Britney, every cent, or the world will know you are a worthless, conniving old bitch. Sell that silver centerpiece, sell whatever you have to, and give her back all the money you stole from her—and you did steal it, Amanda."

For once, Amanda was silent. Then she grumbled, "All right."

"Thank you." I hung up on her before she could hang up on me. I took a long drink of my tea. "Amanda was her lovely, sympathetic self."

"I heard every word," Jerry said. "Nice job."

"Worst client ever. But her evil influence still lingers. What I read of Constance's play was so much better than Amanda's version. In a strange way, I feel like Amanda's getting away with murder. Theatrical murder."

Jerry's smile was full of mischief. "Well, there may be a way to fix that."

Uh, oh. Did I see a con on the horizon? "What do you mean?"

"Amanda's finances are low, and when she's not extorting money from high-school girls, she's depending on contributions from the rich women in town to underwrite *Flower of the South*."

"That's right."

"What if they withdraw their support?"

"At one time, I thought they might, but then this rivalry with Rossboro fired them up."

"Then they control what happens."

"They're all so timid, though. It's as if Amanda has this secret power over them."

"Maybe they don't understand if they control the money, they have the power, not Amanda. It's not something she'd want them to know. But we could tell them."

"I just told Amanda if she pays Britney back, I wouldn't tell anyone she's broke."

His smile widened. "You won't have to tell them she's broke. They only need to know they're rich."

Chapter Twenty-four

I saw my chance the next morning at Deely's when the older remaining members of the Improvement Society, including Eloise Michaels, came in for breakfast and sat in their favorite booth. Jerry took a moment from his cooking to join me as I explained to them what had happened with Constance. The real version, not Amanda's.

I knew the women would be curious. They were shocked that someone like Constance would commit murder, and unlike Amanda, they expressed pity for Megan and were happy the whole ordeal was over.

"Amanda, of course, is upset," I said, leaving out *and hopes Constance gets the chair.* "Jerry and I were hoping to clear up some things about *Flower of the South*, so maybe you can help us. You've got the cast you wanted? Everyone happy with their parts?"

The women exchanged glances. "Well," one said, "we're having trouble finding someone to play Mrs. Ross. Since Amanda's playing Emmaline, we have to find someone who looks as if she's old enough to be Amanda's mother."

"Why not go with a younger Emmaline?"

"Amanda's Emmaline, or there's no show."

"Here's the thing," Jerry said. "You ladies put up the money for the show, right? That means you're in charge. If you don't like something, then you withdraw your support."

"But that means Rossboro wins," another woman said.

"No, that means if you play your cards right, you get the show you want."

There was silence around the table.

"What does Amanda have on you that makes you do whatever she says?" I asked, then answered: "You're all very wealthy, very influential women. You control *Flower of the South*. Even if it's Amanda's idea." And it was Constance's idea first, I wanted to say. "Amanda can't have the show without you. If I were you, I'd look into this one-hundred-thousand-dollar grant she received and make sure it has the Society's name on it and not hers."

"The signature card…" Eloise said in alarm, and the other women gasped. "Has anyone looked at it lately?"

"Signature card?" I asked.

"For the Improvement Society bank account. The bank requires names of persons who can sign the checks for the organization. If Amanda's name is on the card, she can withdraw funds. She could say it was for general operating or production costs or a consulting fee and put it right into her pocket."

I'd wondered how Amanda was going to get her hands on the cash. "That's how she can siphon off all the grant money." I let that sink in for a moment.

There was another long uncomfortable pause. Then Eloise met my gaze. "Could we have a few minutes to discuss things privately?"

"Of course."

Jerry and I retreated to the kitchen. "I can't believe they're just now figuring that out."

"We incredibly wealthy people have trouble dealing with ordinary problems."

I laughed and gave him a push. "You gave up that wealth."

"And now I can deal." Then he started laughing.

"It wasn't that funny," I said.

"No, you reminded me of something. At the theater when we caught Megan, you pushed the witch into the oven—well, technically it was a pit, but that's how you got her."

"We got her. That was some sneaky ankle-grabbing."

"Let me grab your ankles."

"No! You know I'm ticklish down there."

"Madeline," Eloise called, "we've made a decision."

We returned to their booth. The women were all smiles.

Eloise had gained a new spirit. "We've decided to take control of the outdoor drama. I'm going to the bank right now and change the signature card. Then we're going to write down our demands, and if they aren't met, Amanda will be thanked for her efforts and dismissed. We still have Jerry's songs, and we're going to ask one of the younger women who auditioned to be Emmaline. It's much more historically accurate." She added slyly, "And if Amanda wants to be in the show, we have the perfect part for her. *She* can play Emmaline's mother."

Jerry and I left the Improvement Society congratulating themselves and planning their next move.

"Ding, dong, the witch is dead?" Jerry said.

"I wouldn't put it past Amanda to have another scheme up her sleeve. She'll find a way to take the grant money and run."

Annie approached, her expression unreadable. "Can I talk to you, Madeline?'

"Of course."

Orders had piled up, so Jerry hurried back to the kitchen. Annie and I sat down in the same booth we'd chosen for our earlier conversation.

"Britney wanted me to talk to you. She wanted to thank you for not saying anything to her mother."

"I told her I wouldn't."

"She's heard all this about Constance Tate. She knows once all this dies down, it's only a matter of time before the police come asking about Eric."

"She told me she was with you that night."

"That's true, Madeline." Annie looked down at the table, took her cloth, and wiped up a circle of water. "He wanted me to go with him one time. I said no. I knew what he was doing. I told Britney, but she laughed and said she didn't care."

"She cares now."

"Yeah, she does."

"Will she be able to talk to her mother about this?"

"Her mother is so overprotective, I doubt she will."

"What about Eric's phone? Britney was very concerned someone else might find it and use that video against her. Do you know anything about it?"

"It has a bright yellow-green cover with skulls on it." She took a deep breath. "I've seen it, Madeline. I know where it is."

◇◇◇

Lauren Garrett's office was still orderly, the Bibles and books on religion still straight and neat on the shelves. The stained-glass picture of Jesus still smiled peacefully down on the lambs.

Lauren looked up from her computer. Her expression hardened as she stood. "I need to have a word with you. I do not appreciate you accosting Britney at school. If you don't leave her alone, I'll get a restraining order."

"Did she tell you I came by?"

"She didn't have to. Several people called to let me know you were in the parking lot."

Did Lauren have a spy network to help her keep an eye on Britney?

"Why would you want to talk to her? She had nothing to do with Harold Stover's murder."

"I wanted to ask her a few questions about Eric Levin."

"She doesn't know anything about him, either."

"Maybe not. But you do." I took the bright yellow-green pieces of plastic from my pocket and put them on her desk. The pattern of skulls grinned up at her.

She recoiled. "Where did you get that?"

"In your garbage." *Check the trash cans, Annie had said. When I helped Britney with her chores, I saw the broken phone case. I knew it couldn't be Britney. That left only one other person.* "I guess you smashed the phone. I don't blame you."

She sank back into her chair. "I always check on Britney's friends. When I found out that little creep was bragging about his conquests on Facebook, I told Britney she would be next and to stop seeing him. She didn't listen to me. Then Clover's mother told me she'd overheard Britney telling Clover what a wild time she'd had in the woods with Eric, and Clover warning her that Eric had made sex tapes of former girlfriends. Now Britney is pregnant with his child! I did what I had to in order to protect my daughter."

"You cooked up rhododendron leaves."

"I remembered something useful from my coven experience, yes."

"And the symbols were to throw suspicion on the Parkland Coven."

"Why not? Our old coven was disbanded, and we certainly didn't have that kind of thing going on in Celosia now. Of course the police would think it was the Parkland Coven."

"Why the vineyard?"

"It's a nice quiet place, a very large place. I told him to meet me there. I said I would pay him whatever he wanted for his silence. The greedy little bastard believed me." A wry smile twisted her mouth. "He got his money, all right. I put money symbols all over him. Then I took his phone."

"How did you poison him?" I couldn't see Eric Levin munching on rhododendron leaves.

"Our first meeting was here in my office around five-thirty. I'd noticed before he always carried a certain brand of sports drink, so I had one handy while we discussed how much money he wanted to keep quiet. It was a simple matter to add rhodo-dendron nectar, just enough to make certain he wouldn't give me any trouble later."

"Later?"

"I said I'd get the money and bring it to him, but not at the church. Somewhere more private. He agreed to the far side of the vineyard as a meeting place where no one could see us. It takes about six hours for the poison to take effect. By ten-thirty, he was beginning to feel it. He was no longer a threat."

"That's when you stabbed him."

"I wasn't sure the poison would do the job. Britney knows nothing about any of this. I made sure she was at Annie's with Clover."

Lauren had ruthlessly planned every step. "Have you always controlled every aspect of Britney's life?"

"What else could I do? Her father left when she was five and gave me no help whatsoever. I know the dangers a young girl faces in this world." Her voice became bitter. "Even after all my vigilance, she runs off into the woods with this idiot and now she's pregnant."

Britney had been so careful not to let her mother know any of this. "How did you find out?"

"Clover's mother overheard them talking about a trip they made to Parkland. Whoever they met there had given them a list of abortion clinics and the number for Planned Parenthood. They were discussing what to do."

Clover's mother was as overprotective as Lauren. "Did she also know Clover was lending Britney money to pay for Amanda's silence?"

Lauren sat up straight. "What? Amanda's silence? What are you talking about?"

"Eric Levin wasn't the only one blackmailing Britney. Amanda knew about this video."

She slowly got to her feet. "So I guess I'll have to get rid of both of you."

This time I did not have Jerry hiding in the closet. "Why don't I call the police and let them sort this out? Chief Brenner likes to solve these cases himself. He's told me not to interfere, so I doubt he'll believe a word I say."

She reached into her desk drawer and pulled out a gun. "No, I think we'll say Amanda shot you. That'll take care of both problems."

"You have a gun at church?"

"We've been broken into a couple of times, and I'm often here alone. I decided I needed a little protection." She motioned toward the door. "Let's go."

During my pageant days, I'd once broken up a fight between Miss Roadway Diner and Miss Sweet Potato Pie by grabbing Miss Congeniality's overlarge trophy and whacking the two queens apart. I didn't have a trophy handy, but I did have the statue of Jesus on the little table by the door. Assuming a posture of defeat, I made my way slowly to the door, then quickly snatched up the statue and swung it, sending Lauren's gun flying in one direction and Lauren in another. She fell with a groan and didn't get up. I scooped up the gun and returned the statue to its place.

"Thank you, Lord."

Lauren rolled over on her back, her voice choked with tears. "Madeline, you have to understand! I had to protect my daughter."

"Next time, try talking to her instead of everyone else," I said. "Only I don't think there'll be a next time."

At Deely's that Saturday, the news of Lauren Garrett eclipsed Megan's attack on Amanda and Constance as Harold's murderer.

Waffles were on the menu today, and Jerry brought me my order. "Word is already out that Amanda turned down the role of Mrs. Ross and is currently in negotiations with the Rossboro Arts Council to play Emmaline in their production."

"Taking advantage of Joanie's accident."

"We'd be surprised if she didn't, wouldn't we? Did she pay you?"

"Yes. I found an envelope under my office door this morning with a check and a curt thank you note. I'll bet that check bounces."

"Better not. Do you suppose she suspects that you were the one who set the Improvement Society on her?"

"No, I think Eloise set her straight."

Jerry returned to the kitchen. I listened to the hum of voices around me, the clank of silverware, and the occasional complaints from the Geezer Club in the corner. Amanda's plans were finished in Celosia; Constance was in jail for murder; Lauren was in jail for murder; and as for Megan, Amanda dropped all charges against her sister. Megan was under psychiatric care and responding well to medication. At least Harold's money would benefit all those charities. That was the only good thing I could think of to come out of all this mess.

I surveyed the diner, wondering which one of these people would be the next to snap. I had my work cut out for me here in Celosia. Now if I could think of a way to control everyone's emotions, there'd be no more murders. No, wait. Isn't that what got Lauren into so much trouble, trying to control Britney's every move? Britney. I couldn't think of her without feeling I'd let her down. Her father appeared from wherever he'd been all these years and took her with him, sparing her any further embarrassment. I hoped she would be able to make the right decision regarding her unborn child.

"Ready?" Jerry asked, breaking into my thoughts.

"Ready."

We had decided to go to Peaceful Meadow, find a nice spot in the woods, and bury the baby rattle. The meadow was filled with flowers and sweet smells. I picked a handful of daisies. The forest was cool and filled with patterns of light from the green leaves. We found a place in a grove of pine trees. Jerry had brought along a trowel, and he dug a hole at the base of one of the trees. I placed the rattle gently on the soft earth. He covered it, and I spread the daisies on top. We stood for a while, not knowing what to say, until Jerry began to softly sing the angel lullaby from *Hansel and Gretel*, adding his own words.

> *When at night I go to sleep,*
> *Fourteen angels watch do keep.*
> *Angels all around me,*
> *Now at last have found me.*

We walked back through Peaceful Meadow to the Jeep. Jerry got in, but I stood for a while and looked out across the waving grass, trying to imagine a happier time when Megan wandered the meadow, gathering her plants and flowers, when the young

Joanie and Lauren and Constance laughed and played silly spooky games in the woods, when Britney and Clover and Annie and their friends thought they'd try some magic spells just for fun. When careless love led to little lost souls. They all believed they were in control of their lives, but no one truly was.

Stop trying to control things. Life will happen. It will happen when you least expect it.

And what about Big Mike? I hadn't forgotten the favor I owed him.

When I slid into the passenger seat, Jerry eyed me. "Okay, what's up? You look like you're trying to solve the world's problems."

"That's exactly what I'm doing."

"Well, stop. You solved Harold's murder and Eric Levin's murder and saved *Flower of the South*. What more do you want?"

What was I thinking? I had Jerry. That was everything, wasn't it? I laughed and reached for his hand. "Where would I be without you?"

He gave me the full force of those warm gray eyes and leaned over to kiss me. "Lost in the woods."

To receive a free catalog of Poisoned Pen Press titles, please provide your name, address, and email address in one of the following ways:

Phone: 1-800-421-3976
Facsimile: 1-480-949-1707
Email: info@poisonedpenpress.com
Website: www.poisonedpenpress.com

Poisoned Pen Press
6962 E. First Ave. Ste 103
Scottsdale, AZ 85251